King the Wonder Dog

Published in 2026 by
She Writes Press, an imprint of The Stable Book Group

32 Court Street, Suite 2109
Brooklyn, NY 11201
https://shewritespress.com
Library of Congress Control Number: 2025927298
ISBN: 979-8-89636-114-5
eISBN: 979-8-89636-115-2

Interior Designer: Tabitha Lahr

"Moon in the Morning" first appeared in Failbetter, April 6, 2023
"Normal People" first appeared in Hamilton Stone Review, Spring 2023
"John and Pablo Meet Their Neighbors" first appeared in 34th Parallel Magazine, June 2023
"The Alcoholic Mariannes" first appeared in Woodcrest Magazine, July 2023
"Old Dogs" first appeared in Hamilton Stone Review, Fall 2023

Printed in the United States

King the Wonder Dog

and other stories

ELEANOR LERMAN

SHE WRITES PRESS

CONTENTS

THE ALCOHOLIC MARIANNES

Laura is having trouble sleeping. She once read in some magazine that this is the curse of growing older: to be an unwilling companion of the moon, up before dawn and wondering how to fill the empty hours ahead. But over the years that she's been retired from her job as an office manager, Laura has come up with strategies to cope with the loss of structure that going to work five days a week had provided, which means that almost every day she has some task she has assigned herself to fill the days and pass the time.

So she gets out of bed, because there's no point in trying to go back to sleep. Five a.m., six, six thirty. She makes herself a cup of coffee and sits on her terrace for a while, watching the dawn come and go. Stars fade, the sun rises. She goes back inside and turns on the television to watch the morning news. Then she showers, dries her hair, and gets dressed. Finally, out the door she goes, on her way to walk the few blocks to the local branch of the Queens library where she intends to browse through the new books that have come in and pick out something to read. She also likes to comb through the used book bins that the library is always adding to, selling old duplicate volumes pulled from the shelves to raise money for their educational programs.

Under a cool, gray sky laddered with clouds, Laura walks up Queens Boulevard, struggling a bit because pain has set in. A few years ago, Laura had thyroid cancer, and while she's free of the disease for now, she has developed chronic neuropathy: painful tingling in her hands and feet resulting from the nerve pathways damaged by chemotherapy lighting up with their complaints. But she continues on, waiting for the pain medication she took before she left the house to start working. It's strong stuff, and she has taken only half the dosage she's been prescribed because even that small amount often makes her feel like she's in a fog. But she will fight against that if it happens today.

As Laura approaches the library, she notices that there's a van belonging to a local animal rescue group parked at the curb. She stops to look at the mural painted on the outside of the van, which shows puppies and kittens sitting under a rainbow with smiling children running toward them and happy adults gazing at the heartwarming scene. When Laura was married, she and her husband had a dog they had adopted from an animal shelter, but the husband claimed ownership of it in the divorce, and Laura was too heartsick about everything, then, to argue with him. But lately, she has actually been thinking about getting another dog. Walking the dog, feeding it—and having its company, another living being to spend time with—can only be a good thing. Not that she doesn't have friends—she does, other women around her age that she sees from time to time—but caring for a pet is a full-time job and she thinks she's finally ready, once again, to take it on. And perhaps the rescue group being right here today, in front of the library, is just the push she needs to actually do something about finding a dog to adopt.

So she steps inside the van, which is a busy place. There are quite a few young couples here, some with children, and some of the adults are already filling out the paperwork needed to adopt one of the cute, energetic kittens or puppies in the cages. As Laura looks at these people, it occurs to her that a puppy might actually be too much work, and so an older dog would be a better fit for her because it would require less constant attention. After all, she often does have to be out of the house—the friends always have some outing planned, like going to a movie or a restaurant—and she also has volunteer work that she does.

So she walks down the row of cages that hold the puppies, but none seem to be more than a few months old. Then, finally, at the end of the row, she sees that there is one older dog here, a skinny brown mutt with the curled tail of some wild pariah ancestor sitting quietly in the back of its cage, staring down at the floor. But as Laura stands nearby, watching him for a while, he raises his head and looks up at her. And that's it, that's all it takes. She can see that he's scared and he's defeated; he knows he's lost and thinks that he will be forever. How can Laura just turn away? She holds a brief debate with herself, but she already knows which way it's going to end, so she walks up to the front of the van, gets the form she needs in order to apply to adopt the dog, and fills it in.

There is a young woman sitting at a table at the front of the van processing the applications. She tells people handing her their paperwork that it will be reviewed in the next few days and then they will hear from the rescue group. When Laura's turn comes, she hands in her form and waits while the woman reads what she's written down.

"Um," the woman says, "I'm afraid there's a bit of a problem with your application."

"What problem?" Laura asks. "What are you talking about?"

"Well," the woman says, "we have a policy that prevents us from accepting applications from anyone who is seventy or older. And you've listed your age as seventy-one."

"You're kidding," Laura says with true astonishment. "You must be. The information card on the dog's cage says he's about six years old and was found wandering in the street. He's just a stray dog. It's not like I'm asking you to give me a purebred puppy."

The tight smile on the young woman's face compresses just a little bit more. "I am sorry," she says, "but we have this policy in place for the benefit of the animals. We wouldn't want to release a dog or a cat to someone who might not be able to provide them with long-term care."

Laura's face reddens; her heart crashes around in her chest. She feels as if she's heard some terrible secret about herself spoken out loud, her own punishing thoughts read back to her. After all, there are days when *she* can't believe that she's as old as she is. That she's suffered from a disease that nearly killed her and left her with damage that will never heal. Getting older, getting sick: These are conditions that seem to go hand in hand if you think about them too much, and Laura does, sometimes. Think too much and worry. Still, weakly, she protests. "I know what you're telling me—that because I'm over seventy, the dog might outlive me, and then what would happen to him? But what will happen to him now? I can't imagine that there are other people rushing to adopt him."

"I am sorry," the woman says. "But please, there are other people waiting behind you."

Still wanting to argue, Laura goes on standing in front of the woman in charge of the applications, who just continues to smile. Finally, another woman reaches around Laura to place an application on the table and then adds to the pool of smiles directed at Laura that have only one message: *Go away.*

Shocked and beaten down, Laura leaves the van and walks into the library. She feels like she can hear the buzzing of the fluorescent lights hanging from the ceiling, and the sound reverberates in her head. Her eyes are blurry and she's afraid that she's going to cry, so she hurries to the bathroom, where she stands over the sink and splashes her face with cold water. Then she looks up and sees herself in the mirror.

I don't recognize you, she tells herself, but this is not a new thought. Even though she knows she shouldn't be, Laura is baffled by the fact that when she looks in a mirror, she still expects to see a younger person—not a girl, necessarily, but someone in her forties or fifties with a few lines around her eyes and some puffiness where there used to be taut skin, but a pretty woman nonetheless, with waves of brown hair complemented by hazel eyes. But instead, her own grandmother seems to haunt her features: an elderly woman, thin as a bone, who was born in a country that no longer even exists on modern maps.

Laura does her best to collect herself, but the pain in her fingers and toes is firing up again with renewed ferocity. So, without even looking at any of the books on the shelves, Laura leaves the library and limps home. She has lunch. She has dinner. She watches a movie on television, then watches another. Then she watches the late news and goes to bed.

The next morning, Laura is expected at the local food pantry where she volunteers a few days a week. The pain is a little better, something of a double relief because she has to forgo taking any medication when she does her volunteer work, which involves driving around the borough of Queens, stopping at local restaurants to pick up leftover food and produce that would otherwise go to waste. But when she arrives at the food pantry, Roger, the man in charge, asks her for a favor.

"Look, Laura," he says, "do you think you could drive into the city for us today? A friend of mine did a catering job at some big event last night, and he said they've got tons of food left over. Platters of cold cuts, all kinds of meat and seafood on ice. It was for some kind of fundraiser so either they over-ordered or the event was a bust, but one way or another, all that food's going to go to waste if we don't pick it up."

"I can't believe there's not someplace in Manhattan that will gladly take it," Laura tells him.

"Sure there is," Roger says. "But we've got first dibs if we can get there this morning. So can you go? You'll have to drive the panel truck instead of the minivan, and you're the only one I trust with it."

"Where is it? I mean, where would I have to go?"

"Someplace in the Village. Bethune Street, I think."

"No," Laura says automatically. "I don't think so."

Roger, who has been stacking cases of canned vegetables, stops what he's doing. He takes off the heavy canvas gloves he's wearing as if he needs his bare hands to help him make gestures that will emphasize the importance of what he's asking. "Why not? Are you worried about driving into the city? I know the truck needs work but it's in decent enough shape to make the trip."

"It's not that. It's just . . ." *Just what?* Laura knows how to fill in the answer to that question, but she doesn't want to. She doesn't want the feelings she's having to be given a voice.

"Please," Roger says. "I don't have anyone else who can do it today. I'd go myself, but you know I have to stay here. People expect the doors to be open by nine a.m."

Laura sighs. She hears the sound of her own breath leaving her body and thinks of it as a kite sailing away. Something that can never be retrieved. "Alright," she says. "Just give me the address."

She climbs into the truck and steps on the gas, heading toward Queens Boulevard, which slices through the borough heading straight for Manhattan. It's a hard, mid-morning-in-New-York-City drive, with aggression seemingly boiling in the veins of everyone with their hands on the wheel of a vehicle. Trucks, cars, taxis, motorcycles—everyone cuts everyone off, everyone has their radio pounding out the tunes, everyone is in more of a hurry than everyone else. Laura can deal with that. She's a good driver, and she can navigate the river of crazy traffic without thinking about it too much, but today, she makes herself think of nothing else because she's on her way to Greenwich Village, a part of the city where she used to live but that she has purposefully stayed away from for a long time. *No*, she tells her thoughts, her memories, if they even dare to wander down that way. *Go away. Fly away from me.* But do they? Probably not.

The address Laura has been given takes her to an imposing glass skyscraper on a street where nineteenth-century brownstones used to sit quietly side by side. These buildings are now all gone, replaced by sky-high towers built for the wealthy to stride around in as they gaze out at a city they have many reasons to believe that they own. Laura double-parks outside and runs in to ask where she can leave the truck while she goes up to the penthouse. The building's concierge directs her to an underground garage where she can park and then take an elevator upstairs.

Following these directions, Laura soon finds herself stepping into a vast space with tall windows spilling golden sunlight onto hundreds of spindly gold chairs stacked around tables covered with wine-stained linens. Men and women are moving back and forth across the floor, carrying trays of used plates and dirty glasses, mopping up messes of food and drink. Someone is playing a radio. Someone is calling out orders to the workers. It's very noisy.

Laura finds the man she's been told to ask for, and he sends her off to the kitchen, marching behind her as he tells her his troubles, a story that snaps and crackles with annoyance at how the event he catered here last night was supposed to be attended by far more people than actually showed up, forcing him to move tables and decorations around at the last minute to make it seem like this huge space was actually crowded with guests. Roger, he says, is a saint to take all the extra food off his hands because otherwise he would have to bear the sin of so much waste. And, as Laura enters the kitchen, she sees that sin would indeed abound if all the coolers and crates stacked near the service elevator are what she is meant to drive back to Queens. And yes, they are. The food pantry will be well stocked tonight.

Once everything is brought downstairs and loaded into the truck, Laura steps up into the driver's seat and tells herself to turn the key in the ignition and head straight back to Queens. But she can't do it. She can't leave. Not yet. And this is just why she didn't want to come here, to be back in the Village: She was afraid that she was going to do just what she thinks she is going to do now—no, what she *knows* she is going to do—because there is nothing to distract her. Nothing to keep her away.

Ah, well, she thinks. *Ah, well.* She still wants to argue with herself, even as she steps out of the truck, leaves the garage, and starts walking along Washington Street. Here, change is also evident: The old, familiar apartment buildings and quirky Village stores are gone, the new ones having staked their claim, glowing and gleaming in the sunlight. It's a mild spring day, and people are out strolling around. Some are going in and out of the high-end shops selling designer goods and other luxury items, some are pushing babies in carriages or walking with a friend. It's a pleasant scene but has nothing to do with Laura's memories of the Village, which go back so far that they start in another century. *Another century!* As if when Laura lived here it was the time of pioneers in covered wagons instead of streets crowded with coffee shops and gay bars and stores that sold sandals and bongs and decks of tarot cards; a time of head shops and posters and pot. *Maybe this is just the way things work,* Laura tells herself. Time flows along and everything is different than it was before. But as Laura walks on, she grows sadder and sadder. *This is loneliness,* she tells herself. *This is grief.*

Soon, she is standing at the top of a cobbled lane, an anomaly in a city of wide avenues and concrete sidewalks. She takes a breath and then a step. Two steps, three. Down the lane she goes.

When Laura was eighteen, this was the place where she was able to afford the rent on her first apartment—just a small studio, actually—on the top floor of an old carriage house dating back to the mid-1800s. But just like almost everywhere else in New York, this area is now an extravagantly expensive place to live. Duplex condominiums have risen on either side of the lane, but it's still quiet here, and shady. Trees have been planted around the duplexes and flowers have sprung up.

When Laura lived here, she had worked as a housecleaner. There really weren't many other types of jobs she could get as a teenager from a rattletrap New Jersey suburb who came to the city with a high school diploma and little else. The company she worked for called their cleaning people "maids" and sent them to residential buildings in Manhattan. Laura cleaned townhouses and huge Upper West Side apartments, but also lofts and brownstones in the Village, which are the places she remembers most clearly. There always seemed to be drama in these apartments, people swanning around in beautiful bohemian clothes, trailing cigarettes and scarves, nannies and babies. The husbands always seemed to be older, the wives younger, and everyone did drugs, had dangerous affairs, broke things. They argued about who spent too much money, acted too foolishly. Sometimes the husbands shouted, the wives wept. They accused everyone they knew of being an alcoholic, but then confessed—sometimes to Laura, who was no one, just the cleaning lady, the convenient person in the room—that they were too. Only the wives made the confessions. The husbands stormed out of the house. Laura doesn't recall any of the husbands' names, but in her memory, the wives always seemed to be named Marianne.

Occupied by these thoughts, Laura suddenly finds herself standing by the front door of the carriage house. She knew the building would still be standing here because a few years ago, she looked it up online and saw that it had been gutted and remodeled, then sold more than once, most recently to a wealthy European family who only stay here from time to time. Now is not one of those times—it can't be, because as Laura lifts her hand to touch the door, a thick slab of wood with iron fittings, the house radiates emptiness. It speaks of deep silence. Then, as she closes her eyes, she also feels the vibrations of time, the years of sleeping and waking and going from place to place. Of changing clothes, making plans, being and doing and running around. And she remembers that it was here where she finally changed her life by taking a typing course and finding work in offices, where she did well. She liked her work, was often promoted, saved some money. And here she married, moved away, then got divorced.

But mostly, she finds herself remembering the alcoholic Mariannes. And she wonders if there wasn't something that she always thought was inevitable about them, those slim, delicate women with their middle-American beauty and fashionable weakness for self-destruction. Their air of being obedient to the carelessness of fate, running toward it as if there was nowhere else to go. Because as she stands here now, Laura, with her hand on the door to the place where she started her adult life—where she believed that the future would go on and on and things could always change, get better, that time was inconceivably eternal—she thinks that maybe what she was really doing all those years and in all the years that followed was hoping for something hidden inside a whirlwind to explain itself. For something to break wide open right before her eyes.

And yet. If she could, if she didn't think that anyone would see her, she would press her body against the door and let herself pretend that she could pass through the wood and iron and melt back into the past. Climb back into her bed again, the mattress on the floor with its bedspread from India laid out beside a dresser rescued from the street, where candles were burning, where posters of angels and winged horses were hung up on the walls. Where she would be young. Safe. Starting all over again.

Hours later, back in Queens, after she stops at the food pantry to drop off the truck and its contents, Laura finds that she can barely walk the few blocks home because the pain is back again, and this time it's really bad. At home, she takes the full dose of her medication, a powerful opioid, which eases the pain but also has the effect of making her feel like she is being peeled away from the core of herself and that what is left will soon become unmoored from life, from living; a poor wraith, lost and alone. The night is a cage, and she is a prisoner, with no one to help her or speak on her behalf. Soon, she falls into a long, drugged sleep.

When she wakes up in the morning and drinks enough coffee to begin to clear her head, she slides open the door to her terrace and sits outside for a while. She lives on a high floor of her building so she has a view that stretches off toward the horizon. As stars fade and the sun rises, she sees houses and clouds, trees and cars, endless highways wandering from one place to another and then back again. Laura's thoughts wander as well, leading her back to yesterday and the day before. Then going forward: What will transpire in the days ahead? The weeks, the months, the years? Only time will tell. And time is pushing her along. Day after day she is growing older. Older and older—but that's what happens, isn't it? That's what happens to everyone, human and animal, all who inhabit this one known world.

So Laura goes to her closet and pulls out a skirt and jacket, clothes she used to wear when she went to work, because her first thought is that she needs to look poised and professional for what she has decided that she will do today. But then she thinks, *No, the hell with that. I don't have to dress up for anyone anymore.* So she puts on the clothes she usually wears these days: a T-shirt, jeans, her old Frye boots. And then she leaves her apartment and walks out into the sunshine. It's warmer today than yesterday; spring will soon blow away and summer will heat up the city. It will be air-conditioning weather but still a good time to walk a dog.

First, however, she has to get the dog. So she walks several blocks, heading for the neighborhood office of the local congressman who represents her district. She's voted for him in two elections, which should count for something, but even if it doesn't, Laura believes that she can make her case. Maybe she was too shocked to say anything, too overcome with embarrassment or shame or whatever it was that sent her limping home from the library after the pet rescue group sent her away, but she feels differently today. She has intent and she has purpose. She knows what she wants to do.

It doesn't seem particularly busy in the small branch office of the congressman, which is located in a storefront between a hardware store and a pharmacy. A young man is sitting at the front desk, typing away on a computer. He looks up when Laura walks in, smiles, and says, "Hi. Can I help you?"

"Yes," Laura says. She introduces herself and then gestures to a chair by his desk. "May I sit down?"

"Sure," the young man says. "I'm Randy," he tells her and asks if she lives in his boss's district. Laura says that she does and then adds the part about having voted for the congressman every time he's been up for election. "That's great," Randy says. "Now, what can we do for you?"

"The other day," Laura begins, "I wanted to adopt a dog. Not a puppy, an older dog—but the rescue group that has him said they wouldn't even consider my application because I'm seventy-one."

"I don't understand," Randy says, sounding genuinely surprised. "What does your age have to do with it?"

Laura smiles. The smile is meant for herself. And she thinks, *Of course he has no idea. He's too young to even consider the possibility that he will ever die.* "Because of my age, they think I might get sick at some point soon or maybe not even live long enough to properly take care of the dog."

"Really?" Randy says. "Wow." To Laura, he sounds like a teenager, a little out of his depth to deal with what she's telling him. But he redeems himself by offering what Laura, with wry amusement, understands that he must mean as a compliment. "By the way," he says, "you don't look your age. I really mean it. You could have just told them you were, like, fifty."

"But I shouldn't have to do that, should I?" Laura says.

"Absolutely not," Randy replies. "It's age discrimination." He asks the name of the rescue group, and after Laura tells him, he turns and calls into the next room. "Hey, Angela, would you come out here?" In response, a woman walks out of a back room. She's a little older than Randy, tall, sharp featured, and dressed the way Laura would have been if she'd opted for office attire. "Have we ever done any work with the Queensway Friends of Animals group?" Randy asks her.

"Yes, we have," Angela replies. "Janet Kellogg is the name of the woman who runs the group. A few months ago, we helped her get a permit to expand the number of kennels she has. Why are you asking?"

"Well, this is Laura," Randy says, sparking a quick exchange of greetings between the two women. "She wanted to adopt a dog from Queensway, and they wouldn't let her because they said she's too old. They can't discriminate like that, can they?"

"Unfortunately," Angela says, "since Mrs. Kellogg is running a private organization, she can make her own rules about who she lets adopt the animals she fosters. We actually have had other complaints about her, but usually it's from younger working people. If both people in a couple work full time, she refuses to let them have a puppy because she thinks it won't get enough attention. Personally, I think that's ridiculous, but she's pretty intransigent."

"But Laura didn't want a puppy," Randy explains. "She wanted to adopt an older dog."

Angela sends a sympathetic look Laura's way. "That does seem like it's hardly in the dog's best interests. Do you want us to call her?" Angela asks.

"Would you?" Laura says. And now she's absolutely determined to get the dog. Otherwise, he's going to be sitting in a kennel for the rest of his life because of some random rule that someone she's never met has seemingly made up out of thin air.

"Okay," Angela tells Randy. "See what you can do."

As Angela walks away, Randy looks up the number for the Queensway rescue group, picks up the phone, and dials. As soon as someone answers, his breezy tone turns hard and professional. He asks for Janet Kellogg, and when she gets on the phone, he introduces himself and speaks to her for quite a while, asking how the expansion is going before he gets to the issue of Laura and the dog. At one point, he puts his hand over the phone and, in a whisper, asks Laura if she recalls the name of the dog. And yes, she does, because it was printed on the card that was taped outside his kennel on the day that Laura saw him.

"His name is Buddy," Laura tells Randy, who repeats it to Janet Kellogg.

The phone call seems to go on and on, but Randy knows how to apply the right kind of pressure. Again, he reminds her how helpful his congressman has been to her and then pivots to explain how he's worried that Laura might go to one of the local television stations and get their consumer affairs reporter to do a story about age discrimination in pet adoptions while standing right outside the Queensway kennels. As he tells this fib, he looks over at Laura and winks. Finally, after listening to some long, garbled speech that Janet Kellogg seems to be making, Randy says, "Yes, that's right. We want to do everything we can to help our seniors, don't we?" Laura cringes when she hears this, but never mind: She's decided that Randy can say anything he likes as long as at the end of the conversation, she is able to get the dog.

Which seems to be what's going to happen because finally, Randy says, "Yes, thank you. Thank you so much, Mrs. Kellogg. I'm sure she'll be happy to come over there today." And then he hangs up the phone.

"Well," he says, "she's willing to make an exception and let you have the dog. But you're going to have to pay some sort of special emergency release fee, which I imagine is something she just made up. If that's going to be a problem for you, I'm sure we can find a way to help you out."

"No," Laura says, "that's fine. Whatever she wants to charge, I can cover it. Thank you," she tells Randy. "I really appreciate it."

"Glad to be of help," Randy says, beaming, happy that he's going to be able to tell the congressman how he did a good deed for a voter.

Randy writes down Queensway's address, and luckily, it isn't too far away. Still, Laura opts to call a taxi because pain is creeping up on her again, and she doesn't want to take any medication until she deals with Mrs. Kellogg. But when she arrives at Queensway, it's not Mrs. Kellogg who Laura ends up having to work things out with, it's a woman named Betsey who is hostile enough for Laura to guess that her boss has filled her in on the morning's phone call. Betsey is a large woman with an unkempt puff of blonde curls, wearing a nurse's tunic printed with cartoony images of dancing dogs and cats.

When Laura explains who she is, Betsey says, "I am well aware," and hands her a piece of paper that turns out to be an invoice for $200. This is, of course, an outrageous amount of money to pay for adopting a homeless dog, but true to her word, Laura just hands over her credit card, which Betsey inspects for forgery, perhaps, or theft. But she runs the card and prints out a receipt, which she gives to Laura. Then, without saying anything else, she turns and disappears behind a door that leads to the back area where, presumably, the dog kennels are.

Soon, Betsey returns with the dog, who is following obediently behind her. Betsey is pulling him along on a leash attached to a plastic collar, but his head is still down, the way it was when Laura last saw him. She also notices that his ears, which look like they were chewed around the edges somewhere in his secret long ago, are laid back against his head, flattened by worry.

"Did you bring a leash?" Betsey asks.

"No," Laura replies, caught off guard. Certain that Betsey will use this presumed negligence to cause some delay, Laura comes up with a quick solution. "Do you think that maybe I can buy the one you brought him in with?"

Twenty additional dollars later, Betsey hands over the leash. As Laura takes it in her hand, Betsey says, "Oh, by the way. Just so you know, he doesn't bark."

Laura gets what she's being told: *We won anyway. You bought a damaged product.* "Oh?" Laura says, keeping her voice soft and even. "Thanks for letting me know."

Betsey disappears back behind the door and leaves Laura standing in an empty room, holding the leash. The dog still hasn't even looked up. "Well," Laura says, maybe to the dog, maybe to the air in the room, maybe to herself, "okay then." Taking her first steps toward the front door, she experiences a flash of apprehension. What has she actually gotten herself into with this dog? Soon enough, she imagines, she is going to find out.

The dog follows Laura outside but stands somewhat away from her, not testing the length of the leash, exactly, but still keeping his distance. After a few moments of just standing on the sidewalk together, Laura decides they'd better walk home because she has no idea if the dog would even get into a car with her if she called another taxi. But to make it all the way home she is going to have to take some medication, so she fishes around in her shoulder bag and finds the little metal container in which she keeps the broken halves of pills she carries for those times when she needs help with the pain but doesn't want to feel the full strength of the medication's grip.

And so, off they go. The dog walks silently behind her, keeping his head down, barely looking around at his surroundings. But Laura talks to him now and then, telling him her name, where they're going, saying over and over that he's safe and that his life is going to be better now than it was before. She speaks to him as she imagines she would speak to a worried child. They travel together up and down the hilly streets of the neighborhood where Laura lives, passing through sunlight on the sidewalk and shadows stretching across the path winding through the small park near Laura's building. Once they arrive, the dog follows her into the cool vestibule and up the stairs to Laura's apartment, still without having looked at her, even once.

He takes a few steps inside and then stops of his own accord and sits down. The spot he's chosen is in a short hallway just inside the front door, near the entrance to the kitchen. "Well, that's fine," Laura says to the dog. "If that's your safe place for now, you can just stay there until you feel comfortable walking around the apartment." She takes off his leash and collar and pats him on the head. He doesn't respond to her touch but at least he doesn't try to pull away.

The dog goes on looking at the floor. Then, suddenly, it occurs to Laura that because she had no idea that she would actually be bringing the dog home with her today, she has bought nothing for him to eat and no dishes for him to eat from either. But it's around noontime now and she's hungry, so she decides that what she'll do is share her lunch with the dog in the hope that it will be a first step to showing him that she's his friend.

She has slices of ham and cheese in the refrigerator, so she makes a sandwich and carries it with her to the couch. She sits down and takes a bite. "It's good," she says to the dog. "Would you like some?" She sees his nose twitch slightly, but he doesn't move. So she goes back to the kitchen and puts a few slices of ham on a plate. Then she puts the plate in front of the dog and sits herself back down on the couch. "All yours," she says to him. "Go on, Buddy. Help yourself." The dog waits a few moments, then, finally, he lifts his head slightly to look at her, as if he's checking on whether she means what she's said. She nods, and he gobbles up the food in a few quick bites.

For the rest of the afternoon, Laura goes on talking to the dog as she moves around the apartment. She watches television, does some cleaning, writes out checks to pay a few bills. Then, around four o'clock, she decides it's time to go to the supermarket and buy some things for the dog. After that, she'll come back and take him for another walk.

When she returns from the supermarket, the dog is in the same spot, but he's fallen asleep. She imagines he's exhausted from all the unexpected things that have happened to him today, but he immediately stands up as soon as she opens the door. Once again, he keeps his eyes on the floor as Laura puts his collar and leash back on. When she leads him outside, he continues to walk silently behind her, his head down, barely looking around. But he does pee a few times, the only times he lifts his head, as if he's worried that something bad will happen to him when he's occupied with the functions of his body.

That night, the dog sleeps in the spot by the front door, and that's where he stays for the next few days and nights, though he always follows Laura outside when she puts on his leash and walks behind her with the same air about him of obedience and defeat. Now and then, though, when they are in the apartment, she does catch him looking at her, but if he sees that she's looking back, he puts his head down again. And he continues to wolf down his food as if expecting, always, that it will be snatched away.

Then, one night, Laura is awakened from sleep by a sound she can't identify. It's loud, insistent, like a warning being shouted out over and over again. But once she is fully awake and just about ready to jump out of bed, she realizes what she's hearing: It's a dog barking. *Her* dog. The dog sitting by the front door.

She runs out of the bedroom and sees that the dog is up on his feet. His body is shaking but his feet are flat and steady, and he's pointed himself straight at the front door. His posture makes clear to Laura that he may be frightened, but he's not backing down.

If something on the other side of the door is ready to attack, he's ready to fight.

Laura's surprise at hearing that the dog can indeed bark almost immediately gives way to concern. The lock on the door to the building's vestibule is often broken, so anyone could have gotten in. Anyone could be roaming the hallway outside. Anything could be happening. Anything at all.

So she crouches down beside the dog and puts her arm around him. And with that one gesture, he feels, he learns. He leans his body against her, and his trembling stops, while somewhere inside herself, Laura's own animal heart begins to beat louder. Deep inside, where illness has scratched its indelible record and age is gnawing away at her joints, her bones. And outside, in the unknowable elsewhere, time goes on and on and on. Stars fade, the sun rises. The moon makes an appearance on the earthly plane. There may be meaning to all this, purpose and intent, but who can tell? So Laura listens and tries to learn as the dog goes on barking. On and on and on.

And she will stay with him until he's sure that he's safe here. *Here*: in this one moment, this one place, with this one mysterious creature sitting beside him, still awake and alive inside her human hide.

KING THE WONDER DOG

"Do you think I can come home soon, Paul?"

"I don't know, honey. Do you want to?"

"Yes, but I'm confused. Everyone keeps saying that I need help."

"Then why don't we wait a few days and see how you feel?"

"Maybe. But in the meantime, I'm going to go work on a crossword puzzle."

"You like crossword puzzles?"

"I do. I'm really great at them."

"I didn't realize that."

"There's a lot of things I'm good at that you don't know about."

"I suppose that must be true. I'm sorry."

"Are you sorry enough so that you won't just leave me here?"

"Cassandra. I would never do that. Not in a million years. Okay?"

"Yes, okay. I believe you. Maybe."

Ten minutes later, after saying good night to his wife, Cassandra, Paul Renard is standing outside Lenox Hill Hospital in Manhattan, trying to sort through the conversation they just had. Currently, Cassandra is a patient in the hospital's psychiatric unit. She's been there for two weeks and the insurance policy that Paul and

Cassandra have will pay for a few weeks more—but after that, she has to be released. In New York State, the laws about psychiatric commitment are heavily weighted in favor of the patient, which is sometimes a good thing, and sometimes, not so much. In Cassandra's case, she entered the psych unit voluntarily, and so the decision about when to come home is mainly up to her. Paul has an opinion on the matter, but it's irrelevant, as, over the years, many of his opinions about his wife have proven to be. So he can stand here, paralyzed and miserable as he thinks deep thoughts about his inability to understand his wife, or he can head home, which is where he wants to be after working all day and then spending the evening at the hospital. But before Paul can go home, he has to return to the office because that's where he left his dog.

Paul hails a cab and tells the driver to take him all the way downtown, to an address on the edge of Chinatown. This is where he works, in a loft he rents on the top floor of an old building that was once a sweatshop where immigrant workers sewed shirts and blouses. Once, when Paul tripped on a floorboard that was beginning to warp, he bent down and found a thimble stuck under the wooden planking. He keeps the thimble on his desk now, near one of his computer screens. He often wonders who it belonged to, and sometimes, when he works late at night, he finds himself imagining that a ghost may show up to reclaim its lost possession. So far, thankfully, that hasn't happened.

Paul is a graphic designer. He's had a successful career, but he's sixty-eight years old now and he's trying to wind down his work. The last thing he has to complete is an annual report for a chain of department stores. It's a big job, and while it comes with a significant paycheck, Paul will be glad to be finished with it. After that, his plan had been to declare himself officially retired and stop accepting outside commissions in order to begin to work on his own projects. The one thing that he wants to do most is to write and design a graphic novel. Over the years, he's become intrigued by this form of storytelling, and even though he's not sure that he has the necessary skills to both write and illustrate an entire book, he'd like to try. The main problem with this idea—and it's a big one—is that he hasn't yet been able to come up with anything even approaching the outline of an original story. He hoped that once he no longer had the pressure of trying to meet clients' deadlines, it would be easier for him to let his imagination have free rein, and then finally, something would come to him. But now, because of what happened to Cassandra, her nervous breakdown—which, he was told by a disapproving nurse, was a term no longer in favor so he should instead refer to his wife's condition as a "manic episode"—he assumes that once she's home he's going to have to devote himself to taking care of her, and that is probably going to leave little time for anything else.

For now, Paul climbs the stairs to the loft, which is a long, narrow space that gets little natural light. There are only two windows at the front of the loft, and they look out on a blank brick wall, so lots of electric light is necessary to keep away the gloom. When Paul first rented this place, the neighborhood was in flux; squatters were taking over the abandoned factory buildings on the surrounding blocks and the illicit drug trade was thriving on the streets outside. Times have changed, though, and these days, the area is both fashionable and expensive. Eventually, Paul knows that he's not going to be able to afford the rent anymore because it's been rising every year, but he's trying to hold on. He loves the loft, loves how quiet it is when he walks in and closes the door behind him, and he loves the fact that it's his private space. He likes being alone when he works—except for his dog, whom he brings to work every day.

Paul's dog is a big German shepherd named King. Really big. He's twenty-six inches at the shoulder and weighs about ninety pounds. For the past few hours, King has been lying by the front door of the loft waiting for Paul to return. When he does, the dog watches every move he makes as he gathers some papers together, zips them into his backpack, and turns off the lights. Then out they go, into the golden evening. Stars are beginning to appear in the sky, scattered like pins. Drifting clouds look like blue mountains; the moon is a thin crust of light rising in the east.

Paul and his dog are heading toward the Brooklyn Bridge, using an underpass that runs beneath a nearby roadway instead of the more heavily trafficked entrance near the downtown municipal buildings. Unless bad weather forces Paul to call a car service that allows him to take his dog with him, he and the German shepherd walk across the bridge twice a day as they travel back and forth between Manhattan and Brooklyn, where Paul lives. Most of the time, the pedestrian walkway across the bridge is crowded with tourists who come to admire the famous view of the city skyline. At this hour, the borough of Manhattan is a thrilling sight, brilliantly illuminated by the lights coming on in its skyscrapers and apartment towers, but Paul barely glances at anything other than his feet as he and the dog head home. He's very tired. All he wants is to get something to eat, maybe watch television for a while, and then collapse into bed.

His apartment isn't far from the other side of the bridge, on a quiet street in a Brooklyn neighborhood that has not yet been remade by developers. That will come, but maybe not for a while yet. Paul and Cassandra have lived here since they were married twenty-seven years ago. He was forty-one; she was twenty-five and absolutely the most beautiful woman he had ever seen. Tall, slender, with long, dark hair and eyes so blue that looked like they could see forever, Cassandra was the woman everyone turned to admire wherever she went. Paul didn't care about the age difference between them, and he took much of the other information she shared about herself—including that she'd already been married and divorced, that she had no steady job, that she took two different medications at night to treat her chronic insomnia and another to deal with anxiety—and filed it all away in the back of his mind. Whatever problems she had, he intended to help solve them, and he's been working on doing that since the day they got married. His guess, now, is that he's been largely unsuccessful.

When Paul finally gets home, he removes the dog's collar and leash and then walks toward the bedroom. The apartment has arched doorways and the paint on the walls is a color called summer peach that took Cassandra many months to settle on. There are soft, billowy curtains on the bedroom windows that look out on the building's interior courtyard; the living room windows face the street. In the bedroom, Paul changes into sweatpants and a T-shirt, then goes to the kitchen to feed his dog, who has been following him step by step through the apartment. Then, as Paul is standing in front of the refrigerator trying to decide what to feed himself, his cell phone rings. As he reaches for the phone, the many possible identities of the caller are already pinging through his brain: *Is it the hospital? My department store client? My client's boss?* But instead, the person who wants to speak to him is his brother.

"Hey, Danny," Paul says. He talks to his younger brother often, but dinnertime on a weekday night is an odd hour for the call, so he's worried that something's wrong. "What's up?"

"So listen," Danny says, "is Cassandra there?"

"No," Paul answers. He hasn't told Danny anything about Cassandra yet, but he's guessing that whatever his brother is going to say next won't be good. "Why?"

"Well, I need to talk to you about her, so I wouldn't want her to overhear our conversation. I'm not sure what all this means, but she's been texting me maybe ten, twelve times a day and sending strange stuff."

"Like what?"

"Oh, links to different songs that she says will change my life, quotes from the Dalai Lama, copies of tweets from Taylor Swift, and other things that are just kind of random nonsense. It's like she thinks that what she's sending me is profound and important, but it doesn't really make any sense. And I guess maybe you haven't looked at her Facebook page in a while, but she's changed the whole thing. Now it says that she went to Harvard, that she lives in Nome, Alaska, and that she's in a rock band called The Beatles Number Two. Is something wrong, Paul? I mean, it's pretty clear that there is."

Paul sighs, sits down on a chair. The dog quietly pads over to him and slides his head under Paul's hand. "She had some kind of breakdown about two weeks ago, and I had to take her to the hospital. She's still there, but probably not for too much longer."

"Jesus. What happened? I mean, do you know what brought it on?"

"Not really. I came home from work one night, and as soon as I walked into the living room, she looked at me and started screaming. She said she finally had to shake off the memories of all the people who had ever hurt her so she could become the woman she always wanted to be. She was making so much noise that one of our neighbors knocked on the door because I guess he thought I was trying to kill her. I couldn't get her to stop screaming until I asked her to name the people she was talking about."

"And?"

"And she had quite a list. Her father, her older brothers, some kids at a summer camp she went to who bullied her, people at different jobs she had—there were also some people who I think were . . . well. I think she imagined them. But maybe not. I don't know."

"You've told me that her father was pretty violent with her."

"He was, yes. He broke her arm, her ribs—I don't really know the extent of what happened, but it does seem like her mother never did much to intervene. And when Cassie was around fifteen, her younger sister died. Lisa. She had leukemia and she was sick for a long time before she passed. Cassie was the one who took care of her for all that time, and the bond between them was the most important thing in Cassie's life. I don't think she's ever really gotten over how all alone she felt after her sister died. Lonely and abandoned. She left home when she was eighteen and lived on her own, but it wasn't easy for her. The way she looks—well, you can imagine. People were always attracted to her, and I guess she knew how to use that to get her way, but, in the end, things always seemed to go wrong, especially at work. She's never stayed very long at any job she's had. She gets bored with the work or she just can't get along with the people she works with. I suppose that's why she doesn't really have any friends—she never seems to like anybody very much."

"Except you."

"I'm not even sure about that right now."

"Do you know that in all the years you've been married, that's the most you've ever told me about her? And about how things are between the two of you? All I ever hear is that everything is great. Just the usual ups and downs."

"I know," Paul says. He's too tired, too battered and bruised by how his life has been, not just for the past few weeks but maybe longer too—maybe a lot longer—to keep trying to pretend that everything is fine, absolutely fine and dandy. "I'm sorry."

"I'm your brother," Danny says. "You can tell me anything. You don't have to be embarrassed."

Is that how I feel? Paul asks himself and knows that the answer is *yes*. There's a lot more, but *embarrassed* is close to the top of the pile.

"Everybody's life is fucked up sometimes," Danny says. "Take me, for example. How old was I when meth hit the East Coast? I mean, I had been cruising around forever as a happy hippie pothead, and then the master class began in how to turn a perfectly good life into a raging drug addict's journey of debt, divorce, and destruction. What kind of person decides that he's found the greatest love of his life the first time he tries crystal meth?"

"But you turned things around a long time ago."

"Yeah, but I know that I could slip up and head right back into disasterville at any time. Not that I intend to, of course. I mean, I'm sixty-two years old, for shit's sake."

"That means you're a baby. Think about it: I'm almost seventy."

"So what about that? Are you angling for me to buy you some special present or something? Some nifty old man gear?"

Paul laughs—and it feels like he hasn't done that in a million years. "Yes," he says. "That's exactly what I want."

"Seriously, Paul. What are you going to do?"

"I don't know. If I had the money to get her into a private clinic, that would probably be the best thing, but I can't afford it, and the insurance won't pay for it."

"Yeah, that sounds familiar. In my world, it's cigarettes and coffee at Nar-Anon meetings in the ratty basement of some church or you're back on the street. So listen, if there's anything I can do . . ."

"Just ignore whatever she texts you. But if it gets any worse, let me know."

"Okay, will do. I love you, brother."

Paul is almost too surprised to respond. He can't remember the last time he and Danny said anything like this to each other, but he manages to repeat the same words. "I love you too."

A few days later, after being summoned to a meeting with the social worker who is part of the team trying to decide what's best for Cassandra, Paul finds himself sitting in her office while she leafs through a folder full of papers lying open on her desk. As the woman starts speaking to him, Paul's gaze keeps drifting off to the window behind her. There are bars on this window, just as there are bars on all the windows in the psychiatric unit, but he can still see the street outside, see the crowded city street where sunlight shimmers on the path where free people walk, busy people, men and women in light, spring clothes—linen, cotton, airy shirts, pretty shoes.

"Mr. Renard?"

"I'm sorry. What did you say?"

The social worker frowns at Paul. "I was telling you that according to your wife's psychiatrist, it's best to let her go home. I spoke to Cassandra this morning, and she said she feels much more stable now, that her thoughts aren't racing, and her mind is clear. She definitely wants to be released."

"Oh?" Paul says. "She didn't seem so sure just a few days ago."

The frown on the social worker's face deepens. "Well, from what I understand, the consensus among all her doctors is that keeping her in the hospital isn't going to make a qualitative difference. The medications she's taking are a key factor in how well she's doing, so just make sure she takes them. And I see that the dosage of her mood stabilizer has been increased, so that should help to optimize her recovery."

"*Will* she recover?" Paul asks.

"Your wife has a great deal of trauma that she has to process. We'd like her to come back at least twice a week to continue treatment on an outpatient basis with the therapist we assigned to her. Your insurance will pay for that, so can you make the arrangements?"

"Yes," Paul says automatically, as any good husband would, but in actuality, his own mind is racing now because he has to figure out the logistics of taking Cassandra back and forth from Brooklyn to Manhattan while still trying to manage the ever-tightening schedule for the project he's trying to complete. "I'll take care of it."

Cassandra is officially released from the hospital by early afternoon. Paul takes her home using the same car service that permits pets because once again, he has to retrieve King from the loft before they head back to Brooklyn. Cassandra barely acknowledges the extra stop they make before the car continues on, driving across the bridge. All the way home, she chatters on about things that don't make much sense to Paul, but he isn't really listening to her because he's still thinking about his schedule. His game plan for the rest of the day is to try to work at home and let Cassandra settle back in, but as the car turns onto his block, he's already beginning to feel . . . well, what's the right way to express it? Uncomfortable? Out of sorts? No, probably *out of place*. He doesn't belong at home on a weekday morning—he should be in the loft, where he has two large computer screens that can show him full-size page layouts and the bright, artificial light feels like it holds him in a bubble of focused attention.

Back at the apartment, Cassandra twirls around the living room, exclaiming that she is happy, really happy, to be home. The dog lies down in a corner and stares at her, clearly spooked by her behavior. Paul calls to him, meaning to take him into the kitchen and give him one of his favorite dog biscuits, hoping that will make him feel like things are more normal around the house today than they really are.

With the big German shepherd following warily behind him, Paul gets as far as opening the door of the kitchen cabinet where he keeps the dog's treats before he hears a series of loud crashes coming from the living room. Running toward the noise, he sees Cassandra standing in the middle of the room holding a heavy glass vase in her arms. All around her are shards and slivers of things she's managed to break in what seems like an instant, including a picture frame, a lamp, and a stained-glass panel that hung in one of the living room windows. Stunned by the sight of all this damage, Paul stands frozen in the kitchen doorway, just long enough to see the dog go streaking past him, heading for the bedroom.

"Where are my bracelets?" Cassandra screams. Her demeanor has completely changed: The unbridled joy she seemed to be experiencing as she danced around the living room has metamorphosized into anger. No—more than that: into rage. Dark, all-consuming, dangerous rage.

"What bracelets?" Paul asks. He must know what she's talking about, but his mind is blank. *What bracelets? What does she mean?*

"The gold cuff bracelets that I bought for myself before we even met. I always wear them." Suddenly, the look on her face is contorted with disgust. "I remember now. You took them from me!"

Now, Paul remembers too. "No, Cassie, it wasn't me. At the hospital, they made you take the bracelets off. I brought them home and put them in your jewelry box."

"I don't believe you!" Cassandra lifts the glass vase over her head and lets it slide out of her hands. It crashes on the wide oak floorboards and shatters, leaving broken pieces that look like long glass knives scattered all over the floor.

"I'll get the bracelets," Paul says. "I promise. Just give me a minute."

He runs into the bedroom and sees that the dog has somehow managed to wedge himself under the bed. "Good boy," he whispers. "Just stay where you are." Then he crosses the room and opens the lacquer jewelry box that stands on Cassandra's side of the dresser. Her gold cuffs are right on the top of a massed pile of bracelets, rings, and necklaces that she has collected over the years. But the cuffs are special, and she's right: She has been wearing them for as long as Paul has known her. When they first met, he joked about how they looked like Wonder Woman's bracelets. He carries them back out to the living room and hands them to her.

"Here they are," he says. "Safe and sound."

Cassandra slips her hands through one cuff and then the other. Almost immediately, her mood changes again; the anger disappears, and happy, smiling Cassandra returns. "I saw that you were on your way to the kitchen," she says. "Were you going to make something to eat? That would be great, Paul. I'm really hungry."

"Yes, sure," Paul tells her, trying to conjure up an image of whatever food he may have in the house because he hasn't been shopping lately. He hasn't done much other than work and visit his wife in the hospital. *Soup*, he thinks desperately. *Bread and butter.* "Coming right up."

For the rest of the day, after making a show of seating Cassandra at the kitchen table and serving her the meal he's managed to pull together, Paul tries to work, but it's impossible. After she finishes eating, Cassandra can't sit still no matter how Paul tries to distract her. He turns on the television, but she only watches for a few minutes before she starts walking around the house, looking at the pictures on the walls, the books on the shelves, as if she's never seen them before and questions Paul about where they came from. Then she's in her closet, pulling clothes off their hangers and trying them on, wanting Paul's opinion about how she looks in this dress, that shirt, this pair of jeans. Finally, he gives up, closes the laptop he's been working on, and spends the rest of the day with his wife, following her around the house, answering her random questions, agreeing with opinions she offers on various disconnected topics, and just generally trying to keep her calm. The dog remains under the bed.

Late in the afternoon, as Cassandra is sitting on the couch, suddenly quiet, suddenly tranquil, as if she's emerged safe and sound from a passing storm, she holds out her hand and asks Paul to come sit beside her. When he does, she turns to him and says, "I remember what happened, what started all this. Do you know what I mean?"

"Why you had to be in the hospital for a while?"

"Yes. I remember how I was standing in the middle of the living room, just screaming and screaming, and I couldn't stop. What happened was that I was thinking about Lisa."

Paul almost says, *Yes, just the other day I was talking to my brother about her*, but he stops himself. He has a feeling that if he tells his wife that he was discussing her sister with Danny, she will blame him for being insensitive or gloating that his brother is still alive and well while Lisa is long gone. Maybe he's being a little irrational, but Paul isn't sure how Cassandra will react to anything right now, so he keeps silent while his wife continues to talk about her sister.

"Something reminded me of her," Cassandra says. "Maybe just because it's spring. I was remembering how it was her favorite season and then it occurred to me that I hadn't really thought about her much in a long time. I felt like that was awful of me.

How could I forget her? I loved her so much. She was like my baby, you know? I was the one who took care of her more than anybody else—certainly more than my mother. I think she was actually angry at Lisa for being sick." Cassandra squeezes Paul's hand, looks straight at him with her extraordinary pale blue eyes. "You're not angry at me, are you?"

"Of course not," Paul says, though he wonders if he's lying. He really isn't sure.

He orders a pizza for dinner and then drags King out from under the bed to go for a walk. It's a real tug-of-war because the dog doesn't want to move, but Paul finally manages to get his leash on and pull him out of the bedroom, enticing him with a slice of the pizza. When Paul finally has the dog ready to go out, he asks his wife to come with him.

They head for a small park just a few blocks away and stroll down a path lined with cherry blossom trees. The evening breezes are sending showers of pink petals down on their shoulders, and Cassandra laughs with delight. She's wearing a soft suede coat and has a blue scarf tied around her throat. *We look like a normal couple,* Paul thinks. *A happy couple, just out enjoying the evening while we walk our dog.*

Later that night, after they've settled themselves into bed and King has arranged himself at Paul's feet, as he always does, Cassandra suddenly points to the dog and says, "You weren't angry at him when *he* was sick."

"What do you mean?" Paul asks. His eyes are closed and he's already half asleep, but he makes himself wake up. He makes himself pay attention to his wife.

"You remember. When your dog was a puppy. You told me that you were on Craigslist looking for a second printer to buy for your office when you accidentally ended up on the page where people were selling puppies. You said there was a posting that offered a six-week-old German shepherd puppy for free except that he was sick, and if someone didn't take him that day, the owner was going to have him euthanized. You didn't even ask me—you were already at work, so you just called me and said you were going to get the puppy. You had to take the train all the way to New Jersey to pick him up."

"I remember. I don't know what it was—maybe I thought it was my good deed for the year—but I couldn't just scroll past that post once I saw it. I hadn't had a dog since I was a kid, but... well. My plan was to get the dog, bring him to a vet and board him there until they treated him for whatever was wrong, and then find a shelter that would take him in. But it turned out he had parvo, and it was going to be a while until he recovered—*if* he did. It wasn't a sure thing, so—you must remember all this—I had to bring him home for a few weeks and take care of him myself. I had to get up at night to give him medicine, and then he'd fall asleep in my lap. He was really just a baby, and he was so weak, so sick, that I'd sit with him, holding him, trying to make him feel safe. That was it, I guess. I got attached to him and couldn't give him up."

"So, see?" Cassie says, patting Paul on the back as if she had just concluded teaching a lesson to a particularly dull student. "You weren't mad at your dog for being sick."

"I told you, Cassie," Paul says. "I'm not mad at you. Really. I'm sorry if I ever seemed like I was."

This time, he probably means what he says. But now, *he* can't fall asleep while Cassandra quickly dozes off. One of the effects of the medications she's taking is that she sleeps deeply, drifting off to dreamland with no trouble at all. Lying beside his wife, Paul thinks about all the grief she carries, all the anger that rages inside her. Old grief about her sister, old anger at her parents, at long-gone boyfriends and lovers. *And at me too*, Paul thinks. *She probably has reasons to be angry at me too.* He's already declared that he holds no anger toward her—but what about love? After all these years, after all that's happened—does Paul still love Cassandra? Does the sleepless husband still love his wife?

Looking over at Cassandra, in his mind's eye, Paul sees another woman in her place: the cool, captivating beauty that a friend introduced him to one long-ago night. The beautiful woman with those extraordinary blue eyes who knew the power of her appearance. But now, in this moment, this sleepless, late-night time of revelations, it occurs to Paul that the power Cassandra once had is gone. The pretty girl, the beautiful woman who relied on her beauty to hide her insecurities and to get the things she wanted even when she wasn't sure what those really were, is gone. Gone for good. Now, she's just a middle-aged housewife with dark brown hair that's been trimmed short and dyed once a month at a beauty parlor—which Paul is not supposed to know about—and a slimness that is beginning to look fragile, almost breakable. So he asks himself again: Does he still love this version of Cassandra? If he loved her through all the years that she was beautiful *because* she was beautiful, then he deserves every horrible recrimination that he can hurl at himself. But even if he doesn't love her anymore or love her as much as he once did, there is no question that he is a married man who will always be married to this woman—not only because that was a vow he made years ago, but because—*let's face it,* he tells himself—he's getting old. No, maybe not *getting*—he *is* old. So what is he supposed to do? Pack a suitcase, whistle for his dog, and walk out of the house to look for another great love that will strike him blind with desire? And then what happens after the door closes behind him? Does he just leave his poor, damaged wife to fend for herself?

Maybe. Or maybe something like that. If this was a movie, it wouldn't matter how old he was because, on film, he would still be handsome and strong—the man who once wooed and won the beautiful Cassandra. And that man would lie; he would ask a neighbor to come sit with his wife for a while and then yes, hurry downstairs, where a convertible would be parked at the curb—a gorgeous car, something European, sleek and fast. He would jump in, and with only the dog beside him and the suitcase in the back seat, drive off into the sunset to start a new life.

But for Paul, a man who carefully plans every step he takes and only once acted on the forces of uncontrollable passion—his passion for Cassandra—the practicalities of the driving-into-the-sunset dream immediately arise. For example, where is the man in the convertible actually headed? And what is he going to do as night falls—find a motel that permits guests to share their room with a huge dog? And how is he going to fund this escape? Is he going to live on his savings? On Social Security? Or is he going to get a job as a lumberjack in Montana? Work in an oil field in Alaska? Not at his age, he's not. And what will happen to his wife once the neighbor realizes that he's never coming back? Would Paul suddenly remember a large inheritance he'd received from a long-lost aunt and use it to set up a lifetime trust for Cassandra so she'll be taken care of whether or not she recovers from her breakdown? *No*, Paul reminds himself, *her manic episode*.

He reaches over to his nightstand and picks up his phone. Texting his brother, he asks, *Are you awake?*

Yes, Danny replies. *How's Cassie?*

She says she's okay, Paul types, *but it doesn't seem like she is.*

And she probably isn't, Danny replies. *Don't believe anything she says. I know how these things go. Some days are good, some days are bad. Very bad. That's how it'll be for a while. Maybe forever. It's impossible to predict.*

She's not an addict, Paul types. *That's what you mean, isn't it? That's how things are for you.*

I see the similarities, Danny messages his brother. *Even in recovery, every day is scary.*

But life is scary in general, don't you think? Paul replies.

Worse when you feel crazy, even if you don't know that's how you feel. And even if you do. One way or another, we're all headed for a breakdown, even if it never happens.

Well, that's comforting.

You're being sarcastic, but that's okay. I'm still here if you need me. Always. You know that.

So is this role reversal? Do you want to be the older brother now?

It could be time for that. Why don't we try it for a while?

Danny ends the conversation with a smiley face emoji and Paul turns off his phone. At the foot of the bed, the dog sighs in his sleep. *Follow him*, Paul tells himself. *Go to sleep.* Eventually, he does.

The next day, Paul decides that he has to go back to the loft. He just can't work at home; it's the wrong place, the wrong environment, but he's going to have to take his wife with him because he knows that he can't leave her alone in the apartment all day. He makes coffee for them both as he listens to the radio, listens to voices that travel on invisible airwaves to bring him news about the traffic, the weather, the state of the world. Cassandra is mostly quiet; when Paul asks how she's feeling she says she's fine. The vials of pills they left the hospital with are lined up on the kitchen counter, and Paul is trying to figure out how to suggest that his wife take her medication when she opens the pill bottles one by one and swallows them with her coffee.

"See?" she says as she puts the cap back on one of the vials. "You don't have to tell me. I know what I need to do." She walks over to Paul, puts her arms around him, and lays her cheek against his. "I want to get better," she says. "I know I've been confused."

"It's alright," Paul says. "You'll be okay. We will." Then, as if it's an idea that has suddenly occurred to him out of the blue, he tells his wife that he'd like her to come to his office with him, and she agrees.

"Sounds like fun," Cassandra tells Paul.

"But you know I have to work, right? You can watch TV there or use my extra laptop . . . whatever you like."

"I have a book that I was reading. I'll bring that with me too."

"Great," Paul says. "I'll order an Uber." He picks up his phone to use the app, but Cassandra stops him.

"I want to walk," she says. "I want to walk over the bridge just like you do every day with your damn dog." And just like that, her mood has changed. Now, she's getting angry again: Her breathing quickens, and those remarkable blue eyes darken. Her body tenses as if she's readying for a fight.

"That's fine," Paul says calmly. "We can walk over the bridge. I heard the weather on the radio. It's going to be a nice day."

As Cassandra goes into the bedroom to change, Paul notices that the dog hasn't eaten any of the food he put out for him. Usually, he makes a beeline for his bowl as soon as he hears a can being opened, but Paul realizes that this morning, King has been staying out of sight. He goes to look for the dog and finds him lying on the floor in the hallway, pressed up against the front door. Without saying a word, Paul returns to the kitchen, picks up the dog's bowl, and brings it out to him, then stands by as he eats, gulping down his food as if it's going to be snatched away from him at any minute. *Somehow, this will all fix itself,* Paul thinks. Hopes. If the dog is still this unnerved by Cassandra—which, Paul guesses, must be what's going on with him—how are they all going to get through the rest of the day? And then the next day, and the next?

"I'm ready," Cassandra announces cheerfully. As she walks into the hallway, the dog tries to back up even farther against the door, but Cassandra doesn't seem to notice. "Do you want to get going?" she asks.

"Yes," Paul says. "Sure." He runs around the apartment, grabbing his jacket, his backpack, his keys, and sprints back into the hallway. Cassandra is smiling at him, but the dog is still pressed up against the door. Paul slips on his collar and attaches his leash. "Okay," he says, trying to force a bright tone into his voice. "Here we go." Paul has to tug on the leash to get the dog to follow him, but he wins that battle and is finally able to lead the way out of the apartment and down the stairs to the street. The bridge is just a short walk from their building.

As they near the pedestrian entrance, Paul can see that the walkway is already crowded with people. Some are on their way to work, others are tourists pausing to take pictures or just admire the view of the city and the sparkling river beneath the bridge. So, on this sunny spring morning, it's clearly going to require some patience to get all the way over to the Manhattan side of the span. King is used to the push-pull of crowds on the bridge, but Cassandra isn't, and Paul can tell that she's getting nervous. He's been holding her hand, but as they start the walk across the bridge, he grips it tighter, trying to keep her right by his side.

Over to the west, there's a bank of gray clouds on the horizon, stacked up like bars of lead. Suddenly, the wind begins to pick up, pushing the clouds toward the bridge. Someone's hat blows away, a woman's skirt is lifted by a billowing gust. No one seems bothered by this sudden change in the weather. It's an adventure, a story they'll tell their friends later or entertain their coworkers with when they get to the office. But as the clouds are propelled closer to the bridge, they momentarily block the sun, darkening the sky and casting a deep shadow over the walkway. As the sunlight disappears, Cassandra suddenly pulls away from Paul and falls to her knees. Lifting up her arms, she crosses her wrists in front of her face as if she's trying to fend off some looming danger.

It takes him a moment, but then Paul realizes that's exactly what she thinks she's doing: trying to repel any possible threat with her golden cuffs—the Wonder Woman bracelets, as Paul named them. Nobody is paying much attention to her, though—she's just one more odd person acting oddly as the larger, more interesting phenomenon of sudden darkness falls across the bridge. Still, Paul knows that he can't just let her go on kneeling in the midst of the crowds and the shadows, so he moves toward her, meaning to grab her arms and help her to her feet. But as soon as he touches her, she looks up at him as if she's never seen him before and then, leaning back, she musters all her strength and strikes him in the face with her clenched fists.

He reels backwards, but he isn't really hurt—just stunned, so he starts to walk toward her again. He takes one step, then another, but before he can reach his wife, King suddenly rushes forward and growls at Cassandra. Maybe she hears him, but with all the noise on the bridge, maybe not. The dog quickly positions himself between Paul and Cassandra and won't move. Paul can still feel his fingers gripping King's leash, so his mind can't offer him an explanation for how the dog got away from him until he looks down at his hand and sees that all he's holding is a ragged piece of leather. Somehow, the dog has bitten through the leash and run toward Cassandra, whom he must perceive as a threat to Paul, so he's standing guard in case she tries to hit him again.

King is six years old, and in all that time, Paul has never known him to be anything but passive, gentle. Yes, he's a huge dog, but maybe because he was once a tiny, sick puppy, or maybe simply because it's his nature, he is usually the one scrambling to find a hiding place if something scares him—which can be anything like a fly buzzing around the house or a napkin falling from the table—just as he's been trying to hide from Cassandra since she came home. But today, right now, he's managed to find the courage to try to protect the one person who has always protected him.

Slowly, Paul walks toward King, who keeps his eyes locked on Paul's face. "It's alright," Paul says to the dog. "I'm fine. Everything's fine." He leans down and wraps his fingers around the ragged end of the leather leash that's dangling from the dog's collar. As he does, King licks Paul's face. "Right," Paul says. "Good boy." With the torn leash firmly in his grip, he reaches for Cassandra's hand and starts pulling her up. In the same way that the dog allowed himself to be calmed, Cassandra now permits Paul to help her to her feet. She lowers her arms and the golden cuffs glint and glitter as the morning brightens once again.

The clouds pass, the sun shines, and the tourists keep taking pictures, the men and women on their way to work keep walking toward the great, bright city at the other end of the bridge. Paul follows along, steering his wife and his dog through the crowds, then off the bridge and along the narrow streets at the edge of Chinatown. Finally, after what feels to Paul like a nearly endless journey, they reach his building and climb the stairs to the loft. Once he's back in familiar territory, the dog finds his favorite corner and lies down. Paul takes Cassandra to the other end of the loft where he has a couch and a few chairs arranged around a coffee table, a space he created to meet with clients in the days when he was looking for new work. He asks his wife if she'd like to sit down, and she says yes, the first words she's spoken since they stepped onto the bridge. He helps her off with her jacket, and as she arranges herself on the couch, she asks Paul for the laptop he said she could use. He brings it to her, and she smiles at him.

"I'm going to do some shopping online," she says. "We could use a few things for the apartment, don't you think?"

"Sure," Paul says. "That's a good idea."

Apparently, for Cassandra, what happened on the bridge is over, gone, done—if it ever even happened at all. But when Paul walks over to his desk, which sits between the two windows at the front of the loft, King immediately gets to his feet as if he's waiting for some new threat to appear. "You know where we are," Paul says to the dog. "I'm safe. You're safe." He pats the dog on the head and turns on his desktop computer. The screens light up and Paul opens the files he's working on. Eventually, the dog lies down again and goes to sleep.

Paul tries to work on the department store's annual report for a while, but his thoughts keep taking him elsewhere. An idea has occurred to him, and he decides that he should stop what he's doing to at least make some notes. He opens a new file on the computer and starts typing words, then sentences, until he realizes that what he's doing is putting together a narrative, a story that seems to be writing itself. Excited, he looks through his desk drawers until he finds a pad of drawing paper and begins to doodle. The doodles soon turn into pictures, so he opens a new program on the computer and begins digitally recreating both the text and the doodles until, within an hour, he has begun to sketch out the first pages of the graphic novel that until about an hour ago had existed in his mind only as a hope, a seed. But now, on the computer screen, there are two pages of text and illustrations, the beginning of a story that Paul thinks he'll call *King the Wonder Dog*.

What Paul has drawn is a German shepherd wearing a cape that billows out behind him, lifted by the wind. The dog is standing on a bridge that spans a sparkling river winding around a great city of towers and spires. The dog and his master are the guardians of the city, whose citizens have called upon them to thwart a sinister threat that may destroy everything in its path. Paul hasn't yet decided what the threat is or how to depict the man standing beside the dog, but he's sure he'll figure that out. He's happy with what he's done so far, but he can't spend the entire day working on this—he has to finish the annual report. So, reluctantly, he closes the wonder dog file and goes back to plotting out a graph about the department store's sales projections for next year.

Early in the afternoon, Cassandra tells Paul that she wants to have lunch, so he calls a nearby diner and has sandwiches delivered. When the food arrives, Paul sets everything out on the coffee table and eats with his wife while he also feeds pieces of his lunch to King, who is not quite a wonder dog, but still. Still, he's a living creature, cherished by the man who rescued him from certain death. After they've eaten, Cassandra goes back to her online shopping and Paul spends the rest of the afternoon doing the work that he's supposed to be doing. Soon, he's almost finished—he's almost completed the last pieces of the last outside project he ever intends to do, so he closes the file. He turns off the computer and sits in his chair, gazing out the windows at the front of the loft that look out on nothing but a blank brick wall.

Time passes. The afternoon turns into evening; evening settles upon the busy city as Paul takes out his pencil and his pad of paper and begins to draw again. At first, he thinks that what he's drawing is the man standing next to King the Wonder Dog. But no—that's not it at all. In this last hour of his workday, Paul realizes that what he's drawing is an image of himself, of Paul, tall and lean, gray-haired, a little stooped. Then he adds in his worried dog and his sad, troubled wife, all of them walking toward the Brooklyn Bridge. So this isn't the continuation of the wonder dog story; it isn't a cartoon or a graphic tale. Nope, it's real life. That's the real Paul, the real dog, the real woman, all of them on their way to a bridge that they'll walk across again tonight and then tomorrow and the day after that and, probably, for many days, weeks, years to come, for as long as they are able. Walking together for as long as they can.

LUCKY

The feeling Jeanne had, the sudden comprehension that she had somehow stepped outside of life, came upon her in the dress department of Macy's on 34th Street in Herald Square. She hadn't been to Macy's in many years, and at first she'd been confused about the layout of the store, which was different than she remembered. Even the department where she would go every so often to buy a new handbag, which used to be on the first floor right near the front door, had vanished. Now, the whole first floor seemed to be filled with display cases of perfumes—*fragrances*, as Jeanne heard the women behind the counters describe the crystal orbs and dewy atomizers they were showing to passing shoppers. Finally, she saw a sign near the escalator listing the store's departments and located the floor where she would find dresses, which was what she had come for, so she stepped onto the moving stairs and was lifted upward.

But even the dress department was not as she remembered. In past shopping trips, she had been able to browse through long, orderly racks of dresses arranged by size, but all that was gone. Instead, what she found was a collection of designer shops, each a brightly lit island of silk, leather, and glitter, where slender mannequins were posed to demonstrate how to step out of a limousine or prepare for a night of clubbing. Walking on, Jeanne finally found a small selection of clothes that included the kind of dresses Jeanne might have worn to work in the past, arranged on hangers in a far corner. Jeanne, who was retired from a career as a textbook editor in a publishing house, didn't actually need a new dress, but she had promised herself that she would buy one just as a way of proving to herself that she was still able to do something like this: get on the subway, go to Macy's, ride the escalator to the right floor, and buy something nice for herself.

Jeanne had contracted coronavirus last year even though she had been vaccinated, and she had become very sick. In fact, when her doctor thought she could bear to hear what he was going to tell her, he sat down on her bedside in the hospital where she had been a patient for over a month, wracked with fever, barely conscious, breathing with the help of an oxygen mask that was like half of a hard, transparent plastic egg taped over her face, and explained that she had come close to dying. *But you're going to get better*, he told her. And she did, but now, even though she was arguably "better," she was not completely well. *Long Covid* was the current description for the fact that her lungs were irreversibly scarred and she had to carry a rescue nebulizer with her at all times because when she couldn't catch her breath—which happened often—she had to inhale albuterol sulfate to restore her body's ability to function, at least up to a point: the point at which she would not suffocate in the dress department of Macy's, for example. But so far, though the fatigue that was also one of the symptoms of her illness was beginning its daily invasion of her mind and body, she was at least breathing without too much pain.

So she began to look through the dresses—and that's when it suddenly became apparent to her that despite the promise she'd made to herself, there really was no point in what she was doing. Her working life was over, she had worn nothing but denim and

T-shirts (long sleeves, short sleeves, plain ones, some with slogans that advised fighting climate change or restoring abortion rights—things like that) since she had been released from the hospital, and she could see no reason in this year or any to follow that she would need to pull a dress over her head, put on the high-heeled shoes she wasn't even sure were still stuck in the back of her closet, and do anything that required her to look like someone other than the person she now felt herself to be—an old lady growing relentlessly older, whose sleek brown hair was fading to gray (and sprouted from her head in unruly spindles); whose black eyeliner was probably too black for a woman her age; and who, most of the time, could hardly walk a block without needing to find a bench or a low wall to sit down and take a rest. And whether or not that picture of herself was truly accurate, at that moment, standing by the rack of dresses in the women's sportswear department, it certainly felt like it was. At that moment, she felt that the life she had lived up until then—or maybe up until she had been admitted to the hospital—was over for good, and she had been shoved outside, somewhere else that was parallel to life but was not life itself. It was a dim place where she could still see what was going on inside real life—the more brightly lit place on the other side of wherever she was, much like Macy's islands of fashion—but that she could no longer enter. That woman, in the dim place, standing on the parallel track outside of life, did not need a new dress, no matter how much she had managed to convince herself otherwise. What she did need was to get out of Macy's as soon as possible and go home.

Slowly, being mindful of her breathing, Jeanne walked back across the floor, following the signs that directed her to the down escalator. As she stepped on the moving stairs, she noticed that these were the old wooden stairs that had been carrying shoppers up and down the higher floors of Macy's since the escalators had first been installed back in the early years of the last century. It was the kind of information that only someone who had been born in New York, lived here all her sixty-eight years, and was interested in odd facts and trivia relating to the city would keep stored in her mind. The moving wooden stairs were narrow and felt somewhat unsteady beneath her feet, so Jeanne held onto the handrail of each section of the escalator until smooth steel steps replaced the wooden stairs and she arrived at the fragrant first floor where she made her way to the front door and out to the street.

She headed for the subway and down to the platform. When the train came, she found a seat, then leaned back and closed her eyes, listening to the sound of the subway cars as they rattled through the dark tunnels. The noise was both loud and familiar. When she was a child, the screeching wheels and the sharp metal clanking of the chains that linked the cars together as they swayed and sparked had frightened her, but now they were just the background sounds of the trip from Manhattan to her stop about half an hour away in Queens, and she paid them no attention. But when she opened her eyes and looked around, the feeling of being outside of where she was quickly returned. The people sitting in the hard plastic seats as the cars shuddered around curves or sped along straight sections of track existed as far away from her as the planets were from each other up above ground, beyond the sky, out there in the great mysterious unknown. When the train neared her stop and she stood up to grab onto a pole near the exit doors, Jeanne felt herself begin to gasp for air, so she reached into her purse, pulled out the nebulizer, and inhaled a few puffs of the rescue solution. No one paid any attention. This was New York City; no one would have even batted an eye if she had taken out a needle and shot herself full of heroin. Everyone carried some kind of medicine. Everyone had their own way of getting through the day.

Jeanne only had to walk a few blocks to get home. It was a bright, cool fall day; dry brown leaves crunched underfoot, though the trees were still leafy enough to separate the sunshine into puzzle pieces of light and shadow that fell across the sidewalk. She lived in a co-op apartment in a quiet building where the tenants' mailboxes stood in rows along the wall in the vestibule, looking like safety deposit boxes in an old neighborhood bank. Jeanne let herself in and then took the elevator up to her apartment on the tenth floor. It was a small place: one bedroom, a galley kitchen, a living room with a tiny terrace that provided a view of the rooftops and boulevards of central Queens. But, as always, what Jeanne first saw when she stepped into her apartment was her dog, a ten-pound gray-and-white terrier whose nails click-clacked on the parquet floor as he ran toward her. He was six years old, and his name was Rocket. Jeanne had named him in a fanciful mood, in a time before she knew anything about Covid-19 or could have envisioned herself as a person with a chronic illness that put limitations on her life. He had been an energetic puppy she found in a local shelter just after she retired, and she pictured herself chasing him through a nearby park where there was a lake and walking paths that wound through stands of tall oaks and maple trees. *My little pocket rocket*, she had thought when she first picked him up and he had happily licked her face.

There were times now when Jeanne felt that she was not giving Rocket enough exercise because the park was too far away for her to walk to anymore, so when she took him out in the morning and again in the evening, they usually just strolled along the length of a chain-link fence that surrounded a nearby playground. There were flowery shrubs planted along the border of the sidewalks, and in the playground, there was a red-and-gold-painted dragon with three loops in his long body for children to climb on. So Rocket didn't get to run much when he was outside, but he made up for it whenever Jeanne came home, zooming in from the bedroom where he was usually sleeping, barking like he was ready to go out of his mind, and then running circles around her feet until she lifted him up and carried him around.

For the past few months, Jeanne had been paying a woman named Mona Giddings to come over three afternoons a week to take Rocket for an extra walk. Mona's dog-walking business had been recommended by a friend, and she had also ended up keeping Rocket in her apartment for the month that Jeanne had been in the hospital last year. Mona usually brought her daughter with her when she came to take Rocket for his walk. The daughter, Susie, was thirteen, a somber, dark-eyed girl who seemed to light up when Jeanne handed Rocket's leash to her. Mona said that Susie had come to really love Rocket and enjoyed being the one to walk the little dog, though Mona, of course, was always with them.

Jeanne ate a late lunch while she watched the cable news, though she often asked herself why she subjected herself to this endlessly depressing parade of poisonous politics, decimated nations, and the murder of innocents. Maybe, she thought, it was a way of trying to keep herself connected to the outside world, crazy and dangerous as it was, as her inside world was growing smaller. This apartment, the streets around the playground, the supermarket, the pharmacy—where else did she go anymore? Maybe to neighborhood yard sales in the summer or to local winter festivals where she bought pies she didn't really mean to eat and pumpkins she had no idea what to do with except leave them on a windowsill until she took them downstairs to the trash. And as for the supermarket and the pharmacy, she didn't really have to visit them in person because they would deliver whatever she needed, but she was trying not to cut off those few small trips that she still felt some confidence in allowing herself.

Mona and Susie were due today around three o'clock, and they showed up right on time, as they always did. And Rocket, who seemed to have set a timer for their arrival in whatever part of his brain kept track of that information, happily barked and danced around even before they rang the bell.

"Hi," Jeanne said, smiling as she opened the door. "Good to see you both."

Mona was an attractive woman in her early forties who was always dressed in crisp button-down shirts and fashionable jeans, sometimes carefully ripped at the knee, augmented by denim jackets or bright white puffer coats as the seasons progressed from warm to cool to cold. Susie, on the other hand, was at the age when dressing to meet the pressure of whatever influencers she followed on social media was paramount, so her attire tended to feature specific items like tight black leggings and slouchy hoodies embossed with trendy brand names. Jeanne was amused by Susie's clothes, remembering the kinds of things that were must-haves when she was a young teenager deep into her hippie phase: flowered skirts, go-go boots, wide velvet pants. So, though perhaps in an unexpected way, she thought that she related to how Susie adorned herself because she understood the impulse to dress like your friends and to believe that those clothes made some sort of important social statement. There was a time when Jeanne had a closet full of clothes that represented both how seriously she took her work and yet how much effort she also devoted to her appearance, which included a daily consideration of which shoes, jackets, and jewelry would help to perfect a particular outfit. But those days—as her experience at Macy's had reminded her—were not these days. They were not today, when Jeanne placed Rocket's leash in Susie's hand and said goodbye to the dog walker, her daughter, and the little dog. She also gave Mona a check for $240, this month's fee for taking Rocket on his extra parades around the park, which were meant to last around half an hour, depending on the weather. Even though it could sometimes be a burdensome expense, Jeanne told herself the worth of giving the dog some extra time outside was also worth it to her.

After she closed the door, Jeanne went back to the couch, picked up the TV remote, and began clicking through the cable channels for something to watch. She found a British mystery featuring a troubled detective that she had been following, and that was the last thing she remembered until she woke with a start, looked at her watch, and realized that two hours had passed. *Two hours.* Like some old lady with nothing on her mind but maybe a leftover slice of cake in the fridge or whether or not it was laundry day, Jeanne had fallen asleep on the couch and slept so deeply that nothing on heaven and earth had awakened her. *Okay, fine,* she thought as she stood up and looked around, thinking that something was wrong but unable to figure out what it was, *I'm okay, I'm okay, I just have to get my bearings.*

She took a deep, careful breath and looked around again. *Something is definitely wrong,* she advised herself. *What is it? Think! What's the matter with you?* And then she knew. *Rocket. Where's Rocket? Where's my dog?*

She searched through her memory, which seemed to be struggling to return to her, as if it had taken the shape of a lost creature wandering through a forest who was still collecting the breadcrumbs that would lead it home, and finally recalled handing Rocket's leash to Susie Giddings. After that, everything went blank until she woke up. And now, it was way past the time that Susie and Mona should have returned the dog to her. Maybe they had rung the bell, knocked on the door and received no answer, so they had taken Rocket back home with them. That's what Jeanne thought must have happened, so she picked up her phone and dialed Mona's cell number, but there was no answer. Next, she called the landline in the house, which went straight to voicemail. Jeanne left a message on both phones, apologizing for the mix-up that had prevented Mona and Susie from returning Rocket, asked Mona to call her back, and then paced around the apartment for what seemed like a long time during which the phone did not ring. The silence, though, rang from every corner of the apartment, every corner of Jeanne's mind. It was dinnertime: Unless Mona, Susie, and Mona's husband and son had gone out for dinner, there was no reason that someone wouldn't be home to answer the phone.

And even if they were out at a restaurant, there was still no reason Jeanne could think of that would prevent Mona from giving her a quick call. As time passed, the matter of getting the dog back was swelling to the size of anxiety in Jeanne's mind and then rounding up to a dimension that was getting very hard to contain.

Again, Jeanne called Mona's cell phone and the landline, but no one lifted the receiver or swiped up or sideways or whatever was necessary to connect the call. *I'm sure nothing is really wrong*, Jeanne told herself, and then came up with another theory: *Maybe Mona thinks something happened to me and I was taken back to the hospital, where I am now lying on a gurney in a crowded emergency room, drifting in and out of consciousness, so she isn't even checking her phone to see if I'm trying to reach her. That must be it*, Jeanne convinced herself, because she couldn't imagine what else to think. So, holding fast to that idea, she decided that she was obligated to go to Mona's apartment, apologize in person for the inconvenience she had caused, offer extra payment for the unplanned hours that had been spent caring for Rocket, and then take her dog home.

It was evening now, and the sky had taken on a dramatic appearance, unfurling long, dark blue clouds that flew across the horizon like they were being whipped. The streetlights flashed on, and people hurried home from work, home to their families, but Jeanne felt like she was walking in the opposite direction from everyone she passed, heading not to her own home but to someone else's. And she was walking as quickly as she could without worrying that she might lose her breath and have to stop to use the inhaler—or worse, need to rest in front of some building where a doorman was likely to come out and ask why she was lingering on private property. She thought about doormen because after walking about ten blocks—a long stretch for her—she was now in a more upscale neighborhood than the one where she lived. Here, there were newer high-rises, condominium towers with uniformed doormen who answered only to the title "concierge." In most of the buildings, they stood behind marble desks in marble-walled lobbies barring passage to the golden elevators that leapt upwards to the apartments above. When Jeanne reached Mona's building, she spoke to the concierge who was positioned behind the desk in that particular lobby, where the décor was white marble veined with gold. She told him her name and who she wanted to see.

The concierge picked up the house phone, held it to his ear, and nodded a few times. "I see," he said, and then placed the phone back in its cradle. "Mrs. Giddings said to tell you that she's not available right now."

"What?" Jeanne said. "She has my dog. I just want to go upstairs and get him."

"Well," the concierge said, "maybe you can phone her directly."

"She's not answering my calls," Jeanne told him.

"Then it might make sense to try later," the concierge replied and began busily sorting through some papers on his desk.

Jeanne felt perplexed. She couldn't figure out why Mona wouldn't see her, but she was also confused about why she was having what seemed like an argument—couched in politeness, but an argument nonetheless—with a man in a uniform that meant nothing other than that he was hired to stand here and ask people who they were. Maybe sometimes he also got cabs for people, unless that was just something that happened in the movies, since couldn't people just get an Uber these days? Who needed help to summon a cab anymore?

"I don't think I'll try later," Jeanne said. "I think I'll go upstairs now."

"No ma'am," the concierge said. He moved from the center of the round marble barrier that was his home base, closer to the electric gate near his desk that kept him inside and anyone else out. "I can't let you do that."

"Yes, you can," Jeanne said, "because that's what I'm going to do."

The concierge buzzed the gate open and stepped in front of Jeanne. "I really can't allow you to get into the elevators," he told her.

This whole experience seemed unreal to Jeanne—but also frightening. A man was standing in front of her, so close that she could smell the cigarette smoke on the black wool of his uniform jacket and notice that the gold epaulettes on his shoulders looked greasy. And she still couldn't imagine why Mona wouldn't let her come upstairs. How crazy was all this? *Very crazy*, Jeanne advised herself. *I have no idea why any of this is happening.*

"Look," Jeanne said, hoping that her voice sounded much steadier than she felt, "I am going upstairs because Mrs. Giddings has my dog and I want him back. I pay her to walk him and for some reason, today, she decided to take him home instead of returning him to me, so I came to get him and that's what I'm going to do."

The concierge did not move. "Well, I don't know anything about that," he said and took a step closer, like he was going to do something that involved physical contact.

"If you touch me," Jeanne said, "I will call the police." She quickly scrabbled in her shoulder bag and pulled out her cell phone. "In fact, I may call the police anyway if I don't have my dog back in the next five minutes."

The concierge spent a moment or two thinking about what Jeanne had said, and then, with a sweep of his arm that oozed sarcasm, stepped aside to let her pass. Jeanne pushed the button for the elevator, and as she waited for it to arrive, she heard the concierge whispering into the house phone and assumed he had called Mona again to warn her that the unwanted visitor was on her way up.

When Jeanne arrived at Mona's floor and stepped out of the elevator, she could see Mona standing outside her door at the end of the hallway with her arms folded across her chest. As Jeanne walked toward her, Mona said, "I did send the message that we aren't available right now, didn't I? We're eating dinner."

Deciding she would pretend that nothing out of the ordinary was going on, Jeanne said, "I'm so sorry about that. Really. So I'll just take Rocket and go."

"We did try to return him to you. We rang your bell. You didn't answer."

"Again, I'm very sorry. I fell asleep. That's been happening to me lately . . . I just drop off and I guess, this time, I didn't hear you. You know I was sick, Mona." Jeanne offered that reminder as a plea for establishing a truce because she was getting the feeling that Mona was angry about the situation—much angrier than could possibly be called for but, *Oh well,* Jeanne thought. *Who can understand some people?*

"If you're that sick," Mona said, "maybe you shouldn't have a dog right now."

"I don't understand," Jeanne said. "What are you talking about?"

"Do you know what time it is? It's almost seven o'clock and you've just shown up now. Were you even going to feed that poor dog?"

"Mona," Jeanne began, but before she could say anything else, the door suddenly opened, and Susie slipped outside.

Looking up at her mother, Susie said, "Why is she here?"

Jeanne was beginning to feel even more bewildered than when she'd been talking to the concierge, but now little warning bells were going off behind the feeling of confusion because of the hostility she heard in Susie's voice. It was a sharp sound, much too cruel for a thirteen-year-old to know how to use so expertly. All this was truly inexplicable to Jeanne. Up until today, she had always had a perfectly friendly relationship with both mother and daughter, so why on earth were they behaving as if they barely knew her? As if she were some irresponsible stranger whose dog they had rescued from ill treatment?

"Okay," Jeanne said, "I really don't understand what's going on here, but I'd like you to just get Rocket for me, and I'll be on my way. I'll pay you for the extra time you kept him."

"Don't insult me," Mona said and turned away, as if Jeanne was offering a ransom fouled by her inability to see the error of her own ways.

Clearly, she wasn't getting anywhere with Mona, so Jeanne turned to Susie. "Honey," she said, "I'm sorry if I interrupted your dinner, and I'm sorry I didn't answer the door when you and your mom came by earlier, but I'm here now, so please just go get Rocket. I need to take him home."

"I like him better than you do," Susie said. "I don't think you take very good care of him. You left him alone for a month! And tonight you didn't even want him back."

"Susie," Jeanne said, speaking slowly and deliberately, hoping that would help her not to lose her temper, "I paid your mom a lot of money to take care of Rocket for me during that time, and I'm very grateful for her help, and yours. As for tonight, as I told your mom, I feel asleep, and I'm sorry for that. I'm going to bet that must have happened to you once or twice. Maybe when you were watching TV or listening to . . ." She was going to say *listening to the radio*, but that was ridiculous. Kids didn't listen to the radio anymore, so she tried a generic term because it occurred to her that she had no idea how someone Susie's age would be transferring today's pop songs into her head. "Listening to music," she said.

Suddenly, Jeanne was seized with a fit of coughing. This was also a symptom of long Covid, but it was manifesting itself at a bad time. A very bad time—and it was a very bad attack that was causing Jeanne to feel like she was suffocating. She had to lean against the wall to steady herself as she pulled her inhaler from the pocket of her jacket and breathed in the solution. Then breathed in more.

"See?" Mona said. "You're still really sick. Who knows how much you must be neglecting that poor dog because you should probably be back in the hospital. Or maybe in some rehab somewhere."

As Jeanne continued to struggle to catch her breath, she heard the *ding* that meant the elevator was stopping at this floor. A moment later, the door slid open, and a female police officer walked toward them. She was a squat, squarish-looking woman with white-blonde hair pulled tight behind her ears and fastened into a small ponytail that sat on the back of her uniform collar. She strode down the hall with a hard, sure step that seemed to broadcast the message that she was ready, willing, and able to enforce all sorts of laws that Jeanne had probably never even heard of.

"Hello," the officer said when she reached the end of the hall, where Jeanne was just beginning to push herself off the wall so she could stand up straight. "I'm Sergeant Douglas. I understand we're having some sort of problem here?"

"Yes." Mona jumped right in, speaking first. "I'm the one who had our concierge call, so thank you for coming, Sergeant. This woman," she said, pointing at Jeanne with a finger that displayed the polish of a perfect pearl-colored manicure, "pushed her way past the concierge after I told him to explain that I didn't want to speak to her, and now she's making threats against me and my daughter."

Incredulous, Jeanne looked over at Mona. "Threats? For heaven's sake, Mona, what did I say that sounded like a threat?"

Mona didn't bother to reply to Jeanne's question. Instead, she continued to address the police officer. "This woman has Covid. She's been very sick for a long time and isn't able to care for her dog, so she gave him to my daughter. Then tonight, out of the blue, she just showed up at my door and demanded that we give the dog back to her."

"Oh my God," Jeanne said. Those words just seemed to slide out of her mouth as a replacement for a scream. "I don't *have* Covid," Jeanne said, looking directly at the officer, whose face, briefly, had registered concern before resetting into a pose of stern neutrality. "I am not contagious. No one is in danger of catching Covid from me if that's what she . . . Mrs. Giddings, I mean . . . seems to want you to believe. I have the ongoing symptoms of a bout of coronavirus that I had about a year ago." Taking a deep breath, imagining that she could still feel the nebulizer's calming solution coating her lungs, steadying her, helping her to think, Jeanne said, "I don't understand what's going on here, Officer. I really don't. I pay this woman to walk my dog. She came to my apartment this afternoon, picked him up for a walk, and apparently, when she brought him back, I didn't answer the doorbell because I fell asleep. I tried to call her, but she wouldn't answer the phone, so I came over here to pick up my dog. That's it. That's the whole story. My dog's name is Rocket," Jeanne added, as if knowing that specific bit of information was undeniable proof of ownership.

Susie now decided that it was her turn to make her case to the police officer. Pointing at Jeanne, she said, "She yelled at me. She called me names. I'm the one who walks Rocket. I'm the one who takes care of him. That's why she gave him to me. She said she knew he would be happier if he lived with me and my mom because I love him so much."

"I never—" Jeanne began, but the officer interrupted her.

"Can I see some proof of identity?" she said to Jeanne.

"Of course," Jeanne replied. Her hands were shaking so badly that she had difficulty pulling her driver's license out of her wallet. But in those few extra moments while everyone watched her struggle, Jeanne's thoughts, which had been bouncing around in her mind like useless blobs, suddenly coalesced into an actual conclusion, a trail she could follow that led her to a deduction worthy of any detective in the mysteries she liked to watch on TV: Susie must want to keep Rocket, and Mona wanted to give Susie what she desired. Maybe she had wanted to keep the dog for a long time, and today, Mona must have decided that Jeanne had given them a reason to do just that. Although falling asleep and not answering a doorbell hardly amounted to animal cruelty, Jeanne could see how Mona had figured out that this was a way to prove that Jeanne couldn't be trusted with the dog. Having the police on the scene was a bonus that could be factored into the plan.

"I have some other documents you might like to see," Jeanne said to the police officer as the woman handed back her driver's license. Quickly scrolling through the photo section of her phone, Jeanne found what she was looking for and turned the screen to face the officer. "This is the adoption certificate from the North Shore Animal League, where I got the dog," Jeanne said. "They had emailed me a copy, and I kept it. That was six years ago."

"So what?" Mona interjected. "I never said she didn't originally adopt the dog. But like my daughter explained, she gave him to us because she's too sick to take care of him."

"I am not too sick to do anything I need to," Jeanne said, emphatically enough that she hoped the three people whose faces had all turned to stare at her clearly understood this was more than a passive statement of self-defense; it was a declaration that she would never even contemplate the idea of giving away her dog to anyone, let alone to the teenage girl who had begun to weep in the background the way a victim unjustly accused of malice softly weeps. That was all for show, but Jeanne was worried that Susie might be doing too good a job of selling her distress.

"As I explained before," Jeanne continued, "I pay Mrs. Giddings to take my dog for an extra walk now and then. Here," she said as another idea occurred to her: more evidence to prove that what she alleged was true. She opened the banking app on her phone and pulled up her checking account. "Look at these," she said as she felt Mona staring over her shoulder, trying to get a peek at Jeanne's phone. "These are pictures of my canceled checks to Mona Giddings—*this* Mona Giddings, standing right here—and in the corner it says, 'For dog walking.' As a matter of fact," Jeanne continued, noticing a serendipitous entry that she hadn't expected to be recorded yet, "this is the check I gave Mrs. Giddings this afternoon, which she's already deposited." Pointing to the entry, Jeanne said, "And see where I wrote, again, 'For dog walking, September'? Why would I have paid her for a month's worth of services if I had just given her my dog to keep?"

The police officer studied the images of the canceled checks and then said, "Okay."

Such a noncommittal response was not exactly what Jeanne had hoped for, but she was not about to give up. "So I hope you can understand that I never meant for Mrs. Giddings to keep my dog this afternoon. I'm sorry Susie feels so upset about this, I really am, but I want to get Rocket back right now and go home."

The officer sighed. It was the deep, weary sigh of a person who had been asked to adjudicate too many matters like this, too many disputes over what—given what else she had to deal with on any given day: violence, danger, madness—she no doubt thought amounted to a minor quarrel over nothing.

"Look," the officer said, "this isn't really a police matter. If you ladies feel that you absolutely cannot settle this disagreement between you, then your next step is probably mediation. You can contact the local community dispute resolution center and ask them to help sort this out. Or, if you both think that the dog is worth all this trouble, then you can both hire lawyers, spend whatever it will cost you, and fight it out in court. But I think I've gone as far as I can go with this."

"Good," Mona said. "Thank you, Officer." She smiled at her daughter and raised her hand to push open her front door.

"No," Jeanne interjected. "This is *not* good." She looked straight at the police officer, who appeared in Jeanne's vision as solid bulk, a square blue uniform bisected by a wide waist bristling with weapons: a gun, a nightstick, a radio murmuring static encoded with news of real crimes, real life-and-death struggles taking place everywhere, all around, and said, "I am not leaving here without my dog because this *is* a police matter. That dog is my property, and Mrs. Giddings has stolen it, which is a crime. Officer Douglas," Jeanne added, sending thanks into the ether for the fact that she had remembered the woman's name, "if you don't feel that you can help me recover my stolen property, which Mrs. Giddings and her daughter have more or less admitted is in their apartment right now, then please get someone else to come here and help me because I am not going to be the victim of a crime that the New York City police force doesn't feel is important enough to do something about."

Where did that speech come from? Jeanne's voice was becoming raspy, a warning that she was going to start coughing again, but with what felt like a sheer act of will, she managed to calm her breathing as she recalled the memory of a dispute she had read about online somewhere about whether dogs were pets or property (*both*, was what she remembered as the consensus) that had helped her come up with the argument she'd just made, and it had an effect. The policewoman shifted her weight from one foot to another and adjusted the thin yellow ponytail coiled against the back of her neck. She frowned, but this time, during this pause, she did not sigh.

"Show me the dog," she said to Mona.

"Why?" Mona asked. "He's fine."

"I asked you to show him to me, so you should do that. Now," the officer added as Mona appeared to hesitate before pushing open the door that just a few moments ago she had been eager to walk through.

Finally, Mona looked over at Susie. "Go get the doggie," she said to her daughter, who continued to sniffle and weep as she disappeared into the apartment.

Doggie. Jeanne, whose brain felt supercharged with information, analyzed that sobriquet as a further attempt to claim ownership of Rocket. Only the dog's real owner would be calling him by a nickname, right? *Yes*, she warned herself, but also, *No. It won't work. I won't let it.*

It seemed to take a long time for Susie to reappear, also a ruse, Jeanne guessed, meant to indicate that the poor doggie didn't want to leave his new home. But eventually, Susie returned, holding the little terrier tight against her chest. Rocket knew Susie and Mona well, and he had, in fact, lived in this apartment for that month when Jeanne was in the hospital, so perhaps he should have been unperturbed to be clasped in Susie's arms, but instead, as soon as he saw Jeanne, he began to whine. *That's my good doggie*, Jeanne silently congratulated him as he amped up his discomfort by starting to wiggle and squirm as Susie tried to keep him quiet.

"Put him down," the policewoman said.

"I don't want to," Susie told her.

The policewoman turned to address Mona. "Tell her to put the dog down on the floor."

"But—" Mona began.

"I'm not going to say it again," the officer warned.

Mona puffed out a dramatic sigh but then acquiesced. "Do what she says," she told her daughter.

Reluctantly, Susie bent down and let go of the dog. For a brief moment he didn't seem to know what to do, but then he ran straight to Jeanne, stood up on his hind legs, and began to paw at her. Without even asking if it was okay, Jeanne picked up the dog and held him against her. He panted wildly and licked her face.

The police officer let that scene play out for a moment or so and then looked over at Mona. "Do you really want to go on with this?" she asked. "Miss?" she said, addressing Susie.

"She doesn't take care of him!" Susie wailed in response. "I do. He loves me. What you're doing isn't fair, none of you!" Turning to her mother, she said, "You told me I could have him. You told me! You said she wouldn't want him back."

Susie swiveled around, and her hair, a tangle of long waves, thrashed the air behind her as she ran into the apartment and slammed the door. Trapped outside, Mona glared at Jeanne.

"Why couldn't you just let her have him?"

Stroking the little terrier's ears, feeling his heart thumping against his ribs, her chest, Jeanne said, "Because he's my dog."

Mona tried the handle of the door, but it wouldn't budge, so she began banging on it. Shortly, it was opened by a teenage boy with a set of headphones clamped against his ears. The apparatus looked both too heavy and too complex to be dispensing something as simple as music. "Oh, hi," he said to Jeanne. "What's going on?"

"Hi, Kenny." The boy was Mona's son, whom Jeanne had met once or twice before. "Your mom will tell you," Jeanne said as Mona strode past him and disappeared inside.

The boy shrugged and reached over to pet Rocket. "Hey, fella," he said. "The crazy ladies bothering you again?"

Jeanne found herself wondering if she counted as one of the crazy ladies, but she really didn't care. "Can you do me a favor?" she said to the boy. "Your mom forgot to give me Rocket's leash. Can you get it for me?"

"Sure," the boy said. "It's hanging right here, in the coat closet." He handed over the dog's collar and leash and went back into the apartment. Jeanne heard the locks click behind him.

Kneeling, Jeanne put the dog down on the floor and fastened his collar around his neck. When she stood up again, she saw the officer striding down the hallway toward the elevators, and she followed. Walking beside her, the terrier's nails sounded very loud as they clicked along on the black-and-white tiles. Jeanne imagined that everyone in every apartment on the floor could hear him, so she picked him up again.

"Thank you," she said to the policewoman as they waited for the elevator.

The woman nodded. She wasn't looking at Jeanne, though. Her body was turned toward the elevator, and her eyes never wavered from whatever point on the door with its layers of peeling green paint she was staring at.

"My sister-in-law's mother died of Covid about two months ago," the officer said, "and she had every vaccine available. Shots, boosters—everything. She couldn't breathe, and they just couldn't pump enough oxygen into her, I guess. Everyone says that Covid is just like the flu now—all you need to do is get vaccinated, or not, if you don't believe in it. But Covid isn't like the flu. It kills people." Then, finally, she turned to look at Jeanne. "I guess you're going to have to get a new dog walker."

"I hadn't thought about that," Jeanne said, "but maybe I'll let it go for a while. I'll just walk him myself."

"Probably best," the officer replied.

The elevator bell dinged, the doors opened. Jeanne, the policewoman, and the dog rode downstairs. "Thank you again," Jeanne said when they were out on the street.

The officer reached into one of the hidden pockets of her uniform and pulled out a card, which she handed to Jeanne. "I don't think you'll need this, but just in case you do, here's my number at the precinct. You can leave a message if I'm not there."

The police cruiser was double-parked in front of the building. People passing by glanced at it and then walked on. Some of them were probably curious about why the police had been called to this building; others most likely just wanted to walk on by and keep to themselves.

Even though the night had grown chilly, Jeanne wasn't often out after dark anymore, so it felt soothing to be walking under the high, bright moon and the cold blanket of stars. She followed along Queens Boulevard: eight lanes of traffic as wide as a river of red and white taillights, all sailing somewhere, sailing home. By the time Jeanne reached her building, she was beginning to cough yet again, so she stopped, briefly, to use her inhaler, and then led Rocket inside.

As soon as Jeanne opened the front door of her apartment, the dog peed on the parquet floor in the entranceway, something he never did. He had not paused even once to relieve himself all the way home, so this must have been nervous behavior. He sat down and looked at the puddle, then looked up at Jeanne.

"It's okay," she said to the dog. "No harm done."

He ran off and leapt up on the back cushions of the couch where he could sit and look out the window. Jeanne took off her coat and then went into the kitchen for paper towels. After she cleaned up, she microwaved a frozen meal for herself and spooned some dog food into the terrier's dish. She ate; he ate. Everything was back to normal.

She watched TV for a few hours, steeled herself to watch the late news, and then went to bed. The dog followed, climbing up a small set of stairs Jeanne had bought for him so he could reach the bed, which was higher than the couch—too high for him to jump. He circled around a few times, sighed, and was quickly asleep. Jeanne always waited to hear him sigh because she thought it was sweet and also funny. She checked that she had her extra inhaler by the bedside and put her head down on the pillow. Soon, she too was asleep.

She woke up somewhere in the middle of the night, feeling alarmed. Usually, when this happened, it meant she was having trouble breathing but no, that wasn't it—her breathing was regular, easy. It was the memory of the day's events embedded in an already-vanished dream that had stirred her, the long, troubled hours that had carried her from Macy's to the hallway of Mona's apartment, a span of time when nothing good had happened as she moved from one place to the other. But then she looked down at the foot of the bed where the little terrier was stretched out on his side, fast asleep, and changed her mind about the sum total of the day as she remembered how she had stood in the hallway, laser focused on getting her stolen dog back, which meant that she'd had to think clearly, organize her resources, present her documents to the authorities (like in a spy movie, which she was as fond of as detective stories), and make her case.

So I can still do that, she told herself. Pierce the membrane of pain that continued its campaign to envelop her, part the suffocating clouds that sailed into her view and blocked her ability to see herself as who she was and who she remained: a person, a human being, damaged, worried, caught up in a lingering illness, but still capable of meeting the moment when she needed to and fight for herself, for what she cared about. *And that's a clue*, she told herself, alone in the dark with only the sound of the sighing dog, the companion of human beings a thousand years ago—ten thousand—who lived in caves, who looked into the fire that was their singular defense against whatever beasts lurked outside, in the night, and hoped—believed—that dawn would once again meet them with a gentle and temperate light. Maybe it wasn't much, but yes, these things were a clue to what was still meaningful to her, what she could still do for herself when she had to do something. *One clue*, Jeanne thought: It's like a coin you find in the street and think, *Well, it's my lucky day.* And in the days that follow, you look for more.

ELDER CARE

By the time Carole reached her stop, her only company in the train car were a few pigeons. The birds would get on the train at the station where it emerged from the underground tunnel and began to roll along the elevated tracks all the way out to Rockaway, a long, sandy peninsula sticking off the southern tip of Queens. The birds would make the trip, picking up the bits of food left behind by passengers who'd gotten off earlier, then step off the train once it made its way out to the beach. There, they'd cross the tracks and change for the train heading back to the city. The pigeons were smart—even they didn't want to live in this part of Rockaway—and only made the trip to scavenge for free food.

Carole was seventy years old now, but when she was a teenager, she lived here with her father and stepmother in the time when it had been mostly a dumping ground for low-income patients shunted off to nursing homes and for the poor and indigent living in projects that had been built on the cheap. But in the past decade, some areas—particularly along the beachfront—had been undergoing a sudden spurt of development so that these days, there were expensive high-rise condo buildings out here. In the summer, surfers shared the waves with day-tripping hipsters, and the newly rebuilt boardwalk was lined with taco trucks and pop-up shops selling flipflops and sunscreen. The stop where Carole got off the train, though, was in an area that was still undeveloped. As she walked the few blocks to the nursing home where her father now lived, there was no one on the platform and nothing to see on the streets below except empty lots filled with weeds and garbage. She could hear the ocean crashing against the shore nearby, but she was headed in the opposite direction.

Carole came out to Rockaway once every two weeks or so to see her father, though it was more out of a sense of obligation than anything else. It was also to make sure that he was being treated decently and not being retaliated against because her lawyer had made it clear to the administrator of the facility that they couldn't throw him out. It was a strain on her limited budget to even have a lawyer, but it was necessary to deal with the arcane and often inexplicable regulations that governed how Medicaid-funded nursing homes operated. Before she had hired an elder care lawyer, someone recommended by one of the partners at the law firm where she worked as the office manager, Carole would get phone calls from whatever nursing home her father was housed in at the time—and he had already been in four of them—telling her that because he had developed new symptoms to complicate the advanced heart disease and emphysema he already suffered from, her father was too sick to remain in their facility. She had forty-eight hours to find another place for him that provided what they called "stepped-up care" or they would send him to a hospital where he would be relegated to a corridor in the emergency room and be left there for days until Carole found him a bed somewhere else. The lawyer was able to forestall these ultimatums because he knew more about Medicaid than the nursing home administrators and was able to make them stop threatening Carole by issuing his own threats of elder care abuse.

If Carole's father knew that she had a lawyer who was dealing with the nursing home, he would have been upset with her, since "don't make waves" seemed to be one of the guiding principles of his life. Carole had tried to explain to him that the reason he'd been moved from one place to another was because of Medicaid's ever-changing directives, but he didn't believe her. He was convinced it was because she, Carole, was somehow punishing him for things she had been angry about when she was a teenager. Well, she was still angry, but nevertheless, she was doing what was right for him because she would have felt bad about herself if she was base enough to take a teenager's rage out on a helpless old man, even if that old man was still capable of making her feel like a lot of the things that had gone wrong in his life were her doing.

Leo, Carole's father, was ninety-four years old, and there were two things left in his life that he liked to do: watch television and smoke. When Carole came to visit her father, she always brought him a supply of cigarettes—if she didn't, he would complain so much that she'd have to take a cab to the nearest convenience store to get his Marlboros. So today, she was carrying a tote bag with several cartons of cigarettes for him, but she also had something else with her that she wanted to ask him about. There was no guarantee, though, that he would tell her what she wanted to know.

Once Carole got to the nursing home, she took the elevator up to her father's room, which was located on what the facility called the hospital floor. All the patients there were mostly confined to bed and required round-the-clock medical care. Carole's father shared his room with another patient, but that man was fast asleep and snoring loudly as Carole walked in. But Leo was awake and watching the television that was bolted to the wall opposite his bed.

"Hi, Dad," she said as she walked toward him. "How are you today?"

Before answering, he looked over at what she was carrying to ensure she'd brought his cigarettes. Only then did he look up at her and say, "I'm alright, honey."

Leo used to call Carole "honey" when she was a child, but once he married her stepmother, that stopped. The new wife, Helen, was the only person he called "honey" because he was afraid that she might think he cared about his daughter more than her. Helen was an unhappy, temperamental woman whom Leo had met at an organization called Parents Without Partners and married ten months after Carole's mother died of breast cancer. When Carole's father announced to her that he was getting married, she remembered him saying something like, "Well, I've found you a new mommy," and pretty quickly, Carole, who was thirteen, understood that she was supposed to try to forget about the old mommy and replace her with the new one. This was back in 1965, and there wasn't a lot of guidance for her father to follow about how to handle a child's grief, or his own, or the problems inherent in getting married again less than a year after your wife died. Even if there had been some kind of help available, Carole's father, who didn't know how to write a check or shop for groceries or do the laundry, wouldn't have known where to look for it; instead, he just slotted in a new woman to run the household and went back to his job working on the line of a factory that made machine parts. Carole, supposedly, was already carrying on with her regular life of going to school and reading books about girls who liked horses and mooned over the handsome stableboys, so her father decided all was well. But it was not.

Carole did not get along with the new mommy. She fought with her and made everyone's life hell, including her own. (Not that the new mommy tried to get along with Carole either; most of the time it seemed that the opposite was true.) Carole had been a good student up until her mother died, but after that, she started cutting classes and hanging out with "the wrong crowd," as her father referred to the new friends she had sought out. She smoked pot, she had sex, and many nights, she didn't even go home. On the day she turned eighteen, Carole left her father's house and decamped to the East Village, where she rented an apartment in a rattletrap tenement for $50 a month and got a job making sandals in a store on St. Mark's Place. She was still angry, but at least she was on her own and didn't have to get along with anybody but herself, which worked out better for her. It seemed to calm her down.

Now, as she stood by her father's bed in the nursing home, she made a show of turning to look out the window and forcing a smile to appear on her face. "It's not too chilly outside today," she said. "Would you like to go up to the boardwalk for a while?"

"That would be nice," Leo said, reaching for the tote bag and pulling out one of the cartons of Marlboros. He removed a pack while Carole pushed the buzzer by his bed to call an aide. Carole was going to need help getting him out of bed and into a wheelchair in order to take him outside.

When the aide appeared—a thin, weary-looking woman—she sent one quick glance Carole's way before she turned and walked out of the room. This wasn't surprising. Ever since her lawyer had spoken to Rebecca Conroy, the manager of the nursing home, the staff had clearly been instructed to make things difficult for Carole, although, as far as she could tell, they continued to treat her father as well as could be expected, which meant he got the same poor-quality, minimal services that all the other patients received.

Rebecca Conroy showed up soon after the aide left. Today, she was wearing a black pantsuit and a lot of gold jewelry—*her battle armor*, Carole thought, preparing herself for what she knew was coming. "How can I help you?" Rebecca Conroy asked. Her tone was oily as she clasped her hands before her in a pose of fake servility.

"I need someone to get my father out of bed so I can take him up to the boardwalk for a while," Carole explained, joining in the pretense that this was just a normal conversation between a patient's family member and the woman in charge.

"Well, we don't have anyone available to do that right now," Rebecca Conroy replied.

"That's fine," Carole told her. "I saw a wheelchair down the hall, so I'll just go get it and help my father out of bed by myself."

Time ticked by as Carole and Rebecca Conroy stared at each other. Carole kept a neutral expression on her face while she watched Rebecca Conroy think; every sentence seemed to appear above her head in a visible thought balloon. She knew that she was stymied. Maybe Carole could get her father out of bed by herself and maybe not, but if the effort resulted in an accident, that might be a lawsuit in the making.

"Well, alright," Rebecca Conroy said, finally. "Maybe I can find someone to help you."

Once her nemesis was gone, Carole closed her eyes for a few brief moments. No matter how much she had been prepared for this little scene, it still upset her. It was like having the kind of tug-of-war over nothing—well, usually nothing—that she used to have with her stepmother all day, every day.

Eventually, a different aide returned, pushing a wheelchair. Grumbling, Leo seemed to be confused about what was going on, though once he looked down at his right hand and saw that it was holding a pack of cigarettes, he figured out that he was going to have a smoke and became cooperative. The aide then helped Leo out of bed and into the chair.

Once Carole was able to wheel Leo into the elevator and get him downstairs, she pushed him through the front door of the nursing home and out to the street. It was an almost-warm, almost-end-of-winter day, with high white clouds scudding through a changeable sky. Before they'd left his room, Carole had managed to get Leo into a coat she found hanging in his closet, so she thought he was probably warm enough as she pushed him along the cracked sidewalks, past the empty lots, and up the ramp to the boardwalk.

There was a time when there were arcades along this part of the boardwalk where people played Skee-Ball and bought pizza and ice cream, but that was a long time ago. Now there was nothing here, just a long stretch of deserted beach where herring gulls pecked through the thick strands of seaweed lining the shore, looking for clams. Now, the wind picked up and blew the clouds away. The sun suddenly grew a little brighter, looking like a burnished coin that had been tossed up into the cool gray sky.

Leo's hands trembled so much that he had trouble lighting a cigarette, but Carole knew enough not to try to help him; he didn't like her to do anything to remind him that he needed her assistance. She let him smoke his cigarette in silence for a while, but when he was finished—and before he had a chance to light another—she said, "Dad, I want to ask you something."

"What?" he said, looking out at the gray ocean smacking at the shore with heavy, rolling waves.

"I found a picture of Mom, and I thought you might know when it was taken."

Carole reached into her shoulder bag and slid a deckle-edged photograph out of an envelope she had tucked away behind her wallet. She gave it to her father and made sure he was holding onto it before she let go, worried that the rising wind might pull it from her hands and carry it away.

Leo looked down at the photo, a black-and-white picture of Carole's mother, Lydia. Though she looked young, it was hard to tell exactly what age Lydia might have been when the picture was taken. What Carole did see, though, was a pretty girl, dark haired and trim, dressed in a style that suggested it was sometime in the 1940s. She was walking along a city sidewalk with a bright smile on her face that radiated confidence. And so there she was, striding into the future, not knowing what would happen—that she would die young and leave behind a broken family and a daughter who had lived her life trying to avoid the feeling that she missed her mother. Longed for her comfort, her love. Lately, though, those feelings had broken away from wherever in the back of her mind Carole had managed to keep them caged up and were now roaming free, invading her waking hours and even her dreams in their insistent quest to be recognized.

Maybe, Carole thought, it was because she had retired just before Covid took over the world and found herself pretty much alone all the time now with nothing much to do, nothing to distract herself from her own inner thoughts and feelings, that her mother had decided to step out of that cage and reenter Carole's life, bringing with her both the pain and surprise of her death. Still, Carole couldn't keep from castigating herself about how ridiculous it seemed that at her age, she often found herself suddenly overcome with grief about the loss of her mother, a woman she could barely remember. At this point in her life, when she tried to remember anything at all about her mother, Carole felt like she was trying to retrieve evidence about the life of a ghost.

Now, on the windswept boardwalk, with little whirlpools of sand swirling around the feet of the bench where Carole had found a place to sit, she watched as Leo peered at the photo, narrowing his eyes as if he were trying to identify some hidden message it might contain.

"That's your mother, isn't it?" he said.

"Yes," Carole told him.

"Where did you find this?" Leo asked. He sounded suspicious, as if Carole had attempted to pull a trick on him.

"I was looking through your wedding album a few days ago, and I found it stuck behind one of the pictures of Mom getting dressed for the ceremony."

"Why were you looking through my wedding album?" Leo asked, sounding angry.

In Leo's mind, he probably had a right to be upset, since he still believed that his house and all his possessions were waiting for him to come home and settle in again. In actuality, he hadn't even seen his house in over a decade. It had been sold and the money turned over to the government, which was a requirement of qualifying for Medicaid, the only way someone like Carole could afford nursing home care for her father.

"I was cleaning up," Carole told her father as she took the photo back from him. "You know, spring cleaning. Even though no one's living in the house now, it still gets dusty."

Seeming somewhat mollified, Leo looked at the photo again and then handed it back to Carole. "So?" he said. "What do you want to know?"

"I'm curious about how old Mom is in this picture. And do you know where it was taken? Maybe outside the building in the Bronx where we lived until you got married again and we moved to Rockaway? Or maybe someplace else?"

"I've never seen that picture before," Leo said, "so I can't answer your question. Just put it back where you found it. And don't go through my things!" he warned. These days, when Leo tried to raise his voice, it crackled with phlegm. But that was still enough to make Carole feel scolded—the bad-mommy kind of scolded, as if Leo had learned from his second wife how to make his daughter feel that she'd done something unforgivable.

"Alright," Carole said, lightly. "Never mind." She wasn't going to give her father the satisfaction of knowing he still had any kind of power over her.

She returned the photo to her shoulder bag. She said no more about it to her father, but later, after she'd taken Leo back to the nursing home and was standing on the lonely platform of the train station, waiting with the pigeons for the next train to come rattling down the track, she opened her bag and checked to make sure the photo was still there. She had lied to her father about when she had found it—that had happened years ago, when she was at the house in Rockaway, waiting for the junk haulers she had hired to come and cart away all the old furniture she had to get rid of. That day, Carole had made a pile of the few things she wanted to keep, like the photo albums, and that's how she had come across the picture of her mother. It had been a shock to see her looking so pretty, so alive.

Now, as the train arrived and began its trip across the long bridge that spanned the open water separating the Rockaway peninsula from the mainland of Queens, Carole checked again to make sure the photo was indeed safely tucked away in her shoulder bag. And then, all of a sudden, she found herself on the verge of tears.

It was the photo that often did this to her when she looked at it, and she wasn't even sure why she'd brought it with her today since she could have predicted her father's reaction. But maybe one reason was because it had recently occurred to Carole that she was now many years older than her mother had ever lived to be. Lydia had been forty-eight when she died. Carole couldn't stop thinking about that—how, without understanding why, she had come to a place in her life where she found herself longing for her mother, a woman whose entire life span had been shorter than her daughter's.

The train traveled on. It made all its stops along the elevated section of the line and then headed into a tunnel. So far, Carole had been alone in this car, but once the train emerged from the tunnel and made its first few stops in Brooklyn, crowds of passengers began to get on. It was noisy now. The pigeons were long gone, but people were having loud conversations, babies were crying, and kids were laughing and yelling at each other. Despite the noise, Carole must have drifted off for a while because when she opened her eyes again, she realized that the train had taken her past the stop where she should have gotten off and was now speeding through Manhattan.

She was on an express train, so it bypassed several stations until it finally slowed to a stop in Midtown. The doors opened up and dozens of people pushed their way out through what was now a crowded car, while others squeezed in, elbowing their way off the platform and into the train. The stop was at 53rd Street and Madison, the heart of Midtown Manhattan, and—of all places—the station where Carole used to get off when she was traveling from her apartment in Queens, where she still lived, to the law office where she had worked.

She supposed that finding herself here so unexpectedly, she could have been flooded with memories—after all, she'd worked at this firm for over twenty years and so had been getting on and off at this stop for almost every day of her life for all that time—but that didn't happen. It was a time and a place that was already fading from her thoughts. There were other things, too, that should have demanded at least a passing glance in a parade of memories she should have been reviewing right now, including how hard she'd worked to get the job at the law firm.

She was twenty-one when the sandal shop went out of business. Looking for another job, she saw an advertisement for a course that provided instruction in using the word-processing programs that were becoming widely available. She decided to enroll, and it turned out to be something she was good at. In those days, it wasn't necessary to have a college degree; as long as you could use a computer to type business correspondence, you could get a job in an office, so Carole found work in an insurance agency. She used that experience to change jobs a few times; the last one was at the law office where she had worked her way up from receptionist to office manager. During that time, she had also gotten married and divorced. She had met her husband when she was still working at the sandal shop. He was a musician with the usual dreams that boys with guitars have of being rich and famous—and the usual problems that included alcohol and drugs. But after a few years, when it was clear that he wasn't going to find the life he wanted by playing with pickup bands that couldn't get bookings anywhere except tiny clubs with open mic nights, his drinking and drug taking (heroin, cocaine, crack; whatever else he could get his hands on) increased, so their marriage didn't prosper.

But Carole was busy with work in those days, and she had a group of supportive friends, so she was alright. At least she thought she was until she retired, when suddenly, she didn't seem to have any friends at all. The women she had believed that she was close with had all been people she'd known through her job, and when she wasn't going to work anymore, they suddenly seemed to have little in common. Covid made the situation worse; Zoom calls were not a way to strengthen old bonds or build new ones. Sometimes, the past few years felt more like a movie to Carole than real life, especially when she woke before dawn these days and watched the glowing numbers on her bedside clock tell her that it was an hour when the kind of normal, productive person she used to be would still have been sound asleep, storing up energy for the workday ahead. What was she supposed to do at 3:00, 4:00, 5:00 a.m.—when even her little dog was deep in dreamland, curled up at the foot of her bed—except review her life and find, way back in the beginning, that her mother, the person who should have been most important to her, was absent? In that movie of her life that began flickering behind her eyes during those bleary, predawn hours, there was no one to even play the part of her mother. How could there be when she couldn't remember that woman's voice, or touch, or any conversation they'd ever had?

Carole was thinking about all this as the doors to the train closed and the subway platform turned into a blur as the train sped back into the blackness of the tunnel. She should have already changed trains in order to head home, but she stayed seated. Soon, the train emerged from the tunnel and sunlight suddenly spilled into the car. Carole had now been traveling for almost two hours, the longest distance from one end of the subway system to the other, all the way from Rockaway to the far northwest corner of the Bronx.

The train passed by Yankee Stadium and the Kingsbridge Armory, a huge building with red brick walls and a pair of turrets that made it look like a castle that belonged in another part of the world. Carole remembered this view—perhaps her mother had been erased from her memory but not the landscape of her childhood. It was an urban scene; New York to the core. Blocks and blocks of supermarkets and auto repair shops; gas stations and apartment buildings and playgrounds. Once, this had been the province of immigrants from Eastern Europe, but now the appearance of bodegas and Puerto Rican flags showed that the endless ethnic turnover of New York neighborhoods was still in progress. For Carole, it was a double landscape: She saw all that was new through the train windows and remembered the old—stores and buildings that had stood on these streets in the past. *Home*, she thought, no matter how different it looked. *Home, home*, she repeated to herself.

The last stop on the train was Woodlawn. There, finally, Carole got off and walked through the station and down the stairs to the street. Across the way, there was a huge park where Carole remembered sledding in the winter and playing with her friends in the summer. On the side of the street where Carole was standing, the neighborhood was crowded with old apartment buildings. The marble, concrete, and bricks that had been used to build up this area even before the first wave of immigrants arrived were now in poor condition. The sidewalks were cracked, the buildings seemed to be leaning against one another, and there was trash overflowing the few garbage cans that had been put out for collection. It had probably looked this way even when Carole lived here, but she was a child, so she had no idea that it was anything but perfectly nice, and she was sure that was how it seemed to the children she saw now, sitting on the stoops or walking along with their mothers or their friends.

Three blocks from the train station, she came to the building where she had lived until her father and stepmother had decided to move them all to Rockaway. She remembered her father's explanation: He loved the beach, loved to go swimming—didn't she like it, too, when they used to take the train out to Rockaway on summer days when her mother was still alive and spread out a blanket on the sand and go running into the ocean? Maybe so. She did have some vague memories of splashing around at the shore, but that didn't mean she wanted to leave the friends she had in the Bronx, leave what was familiar to her and move out to what felt like the ends of the earth. Only her father could have been blind to the way Rockaway had declined in the years since they'd been a happy family vacationing at the beach. He was, she thought, a willfully stubborn man who only saw what he wanted to. Perhaps he had always been that way.

Now, as she stood before the building on Barnard Avenue, she wondered if there was still some shadow of her mother here, in this place where she had been her mother's child. Even if she didn't remember the woman, she remembered the apartment: the living room, the bedroom that had been hers, and the kitchen where she could recall an open window with the scent of spring drifting into the room, of grass and dandelions and just-washed laundry hanging on the lines that neighbors stretched above the courtyard below. She remembered looking through a different window—the one in her bedroom—where she could see the train make a wide turn on the elevated tracks just before it reached the station. The sound of the train brakes screeching as the wheels took the cars around the turn had been endlessly recurring in her recent dreams, but her mother remained missing, still a ghost, still forever disappeared. Whoever she was—the bright, happy girl in the photo or Leo's wife—she remained unknown to her daughter. Alone, unloved, abandoned—that daughter, hidden somewhere inside an aging woman, was now standing at the foot of the worn stone staircase leading up to the front door of the building where she had lived as a child.

The staircase seemed smaller than she remembered, though that was all there was to her recollection. She could not recall actually walking up the stairs and through the building's front door. But what she did remember was that the apartment where she lived was on the first floor, across from a line of brass-colored mailboxes. Carole recalled this first-floor hallway as dim and cool, with an overhead light shining down on the mailboxes. She thought of climbing the stone stairs and going to stand before apartment C—the apartment where she returned every day after school or came back to after playing outside—but the front door of the building displayed a serious-looking lock and a buzzer, which had not been in place when she lived here. Carole could not bring herself to loiter near the door and wait for someone to come home so she could follow them in, and anyway, she wasn't sure she wanted to enter the building. On the train, she had fantasized about how she might once again put her hand on the door of apartment C, but maybe it was best to leave that to memory. Let that place live on as whatever paradise she wanted it to be, and just move on.

So she walked away. She continued along Barnard Street for a few blocks and then turned a corner onto Belvedere Avenue, where there were beauty parlors, a pharmacy, a supermarket with posters advertising its weekly specials, a butcher shop, a bakery, and two different bodegas with brightly colored awnings. Women with children in tow were doing the day's shopping as Caribbean music, blasting out of a speaker set up near the entrance of an auto repair shop, thrummed in the air. Everything looked different to Carole—the stores were different, the people were different—until Carole caught sight of something that seemed to look remarkably the same as she remembered it from sixty years ago: a sign that said "Cooper's Toys and Games," surrounded by faded images of little fire trucks, yo-yos, and teddy bears, all tilted sideways to look like they were dancing. She could hardly believe it. Could that same store still be here?

She walked up to the door and pushed it open, trying to remember if what she saw matched up to what she remembered. Maybe so, because although the games, stuffed animals, and toys were clearly all brand-new, the store itself—the display cases, the cash register, the two narrow aisles closely packed with the playthings children coveted—had the feel of a place that had been here forever. As Carole stood in the entranceway, feeling mesmerized by everything she saw before her, she suddenly heard someone call her name.

"Carole? Carole Margolies?"

Looking over toward the counter at the front of the store, Carole saw a plump, gray-haired woman wearing a flowered smock standing by the cash register. There was nothing about her, nothing even slightly familiar, that made Carole think she should recognize her—and yet, she obviously knew who Carole was.

Carole walked up to the cash register and didn't try to hide her confusion. "I'm really sorry," she said, "but you're going to have to help me out. I can't remember your name." The woman frowned. Maybe she was insulted? "I do apologize," Carole added, though she wasn't sure why she was asking to be forgiven. Who was this woman?

"I'm Kathy Collier," the woman said. "You really don't remember me?"

Well, the name was familiar—a little blonde girl named Kathy had lived in the same apartment building as Carole. That particular Kathy had been a few years older than Carole when a few years was the equivalent of a generation to girls under fourteen obsessed with imitating the look, the hairstyle, and the clothes of the dancers and singers they saw on TV shows like *Shindig!* or *Hullabaloo*, where the popular rock bands and pop stars appeared every week. Carole could hardly believe this was the same person but immediately reminded herself that she hardly looked the same way that she had when she and Kathy were neighbors.

"Yes," Carole said. "It's me."

"I thought so. You look just like your mother."

As often as Carole had looked at the picture of her mother that she was now carrying in her purse, she didn't see the resemblance. But maybe here, in the context of the neighborhood she had grown up in, it was possible to discern a similarity that was lost on Carole herself?

"Do I?" Carole asked, still astonished—not just at the idea that she looked like her mother, but that Lydia, who had been on her mind all day (and of course, longer than that), should have turned up in this unexpected conversation. Then she laughed. "Maybe it's because I'm so old now."

"Maybe," Kathy Collier replied.

It was beginning to dawn on Carole that Kathy Collier seemed a little lukewarm about her old neighbor turning up here, out of the blue. So, feeling uncomfortable, she made a show of looking down at the display case under the cash register and was surprised by what she saw.

"I remember those," Carole said, pointing to a row of little baby dolls, each wrapped in a kind of swaddling outfit with a tiny white cap on its head. "I actually still have one."

Carole hadn't thought about that for a long time—the tiny doll that her mother had given her when she was—what, six? Seven? She couldn't remember anything else about it or why it had been given to her, but it was a precious possession, hidden away in a little box stuffed with cotton that she kept in the back of a dresser drawer. The doll had survived what she thought of as a kind of personal holocaust, meaning the afternoon she came home from school and found that her stepmother had thrown away most of her toys, books, and even some of her clothes. The explanation was that Carole had too many things to pack because they were moving to Rockaway in a few weeks and couldn't afford to ship everything her father and the new mommy had bought to the house. It was a story that Carole had almost never told anyone because it seemed too cruel to be true, but it was. It had happened.

"I'm not surprised about that," Kathy Collier said. "Your mother used to come in here all the time. My mom once told me that she didn't like to go shopping with your mom because she was always buying you things, even when she was supposedly just going grocery shopping. Don't you remember that?"

"No," Carole said. "I don't."

"That's why it's so weird to see you turn up here. When I started working in this place a couple of years ago, my mother reminded me about your mother and how much stuff she always bought for you. Even clothes. When we were kids, you always had nicer clothes than me."

"Really?" Carole said, deciding she wasn't going to make any other comment. She couldn't imagine what kind of grudge Kathy's mother—and perhaps Kathy herself—might be holding on to that would spur her to bring up the subject of Carole's mother buying her daughter presents so many decades after the fact. And what about this old toy store—why was Kathy working here of all places, even though it seemed evident that she needed to be earning even the small salary this store could pay? There must be some connection between all these things, especially if, as suddenly occurred to Carole, Kathy's mother was as long-lived as Leo and still renting her old apartment maybe with Kathy as her caretaker. *I don't want to hear about any of this*, Carole told herself. Still, she felt she had to say something.

"I remember your mother," Carole offered, which wasn't really true, but it seemed a neutral enough thing to say. "My father's in a nursing home, and it's a very difficult situation."

"You reach a certain age and everything's difficult, isn't it?" Kathy said sourly.

Carole didn't get a chance to respond—and what did it matter, anyway, since all she could think of was to agree—because at that moment, a woman carrying a plastic dump truck walked up to the counter and made the kind of harrumphing noises that indicated she wanted Kathy and Carole to stop talking and let her pay for the toy. Then, taking the opportunity to move away as another customer came up to the counter and handed Kathy a coloring book and a box of crayons, Carole said goodbye and walked out of the store.

Now, feeling even more disconnected from the busy, bustling life of the neighborhood, Carole walked back to the Woodlawn station, climbed the stairs to the outdoor platform, and waited for the train. There were no pigeons here, just a few small sparrows pecking around the platform, looking for crumbs.

When Carole finally got back to her apartment in Queens, her dog began jumping around with excitement. She had been gone much longer than usual, and the little terrier was glad to see her but also anxious for a walk. Without bothering to take off her jacket, Carole found his leash and brought him downstairs, where they headed toward a small park tucked away in a corner of the neighborhood. In the park, she let the dog chase squirrels through the soft blue light of early evening, then led him over to a bench under a stand of trees just coming into leaf. The dog stood up on his hind legs, wanting Carole to pick him up, so she did, settling him on her lap.

The park, the trees, the evening light. She tried to ease into the mood of peace she sometimes found here, but instead, she started thinking about the dog. He was fairly young—about five years old—and a responsibility she hadn't meant to take on when she happened to come upon him one day at a pet adoption event near this same park and had fallen in love, or whatever emotion it was that overcame her at the sight of what she saw as a poor, lonely little puppy whimpering at her from inside his cage. She had been newly retired then and thinking that she had all the energy in the world to care for a needy puppy. But she felt differently now: She was exhausted from the day, from the travel, the grinding responsibility of dealing with her father, along with the unhappy experience of running into Kathy Collier. So, instead of relaxing, she couldn't stop herself from going over and over everything that had happened since she'd left home in the morning. She tried to tell herself that she couldn't let go because of how unusually taxing the day had been, but she also knew that something else was going on. To begin with, her age was catching up with her: She had health problems that would never just fade into the background—a herniated disc in her spine, a torn ligament in her shoulder—that required monthly visits to a pain management doctor, along with what her primary care physician euphemistically called the "challenges" of an aging body, such as an occasional irregular heartbeat and other issues that resulted in her kitchen counter being lined with prescription bottles. Sometimes she looked at her father in his bed at the nursing home and saw what might lie ahead for her as well.

So, the dog. In the midst of a bleak hour one afternoon not too long ago, she had called a cousin who lived several states away—someone she rarely saw but remained friendly with—and made her promise that if she, Carole, suddenly dropped dead, her cousin would take the dog instead of letting him be carted off to a shelter. But what if she outlived him? Carole knew that she couldn't possibly adopt another puppy if she managed to make it on into the future for at least some measure of time to come. Did that mean she would have to live alone without even a pet for company? To have some living creature with her as she sat in the park and tried to let the soon-to-be spring weather soothe her when she felt particularly gloomy, as she did now?

No, she reminded herself, because she had actually thought about this before. If this dog went over the rainbow bridge (which was the euphemism that she saw people on Facebook used when a pet passed away) and Carole was still able to fend for herself no matter how old she was, then there was a solution: She could adopt an older dog. This was something else she had seen on

Facebook: Pet shelters frowned on the idea of handing over a feisty, energetic puppy to an octogenarian, but there were lots of senior dogs (another euphemism but, oh well) that needed a home. Just recently, she had seen posts from a seventy-six-year-old woman who had adopted a big dog, a lab mix, and was managing just fine with him. There were people who remarked about how maybe it wasn't a good idea for two arthritic creatures, human and dog, to be limping around the suburban neighborhood where the new lab owner lived, but others were quick to point out that the old dog would just languish in the shelter if no one took him home, and what kind of end was that to a life, even if just the life of a dog?

Just. That term had stuck with Carole as she'd read the comments under the short video of the two seniors—woman and dog—slowly making their way along the street. Carole had a genuine affection for her dog and could not imagine that his company had anything "just" about it for her. Granted, it wasn't a substitute for having another person around, but still, even keeping up with her responsibilities to the dog—feeding him, walking him, taking him to the vet for his vaccinations and checkups—meant that she still had something to get her out of bed in the morning when she didn't feel like doing that. When she was feeling almost unbearably blue.

The evening was beginning to turn chilly now, so, sighing, Carole got to her feet and led the dog home. Upstairs, she filled his food bowl and heated up what was left of the Chinese food she'd had delivered yesterday. When she was finished eating, she washed her dishes and went in the living room to turn on the TV.

But in the middle of a British crime drama she was watching, she had another one of those sudden, seemingly out-of-nowhere thoughts that seemed to require her immediate attention. This one, this sudden concern, got her up off the couch and sent her into the bedroom to root through the top drawer of her dresser where she kept various odds and ends. What she was looking for was the tiny doll that her mother had given her so long ago.

She pushed aside scarves, little packages of tissues, lipsticks she didn't use anymore, a pair of eyeglasses with an out-of-date prescription, a glove with a hole in the right ring finger that she kept meaning to mend, and other assorted knickknacks until she found the small white box filled with cotton where she had placed the doll some years ago when she had moved into this apartment. The box had a rubber band around it, which she removed, then lifted off the lid—and there was the doll, safe and sound, looking as new as the day it had been given to her.

She didn't remember that day, but the doll was real, and so was the love that had kept it safe all these years—her mother's love, which Kathy Collier of all people had reminded her of today. Maybe Carole couldn't remember much about her mother as a real person, someone who had once, probably, been the sun and moon of her life, but this little doll was proof that her mother had existed and that she had loved her daughter so much that she so often stopped in a toy store to buy her some little expression of that affection, even if Carole hadn't remembered a thing about that until today.

Carole gently tucked the tiny doll back among the strips of cotton batting that protected it and closed the box, but instead of putting it back in her dresser, she carried it over to her nightstand and put it in the drawer that held a pair of eyeglasses with the right prescription and some other things, like gloves that did not need mending and the book she was currently reading before she went to sleep. Later that night, when she got into bed, she opened her drawer to take out the book and was glad to see the box that held the little doll.

She read for a while and then turned off the light. The dog had already jumped up on the bed and settled himself to sleep near her feet. She looked over at him and found herself silently wishing him a long life; she already believed he had a happy one because he was safe, everything he needed was provided for, and he had someone to love him. Whatever happened that had led to him being abandoned when he was just a few weeks old and ending up scared and alone, that was all behind him now. And even if he didn't understand a word she said when she told him that she loved him, which she did from time to time, it wasn't the language she used that mattered; she knew that. There were other ways to let him know that she was glad to have him with her. Always, come what may.

OLD DOGS

Steven was feeling a little tipsy as he walked down Garfield Avenue in Jersey City, heading home after an afternoon of drinking in a bar near his apartment. He liked the place because it still had a Pac-Man game, so he could sit in the dark for an hour or two and amuse himself, watching a glowing yellow disc devour electronic dots when it was not being stymied by evil little ghost things. The bar was far enough away from the new steel and glass condo towers and rental units being built along the Jersey side of the Hudson River that it still felt like a neighborhood hangout, though its days were probably numbered. The developers were eating up this old industrial city, making it yet another place where only young people with big salaries and hefty bonuses could afford to live. Steven was not one of those people. It had never occurred to him that he was supposed to try to achieve anything like that. Peace, love, and understanding—that was the tune that played in his head when he was younger. It didn't mean anything anymore, but he remembered when it did.

So there he was, Steven, walking along, passing old brick apartment buildings leaning against each other behind their concrete stoops and broken sidewalks, when his cell phone rang. His first thought was that if it was the cleaning service he worked for as a temp, he wouldn't answer because his voice might sound a little slurred, and that wouldn't be a good thing for them to hear. But it wasn't them: It was his sister, Jane. It was okay for her to hear how he sounded, anytime.

"So, what's going on?" Jane asked. "What did the eye doctor say?"

Steven had forgotten that he'd told her about the problems he'd been having with his vision for the past few months. His sight was getting fuzzy and kind of dim, so he'd gone into a cheapo eyeglass store near his apartment and asked to see the optometrist, thinking he probably just needed a new prescription for his distance glasses, but no, that wasn't the verdict.

"I have to have cataract surgery," Steven told his sister. "I've already seen an eye surgeon and he scheduled it for the end of next week. It's no big deal, really—just an outpatient procedure. Medicare will pay for most of it, and all that happens is your eye is blurry for a few days, and when it clears up, bingo, your sight is back to normal. Better than. They'll do the right eye first, then the left a few weeks later. No pain, nothing to worry about. I read about it online, and everyone who's had it says it's an easy-peasy kind of thing."

"Oh, well, if the Internet says so." A dog barked somewhere in Jane's house, then another joined in, and another, along with one or two more. Jane said their names and told them to be quiet, speaking to them as if they were people, saying that she was on the phone and they should cool it for a while, and they responded. They were quiet. "So who's taking you?" Jane asked.

"What do you mean, who's taking me?"

"Come on, Stevie. I'm going to go out on a limb and guess that eye surgery requires anesthesia, which means they're not going to let you have the procedure without someone to take you home."

"Yeah, well, I haven't asked anybody yet."

"Uh-huh. And when you do ask someone, who will that be?"

The truth is, Steven had been avoiding even thinking about this problem—who was going to be the "responsible adult" to accompany him on the day of the procedure, as specified on the paperwork he was given at the eye surgeon's office? One option he was considering was to call the local senior citizen center and see if he could find someone through them—one of the volunteers who baked cookies for the seniors or played the piano for them or something like that. It was hugely embarrassing, but he might just have to swallow his pride, if he even had any of that left.

"I'll figure it out," Steven said.

"No, Stevie, don't figure out anything. I'll drive down and be there with you."

"I don't want that, Jane. It's like a two-, three-hour drive. Besides, what would you do about the dogs?"

"My neighbor will come over to feed them and let them out in the yard. He's a nice guy. I took care of his goats last year when he was in the hospital for a few days."

"Jesus. Sounds like a whole hillbilly thing up there."

"No, just a bunch of old hippies hanging on as best we can. Anyway, tell me what day and I'll drive down the night before."

Steven sighed and gave in. "Alright. Thanks, Jane. I'll text you the info." The barking started again, along with some small yips from what was probably a small dog. Maybe two or three small dogs. Jane usually had an assortment: big dogs, little dogs, some in-between. "I hear your background chorus," Steven said. "How many do you have these days? The dogs, I mean."

"I know what you mean. Seven. All senior citizens."

"Just like us."

Jane laughed. "Yeah, can you believe it? Just like us. Fucking crazy, right? I'm seventy-one years old. How did *that* happen?"

"The same way I got to be sixty-five."

"Alright, old man. I love you anyway. See you soon."

After his sister hung up, Steven realized he'd forgotten to ask her how she was feeling. Jane had rheumatoid arthritis that seemed to get worse year after year, but she never mentioned it unless he asked, and he felt guilty for not even thinking about it. But what always came to mind first when Steven talked to his sister was her dogs.

From the time she was around twenty or so, Jane had lived in the Village, but some years ago she had left the city and moved upstate to a house near Woodstock. She told Steven she couldn't afford to live in the city anymore, and besides, the Village had changed beyond recognition. There were no more cheap rentals, no more dive bars that hadn't been turned into fancy clubs decked out to look intentionally seedy, no more places she recognized, and very few friends left anywhere east, west, north, or south of Christopher Street. She did have some friends living in upstate New York, people who had decamped to the Catskills to mountain towns like Woodstock to get by on just a little money. They sold things they made or drove delivery vans or worked in bakeries or stores that sold rings and candles and tarot cards. Jane had a small pension from the various unionized jobs she'd had in Manhattan's Garment District, rising from seamstress to production manager, and now she had Social Security, so she got by. She and the dogs. Steven couldn't remember a time when Jane didn't have a dog, even when she lived in the city, but this thing with having a house full of old dogs—maybe it was getting to be too much?

He had decided to broach the subject with Jane the last time he visited her, which was about six months ago. He usually took a bus up to Woodstock two or three times a year because he missed his sister when he didn't see her for too long a stretch of time, and she missed him. It had always been easy for them to tell that to each other; they'd been close from the time they were kids and that's how their relationship remained. On his last visit, Steven remembered sitting on the back steps of her house—a 1950s-style ranch house that someone had built at the edge of a woods with a picture window that looked out on a quiet, two-lane road and a wide, grassy backyard fenced off from a meadow full of wildflowers. It was a pretty enough place but was always, always full of dogs. Dogs on the sofas, dogs on the chairs, dogs lying in the sunlight that came through the picture window, dogs in the laundry room, dogs on the rugs. While they were sitting on the steps, watching three of the current bunch of dogs chasing each other through the grass, Steven told Jane that he was worried about how she was managing because of her arthritis. He had watched her struggling with dishing out the dogs' food at their mealtimes. Her hands were beginning to look like the bones inside them were permanently mangled, and her fingers didn't seem to be listening to what her brain was telling them to do.

"I know your heart's in the right place, running this old folks' home for dogs, but doesn't it get to be a bit much sometimes?" Steven had asked. "I mean, you must have fifteen different kinds of prescription dog medicine in the kitchen. And I looked at that schedule you've got on the wall about who gets which pills when. It's a lot to keep track of, especially with the trouble I can see you're having with your hands."

"Ha! My hands," Jane said. "You should see what my back looks like on an X-ray. I think the last one I had even scared my doctor."

"So why keep this up?"

"Because I like dogs. You know that. I can't imagine living without a dog."

"So just have one. Get some nice little puppy . . ."

"Stevie," Jane said, and Steven heard the big-sister sound in her voice, "do you remember after Teddy died? I thought my heart would break. I had him for seventeen years, from the time he was six weeks old. I thought I could never get another dog, but just one day of living here without a dog running around . . . well. It was too lonely. So I drove down to Kingston, to the big ASPCA shelter they have there, and I saw this adorable little brown puppy that I liked right away. I took him into the room where they let you sit with the puppies to play with them and decide if you want the one you've picked out, when it suddenly occurred to me that if the puppy lived to be as old as Teddy, then I'd be, like, eighty-five—*if* I live to be that old."

"Don't say that. Don't say *if*."

"But *if* is the right word. So how could I get a puppy? It might outlive me, and then who would take care of it? And don't say you would. That's not the point."

"But I would."

"And I said, that's not the point. So I put the puppy back in the kennel and went to look at the older dogs. There were a couple of one-year-olds, two-year-olds—those were easily going to be adopted soon enough. But then there was a kennel with a big sad-looking shepherd mix lying against the wall, and there was a sign that said he was eleven years old. Eleven! Lying all alone in a cage, hunched up against a concrete wall. I asked about him, and the lady I was talking to said there was another dog there, too, about the same age. It's a no-kill shelter, thank goodness, but that means that these poor dogs just live in these cages until they die. So I took them both."

"I remember you telling me about that. Roxie and El Paso, right? Those were their names."

"Yes, Roxie and El Paso. A couple of months later, the shelter called me and said some people had dropped off a ten-year-old lab whose owner had died, and no one else in the family wanted the dog, so they asked if I'd be willing to take her. The poor dog was so confused, so terrified when I took her home, but eventually, she figured out someone loved her again. That's how it started, I guess. I became the old lady who takes in old dogs. It's okay with me, to be that person."

"But a lot of them are sick. And even if they're not . . . well, they're old, so they die."

"Yeah, that's what happens when you get old. You have to take a lot of medicine and then you die. But in between, if you're a dog and somebody takes care of you, you get to run around in the grass with a couple of friends if you can, and if you can't, you just hang out, feeling safe and happy. If you're a person, you get to watch a lot of cable TV and eat as many guilt-free potato chips as you want. Did I tell you that's my new thing? I'm eating potato chips for breakfast if that's what I feel like doing."

Steven was thinking about that conversation as he unlocked his front door and walked into his apartment. On his kitchen counter, there were three different bottles of eye drops he had to start taking before the cataract surgery and more drops to take afterwards. And he had to remember to take his blood pressure medicine this afternoon—that bottle was sitting next to the eye drops. Medicine and death—not so different than the dogs. Human or animal, it really was a shitty thing, getting old.

The building where Steven lived was probably a grand place back in the early 1900s when they laid the foundation, but now it was owned by some real estate company that just collected the ever-rising rents and never fixed anything. His apartment was small—just a bedroom, a living room, and a tiny kitchen, but at least it looked out onto a small park so he got to see some greenery at this time of year. Otherwise, there wasn't much about the apartment that meant anything to him—it was just the place where he was living now, in what was considered the "bad" part of Jersey City, meaning the people who lived here were mostly immigrants or they were Covid refugees who'd lost their jobs, or just people who lived on the margins because that's where they'd ended up or where they'd always been. Steven was here because right now, it was what he could afford. By next year, when he got the new lease, that might not be the case, which was why he was still working. Well, sort of.

For over twenty years, Steven had been a steady, reliable member of the maintenance crew that served a number of co-op buildings in an area of Manhattan around the West 40s that used to be called Hell's Kitchen but was now as fancy and expensive as most of the rest of the city. He'd been let go from that job during Covid so, because his sister had urged him to, he'd signed up for Social Security ("For God's sake," she'd said, "take it before the government spends it all and there's nothing left"), but the monthly amount he received was hardly enough to keep him going.

When Covid began to recede and the world started brightening up again, Steven suddenly noticed lots of ads online for temp agencies that were looking for cleaning people. The well-to-do who'd fled their apartments during the pandemic were coming back to the city, and most of them weren't going to do their own cleaning, so Steven decided it would be a good way for him to earn extra cash. What was "maintenance," anyway, besides fixing things and cleaning up? The temp agency he signed up with, the Clean Slate Homecare Service, told him that some customers might be a little uncomfortable with a man showing up (which he heard as *Our customers not only expect women, they expect them to be Mexican or maybe Filipina and not to speak much English so no one has to try to carry on a conversation*), but his solution for that was to wear a big bright rainbow LGBTQ Pride pin on his shirt. Maybe people with enough money to hire other people to clean their apartments would be unnerved by some strange man showing up with a bucket and a broom, but Steven was willing to bet that a gay man would be welcome. Regular men might rape and murder you, especially if you were a woman opening the door to an apartment where you lived alone, but gay men would only shower the place with pixie dust, or something like that. In any case, the Pride pin worked, and Steven was able to clean enough apartments to squeak by in terms of paying his bills.

One of the people he cleaned for ended up becoming a friend. Billy Broome was a sculptor who had a studio in a building off

Canal Street. Most of Steven's cleaning jobs were uptown, so it had been unusual to be sent down to one of the very few areas of the city where there were still cobblestone streets, and the century-old old factory buildings had not yet been turned into upscale lofts. But that didn't mean the neighborhood was an inviting place; instead, the buildings looked heavy and tired, ready to give up. Billy Broome's studio was actually an old warehouse that had served the surrounding factories. He had moved into the space in order to accommodate the sculpture he had been working on when Steven first met him: an angel as tall as a two-story building and weighing about thirteen thousand pounds. The marble block from which the angel had been carved had been hoisted into the building using the industrial-sized elevator that had once been used to lift heavy machinery. That was four years ago. Two months ago, a specialized fine arts moving service had carefully wrapped the finished piece in a bounty of foam, rope, and padding, a process that had taken hours, then built a crate around it and loaded it on a private plane that had carried it across the country to Phoenix. There, the museum that had commissioned the angel was waiting to install it in the entranceway that had been specifically designed for that purpose. The sculpture was an extraordinary achievement: a huge figure with outstretched wings that had required the help of an engineer to figure out how to balance the angel's shoulders with the burden of marble cartilage and feathers that it was going to carry for the next few centuries.

The day after Steven talked to Jane about his cataract surgery, he went to Billy's studio to do his regular weekly cleaning, which was confined to a makeshift living area separated from the rest of the huge studio by bamboo screens. Steven also did Billy's laundry, which meant carrying sheets and towels and whatever clothing Billy had worn during the week to the nearest laundromat, more than a dozen blocks away. But today, since the statue was gone, Steven expected that Billy would finally want him to start cleaning the empty studio space, which was going to be a major job, so perhaps he'd leave the laundry for next week. That was about all that was going through his mind when he rang the bell and Billy let him in.

He looks terrible, Steven thought, which was not what he expected. Billy had actually been gone for the past week; he'd flown out to Phoenix for the celebration that the museum had sponsored to honor both Billy and his work. The event had been covered by the local New York City news programs because Billy, whose real name was William Kunkle and who had been born and raised in Pennsylvania, had been a denizen of New York City for more than fifty years and had taken the surname "Broome" from the first street where he'd lived, just a few blocks away.

With the angel gone, the huge studio looked abandoned. When Steven said hello to Billy, his voice seemed to bounce off the walls. The wooden frame that had surrounded the angel when Billy was working on it had not yet been completely dismantled, but the dozen or so floodlights that hung from the beams were all turned off. The only light in the empty, echoing studio was streaming in from windows high up near the ceiling, light that was bleary, rainy, reminiscent of bad intentions.

"Jesus, Billy," Steven said, "this place looks like someone died here."

"Oh yeah," Billy said. "That would be me."

So it's going to be that kind of a day, Steven thought. Billy had these once in a while, but today had an even worse feeling about it because of all the empty space and the echoing silence. But, meaning to get on with his work, Steven started taking things out of the wheeled case he used to lug around his cleaning supplies until Billy stopped him.

"Not today," Billy said. "Please. I'll sign your worksheet, but let's just have a couple of drinks, okay? I feel like shit, and tidying up this hellhole isn't going to help anything."

He headed toward the old flower-patterned couch that stood near his mattress, a remnant of his old dumpster-diving days, the time before he became famous, which he was, and rich, which he was from time to time, though money seemed to be a fluid thing with Billy. There were accountants who kept track of his finances for him, but he mostly avoided talking to them.

As he walked toward the couch, Steven saw that Billy's steps were wobbly, and he actually looked even worse than Steven thought when he'd first walked in. Billy was in his mid-seventies, small and thin with a nearly concave chest and spindly legs. His hair was still dark, mostly, but gray was quickly taking over, though the grayer he got, the thicker and wirier his hair seemed to become. Today, it was a tangled mess; so was his beard. And the air around him stank from the smoke of the cheroots he favored, which were thin, black cigars he was almost never without.

"Okay," Steven said. "Fine. It'll be a drinking day. But what's the matter? You kept saying you'd be happy to finally be done with Hermione."

"Oh, fuck Hermione," Billy said. "Fuck Hermione six ways to Sunday and back again."

Steven was pretty sure that he was the only person who knew that "Hermione" was what Billy called the angel, with which he seemed to have an ongoing love-hate relationship. There was no doubt that he had loved doing the work, had lovingly held in his hands the same kind of hammers and chisels that Michelangelo had used and employed them with consummate skill. That, after all, was what had interested him in taking on the commission in the first place—the museum had wanted an angel carved from the same Carrara marble as Michelangelo had worked with and with the same tools that would have been available to him in the early 1500s. But there must have been something about living alone with the angel—with Hermione—for four years, day and night, day and night, that had driven Billy around the bend. Not really, but almost. He had done almost nothing but work on it, sleep a little, and work for hours more. Climbing all over the scaffolding that was built up as he progressed had ruined his back; tapping and banging and delicately scraping his tools against the marble had damaged his hands, strained his muscles, and—from a fall high up on the scaffolding—nearly broken a leg. Now, with the statue finished and gone from the studio forever, Billy seemed to have no future plans for himself other than to sit alone in this huge, lonely space and feel shattered to bits. He owned a loft nearby that was his official address, but he had spent almost no time there in the past few years and apparently had no plans to move back anytime soon. And while he stayed here, in the empty warehouse space, there was nobody to come sit with him because he didn't have any friends. He knew people—lots of people—but no one he seemed to be able to stand for more than five minutes, except Steven. There was no explanation for that except that they were two old gay men who had lived in New York for a long time, and, though they'd never met before, Steven had come to clean Billy's place, had been to the same bars and clubs over the years, had lived through the time of AIDS and somehow survived, and now, were feeling like relics.

"I know what you think," Billy said to Steven. "You think I'm depressed. I'm not, really. I just don't feel anything." There was a bottle of Macallan single malt scotch on a little wicker table near the couch, which Billy had been tipping into a plastic glass and drinking from since Steven arrived. The bottle was already half empty. "Want some?" Billy asked, offering the bottle to Steven. "The museum people gave it to me. I'm sure it costs the same as some pharaoh's sarcophagus. They have a couple of those in the museum, along with a giant dinosaur skeleton they insisted on showing me. They call him Mel, but Hermione is going to be the big attraction, or so they tell me. Do you know what I think? I think *Angels in America* ruined the whole idea of angels as any kind of art forever and always, but who wants my opinion? So I spent four years of my life with Hermione, who turned out looking like a judgmental bitch, if you want my opinion, which I don't think is what I intended. But when I looked up at that face in the museum, standing on this kind of plinth they built for the statue, that's what I saw; Hermione has a real puss on. Plus, she—or he; everybody asks me about that, but I say the gender is 'angel,' so shut the fuck up—isn't very interesting. All Hermione is, is big. A big white nothing, representing nothing. Oh man," Billy concluded, leaning back against the couch, "I'm tired."

"Hermione is beautiful," Steven said, stating what he thought was obvious. And the easy compliment was also a way to buy a moment or two until he thought of some better words of praise, all of them meant to be sincere. "What you created is extraordinary. No one could have made as exquisite a work of art as Hermione except you. No one else would have attempted it. You must know that."

"I don't know anything. That's the problem with all this work, that's always been the problem. Once it's done, I don't care anymore, I don't feel anything. And I don't feel like anybody. Not anybody at all."

Steven walked over to the sink, where he found a glass on the counter and rinsed it out. Then he took the bottle away from Billy and poured himself a small drink. He imagined it was supposed to taste like liquid gold or something of that nature, but he couldn't tell. Liquor—no matter how expensive—mostly tasted like penicillin to him, or what he thought penicillin would taste like, so he swallowed what was in the glass and then opened the refrigerator to get himself a beer. There wasn't much else in the fridge except beer.

"So," Steven said, "maybe you should get back to work, and then you'll feel better."

"Work?" Billy said the word like it meant something he had absolutely no knowledge of. "Yeah, maybe, but what would I do? The only thing I've even thought about is making ceramics. Black panthers, like my father used to have on top of the TV when I was a kid. That was a big thing in the fifties: once you saved up enough money to buy a TV in a cabinet—preferably blonde wood, as my father called it—then you had to have some kind of ceramic statue sitting on top of it. My dad had this sleek black panther crouching on top of the TV, with its mouth open in a snarl. I was scared shitless of that thing. I was sure it was going to come to life one day and eat us all alive. So yeah," he said, finally cracking a smile, "maybe that's what I'll do. I'll get a kiln in here and start turning out black panthers. Wouldn't you buy one?"

"Oh, for sure," Steven said. "Who wouldn't?"

"Alright," Billy said, waving the bottle around, "enough about me. So what's going on in your world these days? How's life far across the Hudson in wild and wonderful New Jersey?"

"My sister is coming next week. Remember I told you I need cataract surgery? You have to have someone take you home from the hospital, so she volunteered."

"Your sister? The one with all the dogs? Doesn't she live all the way upstate?"

"A couple of hours, yeah."

Right now, Steven thought, *a normal person who had nothing to do but think about making ceramic panthers would act like a friend and offer to come with me to the hospital instead of Jane*, but he didn't expect anything like that to occur to Billy, and it didn't.

So the afternoon inched its way toward evening. Billy got very drunk, threw up, and then fell asleep on the couch. Steven covered him with a blanket, left the studio, and started the long trip home. He took the subway to Midtown, walked all the way to the far west side, then boarded a ferry and crossed the Hudson. On the Jersey side of the river, he bought a ticket for the light rail, which took him to a stop near his apartment. He was glad to finally make it back, but the time he'd spent with Billy had left him feeling gloomy. *What am I doing with myself?* he kept thinking all evening. *I am so much closer to dying than being born.* He wondered if maybe these were the lyrics to a song he'd heard once, but he couldn't remember what that song might have been. Later, when he went to bed, behind his closed eyes he kept seeing the lights of the city receding into the outlines of skyscrapers, churches, warehouses, and cobblestone streets as the ferry he'd taken home carried him over the river to New Jersey. Then the outlines faded and he fell asleep.

Jane arrived the following week, the evening before the surgery on Steven's right eye. She looked the same as she always looked to her brother: lean and spare, with a bit of a witchiness about her. She had started dyeing her hair jet black when she was a teenager, and it was still the same color, and still long, though now it also had a streak of red in it. She was wearing jeans, a Ramones T-shirt, and had a backpack with her that sported several Grateful Dead decals. *Not a person you would ever think of as an old lady*, Steven reminded himself as he watched her get out of her car. *A tough chick.* Still, the effects of her arthritis were even more noticeable than when he'd seen her a few months ago. The knuckles of her fingers were red and swollen, and when she bent over to reach for something in the back seat of the car, the top of her spine looked painfully twisted, like it was ready to snap.

"Hey Stevie," she said as she embraced him. "You're looking good."

That, Steven knew, was a lie—or maybe it was just the way she saw him. Never mind her own problems: To Jane, Steven was still the little brother, though the man she was hugging tight knew that he was beginning to look a little shopworn, a little thin. His hair was white, spiky but sparse, and his face was becoming mapped with lines. Jane's face was all angles, a few lines, thin lips, hazel eyes that made her black hair look even darker. No one would ever have taken them for brother and sister, and yet this was the one relationship in Steven's life that had never been complicated, never in question. They'd grown up in the Bronx, in a household where their parents' main interest had been drinking, and they often had violent fights. As children, Steven and Jane had been put into separate foster care homes more than once, but each time, Jane had managed to find out where Steven was and had written him letters.

It seemed almost quaint to think of such a thing now—letters! Pen on paper, stuck in an envelope, and mailed with a stamp. But this was in the early 1960s, long before there were computers or email, so if Jane wasn't able to phone her brother, she wrote to him. Mostly, she just wanted him to know that she knew where he was living, that she was keeping track of him and he wasn't alone, even if he felt that way. She had made herself responsible for him from the time they were young, which was what Steven was thinking about now as they sat together in his apartment, working out what they had to do tomorrow, which wasn't all that complicated: just get to the hospital, then get Steven home to rest. After that, if he seemed able to manage on his own, Jane would drive home. She'd come back in a few weeks when the second surgery was scheduled. And then, presto chango: Steven's vision would go from dim and blurry to sharp and bright. *If only everything else could be so easily corrected.* That was something they laughed about, together.

Later, when Steven was trying to turn his couch into a bed for his sister, tucking in a sheet around the cushions and bringing her a blanket and pillows, he watched her open the backpack and saw that it was full of medicine vials. She looked over at him, smiled, and shrugged, because what was there to say? She'd told him all she needed to on the phone, when they had the conversation about how she was too old to have a puppy. Maybe it was unimaginable, but they were both, now, the senior citizens they used to make fun of. Arthritis. Cataract surgery. More was coming, and none of it was pretty.

So, as planned, in the morning, Jane drove Steven to the Jersey City Medical Center, and three hours later he was back in her car. He had been in a twilight sleep during the procedure, so he didn't remember much about it other than a kind of psychedelic light show, and now, the eye that had been operated on was mostly pain-free but very blurry. Otherwise, he felt okay. Good, in fact.

"Listen," he said, "why don't we go sit by the river for a while? I know that I can only half see it, but it's a pretty day."

That it was: a lovely spring day, mild and sunny, with only a few small white clouds drifting through the sky like little boats, little balloons. Jane drove them to Exchange Place, directly across the Hudson from the tip of lower Manhattan, and parked the car. They found a bench and sat together, enjoying the weather, enjoying the view, even if Steven's version of it was less than perfect.

"Even with just one eye," Steven said, gesturing toward the city skyline, "there's nothing like it."

"No," Jane said. "But we don't live there anymore."

"I'm there every week," Steven reminded her.

"Yup," she said. "To clean people's apartments."

"Hey," Steven said, pulling away from his sister, turning so he could face her, but with the effects of the anesthesia he'd been given during the procedure starting to wear off, his vision seemed strange; the eye with the new lens was blurry and the one with the remaining cataract was dim. The effect made him feel like he was underwater. "Are you in a mean mood for some reason?" he asked.

"No," Jane told him. "This is just something I've been wanting to talk to you about." She looked down at her palms as if she'd written some notes there for herself, but then she turned her hands over and placed them both firmly on her knees. "Look, I know that the city was the place we both ran to the first chance we got to be on our own. I did, you did. And we felt like we owned it, like we knew all the secret places, the bad ones, good ones, in-and-out places, gay, straight, and whatever. And we stayed out all night, ran around like crazy people, had all the fun in the world. And dealt with lots of shitty stuff too. But Stevie, I think it's time for you to give it up. I mean, do you see how you end up moving farther and farther away? Like me, first you lived in the Village until the develoers turned it into unaffordable yuppy-ville, then you moved to Brooklyn until the same thing happened, then to Queens, and now you've been pushed out, all the way to New Jersey. I know you're not even going to be able to afford to live here soon enough, and then what? I went through the same thing. You know I did."

"So?"

"So. Maybe you finally need to let go. Fall out of love, Stevie. You could come live with me for a while."

"Oh, really? Maybe you found a way to make yourself believe you're a lady of the mountains or something like that, but no, it's not for me. No fucking way."

"It's the Catskills, for God's sake, not the Alps. Woodstock's a nice place. I have a bunch of friends—people you'd like—so at least you'd have some social life. You don't have anything going on here, so don't pretend you do. Besides, living upstate is a lot cheaper than the city. You wouldn't have to clean anybody's place and you could find something else to do with yourself. Or do nothing. Rest, relax. Commune with nature. Vacation with your sister."

"My sister in the house of elderly dogs."

"You make it sound like a nineteenth-century novel. But there are worse things."

"We were raised in the Bronx, Jane. Apartment buildings, stoops, sidewalks, corner stores. Playing punchball in the street. I can't exactly see myself communing with nature in any shape or form."

"In our case, 'raised' is a theoretical idea, no?"

"Even so. I can't imagine moving away from New York."

"As I pointed out, you already have."

"No," Steven said. He stood up and ran his fingers through his bristly hair—an old gesture, a childhood thing that he did when he was feeling off-kilter. Too late to stop himself, he remembered that, of course, Jane knew what he was doing—and so, what he was feeling—which only made him more annoyed. "Can we go back to my place now?" he said. "I'm beginning to feel really tired. And this thing with my vision—it feels like it's getting weirder by the minute."

"Sure," Jane replied. "I should probably get on the road, anyway. But I hope you don't mind—I have to make a quick stop first."

They went back to the car, and Jane got her phone, typed an address in her GPS program, and off they went. She steered the car down Kennedy Boulevard, heading farther and farther away from the waterfront, from the condo towers, French restaurants, and ironically named bars. Then they passed through Journal Square, where people were selling used clothes from racks they pushed along the street, and every bodega sold single cigarettes or joints. This was old Jersey City, old America, old, poor, struggling USA. Jane finally turned onto a street lined with broken-down trucks parked outside a junkyard piled high with skeletal automobile frames. At the far end of the street was a long, low building with a peeling sign that said it was an animal shelter.

"You're kidding," Steven said to Jane.

"Sometimes I just have to give in to fate," she told him. "I had to get here by three o'clock or there's a dog they have inside who's going to be euthanized."

"How did you even know?"

"Well, online, I keep in touch with someone who tries to save older shelter dogs all over the country. She monitors the shelters' websites and sends out daily alerts, so if there's someone in a particular area, they can try to rescue whatever dogs they can."

Jane went into the building and, twenty minutes later, emerged with a ragged-looking Dalmatian on a leash. The dog's right front leg was bandaged, and he had scars from older wounds on his flanks. Limping badly, he followed slowly beside Jane, keeping his eyes on the ground. He never looked up, not even once. When she finally got him to the car, Jane opened the door and began to pick him up because it was clear that he couldn't possibly climb up himself, but when Steven saw what his sister was doing, he jumped out of the car and said, "Let me help you."

Jane told her brother to put the dog in the back seat, where she had already laid out blankets to make a comfortable bed. As soon as he felt a soft surface underneath him, the dog curled himself up, closed his eyes, and almost immediately fell asleep.

"Jesus," Steven said, looking down at the dog, "is he even going to make it back home with you?"

"There's a vet tech on staff in this place, and he said that the dog looks worse than he is, but he's definitely hurting. The tech gave him a pain shot and a sedative, so he'll probably sleep all the way back to my place, and I'll get him to a proper vet tomorrow. God knows what his life has been like," Jane said, placing a gentle hand on the dog's head, then stroking his ears. Far away, in sleep, the dog let out a deep breath.

"Good boy," Jane said to the dog. "Good Kenny. You're safe now."

"His name is Kenny?" Steven said.

"It is now," Jane replied. "See?" she said when they both got back into the front seat of the car. "This is something you could do. You could join the dog brigade. Don't pretend you don't like dogs because I know you do."

"Who said I don't like dogs?" Steven huffed, but the question didn't need an answer. Jane drove back the way they came, then turned onto Garfield Avenue and pulled up outside Steven's building.

"I'll call you during the week and see how you're doing," Jane said. "And I'll be back for eye number two."

"Okay," Steven said, but he didn't get out of the car just yet. He found himself looking at his sister's hands, still folded around the steering wheel. Her knuckles looked raw today, her fingers were puffy. *There must be times when it's really difficult for her to drive*, he heard himself thinking. Then he finally stepped out of the car but leaned back in and looked over at the sleeping dog, curled into a shape like a crescent moon.

"When he wakes up, tell Kenny I said hi," Steven told his sister.

He stood in the street for a while, even after Jane's car had turned the corner and was out of sight—though "sight," right now, didn't seem like a word that applied to what was going on with his eyes. The psychedelic lights were back, streaking and flashing so much that he was feeling nauseous. One of the nurses in the recovery room at the hospital had mentioned that this might happen, so he went back inside, carefully climbed the stairs to his apartment, and after dousing himself with the various eyedrops he'd been given, stretched out on the couch. As the afternoon changed to evening, the room seemed swept by light from a dying sun: red, fiery, intense. If the light show didn't stop soon, he decided he was going to call the doctor's office and ask them if this was normal—never mind what the nurse had said—but then he fell asleep. He had a dream about the wounded Dalmatian: nothing strange or scary, just that he was riding in the back seat with the dog, Kenny, while Jane drove. The dog had his head on Steven's lap.

When he woke up the next morning, Steven's eye was still blurry, but the flashing lights were gone. And he was in bed; somewhere in the night, he must have gotten off the couch and made his way to the bedroom. Now, he pulled himself up and swung his legs onto the floor, testing that he felt steady enough to stand, and he did. Even the nausea had subsided.

As he headed for the kitchen to start brewing some coffee, his cell phone rang. He knew it was his sister without even looking at the caller ID.

"Good timing," Steven said. "I only woke up a little while ago."

"Well, I'm just checking in," Jane said. "How are you feeling?"

He decided not to tell her about the light show; she might worry, or worse, get in the car and drive right back down to Jersey City. "I'm okay. Tired, but okay. How's Kenny?"

"That's nice, Stevie. You remembered his name."

"Of course, he was my comrade in arms. You drove us both home yesterday. In fact, I had a dream about that. Well, sort of."

"Kenny's doing okay," Jane said. "I'll tell him you were thinking of him."

For the next few days, Steven didn't do much other than sit in the park across the street, trying to enjoy the mild spring weather, but all he managed to feel was lonely—and vulnerable, which he wasn't used to. Unexpected feelings seemed to be creeping up on him these days, and he wasn't sure why. Maybe it was just the cataract surgery because it was the first time in his life that his body had required what he was trying to think of as an upgrade. But the visit to the hospital, the need for his sister to come help him out, and the continued blurry vision, which he hadn't banked on—though maybe the doctor had warned him about this, and he just hadn't been listening, or not listening well enough?—didn't feel like an improvement. Nope. Steven felt like this was the beginning of the proverbial slippery slope and from here on in, there would be more failures relating to aging, more medicines like the eyedrops to keep track of, more weaknesses and pain. *Pain* came to mind because of his sister. The sight of her raw knuckles and bent fingers would not leave him. Maybe the less he could see with his eyes, the more that the images in his mind were taking center stage.

He hadn't even gone to the bar to play Pac-Man because he was afraid that the flashing lights of the game's electronic maze, along with the bouncy, repetitious music, would start up his own behind-the-eyeballs laser light show again. Plus, he was worried about drinking—all he needed was one stumble, one trip, and he might do something to damage the new and still-recovering lens that had been implanted in his eye. So mostly, when he wasn't in the park, he just sat around his apartment. He found that he could watch TV if he wore sunglasses, which darkened everything in a way that seemed to even out his sight so that the problems with it could almost be ignored. Almost.

Toward the end of the week, Steven got a phone call from Billy

Broome. He'd told Billy that he was going to have to skip a week of cleaning, so he was surprised to hear from him.

At first, he thought that Billy had just forgotten that he'd canceled the appointment, but that wasn't it at all. Billy just wanted Steven to come hang out.

"Like last time you were here," Billy said. "Let's just sit around and drink. I enjoyed that. It was like a date."

"Aren't we a little old for that?" Steven replied. He knew that Billy wasn't really serious.

"Of course we are. Come over anyway."

Steven agreed, mostly because he was more than ready for a break in his routine. He took a taxi to the ferry, then another taxi when he disembarked on the west side of Manhattan. These were expensive cab fares, more than he should have been spending, but he was concerned about trying to navigate the subway while his vision was still untrustworthy.

It was late morning when Steven finally got downtown and was greeted by the sight of Billy wearing a silk bathrobe printed with a pattern of water lilies and trailing ashes from his ever-present cheroot. And never mind the hour, it was clear that he was already drunk. That didn't particularly bother Steven, but the huge empty space gave him an odd feeling from the moment he walked in. The wooden scaffolding that had surrounded the angel had now been completely dismantled and carted away, which made the space seem even larger. His footsteps echoed on the concrete floor, and as he headed toward the couch in the back of the studio, Steven felt like he was passing through mountains of swirling dust motes. Long, pale tendrils of sunlight trailed down from the windows near the ceiling, and though, thankfully, this didn't irritate his eye, the dust and the pale sunbeams seemed to emphasize how empty the studio's work area was. Even Billy's mallets and chisels had been put away. There was no work going on here, and none seemed to be planned.

Billy stretched himself out on the couch; Steven sat in an armchair that was another rescue from the streets, as was the small rattan table standing between them. The Macallan was long gone, replaced by a tall, thin, ice-blue bottle of Russian vodka standing too near the table's edge. "Help yourself," Billy said. "You know where the glasses are."

"Thanks," Steven replied. He picked up the bottle to move it closer to the center of the table, but he didn't rise from his chair just yet. He still didn't feel much like drinking.

"So how are you doing?" Billy asked.

Steven realized that Billy didn't remember anything about the cataract surgery, so he didn't bother bringing it up. "Oh, you know. Nothing new. And you? I see you haven't started on the black panther project yet."

"What?" Billy seemed genuinely confused, but then he must have remembered their last conversation. "Oh, ha ha. Right. Nope, no panthers to be seen hereabouts. But I have been thinking about going back to Phoenix to visit Hermione. I hear she's very popular. Maybe I could bring a beach chair with me and sit under one of her wings, signing autographs because I'm a famous artist. I used to be a handsome artist—no, beautiful. I really was a beautiful creature when I was young, if I do say so myself, and I do. I even have the pictures to prove it, but I don't like to look at them anymore. So now I'm just famous and old. Sadly, I have discovered that is not the same thing."

"No," Steven said. "I imagine not." He decided that he did want a drink—this was clearly going to be the kind of conversation that required one.

"Maybe I should get a dog," Billy said as he watched Steven pour himself a dose of vodka. "At least a dog would keep me company when I can't sleep, which is all the time now. Doesn't your sister sell dogs?"

"No, she rescues them. She finds them in shelters and takes

them home with her. Mostly old dogs, in fact, so I don't think that would help you much."

"Jesus, there's no escaping it, is there? Old, old, old, old, old." Billy began waving his hands around, as if old age itself was flying around the studio and he was trying to bat it away.

"She wants me to move upstate with her." Steven surprised himself by saying this. Somehow, voicing the idea out loud made it seem almost reasonable. Almost possible.

But Billy certainly didn't see it like that. "Why in God's name would you want to move *upstate*?" He spat out the word so that it sounded like Steven was contemplating the idea of moving to the underworld.

"Jane has a house near Woodstock. I've been there a couple of times, and it's kind of a nice place."

"What's the matter with you? If the dogs don't eat you—or gum you to death, since I imagine they don't have teeth anymore—then you'll just wither away and die. You're a city boy, Steven. We're both city boys."

"Yes," Steven said, smiling to himself as he heard his own argument presented to him, chapter and verse. But interestingly, hearing these words from someone else made them sound impersonal, like a chant at a protest rally, a slogan on a sign. "I know."

"Besides," Billy continued, "then I'd have to call those Cleany Weenie people . . ."

"Do you mean Clean Slate?"

"Whatever. I'd have to get someone new to come clean this dungeon, and I can't face any new people."

"Oh, well. You might surprise yourself."

Steven stayed with Billy through most of the afternoon, watching him drink the bottle of vodka, but he never refilled his own glass. Finally, Billy mumbled something about wanting to sleep for a while and found his way to the mattress in the corner of the studio that served as his bed. Steven went on sitting in the armchair for a while, watching as the mountains of dust motes, cathedrals of sunbeams, moved across the floor. Then he started the long trip home.

In the evening, back in his apartment in Jersey City, Steven picked up his phone and called his sister. "Hey, Janie," he said.

"Hey, Stevie," she replied. "Everything okay?"

"Sure," he said. "I was just calling to see how Kenny is doing."

"Kenny?" Jane laughed. *Sometimes*, Steven thought, *when Jane laughs, she sounds like the wild child she used to be*. "He's fine. I took him to the vet, got him some meds, and he's settling in."

"So listen," Steven said, "you're still coming the week after next, right? I have to be back at the hospital by nine a.m."

"Of course I'm coming. I'll drive down the night before, just like last time. Don't worry, Stevie," Jane added, for emphasis. "I'll be there."

They talked a while longer, just about this and that, and then Steven left the apartment, heading to the pizza place down the street because that's what he felt like having for dinner. On the way there, standing on a corner while he waited for the traffic light to change from red to green, Steven found himself staring at the light and realizing that finally, the vision in his right eye was beginning to clear up.

No, more than that: It was like the blurry cloud that had obscured his sight for the past few days had scuttered away, leaving a clear field ahead. He could see stars, like tiny drops of light in the soft violet sky, and the leafy trees in the park across the street were so green that they looked almost gold. Raising his hand, Steven covered the eye that was no longer occluded by a cataract so that, for just a moment, he was returned to the dim world that was all his other eye could see. The week after next, when his sister was here, Steven would have his second surgery, and when the blurriness from that cleared up, his vision would be balanced; it would be sharp and clear. All he could think about as he continued on his way was that he should have had cataract surgery years ago, but how could he have known that was a problem he needed to deal with? For the longest time, he didn't know what he couldn't see.

THIEVES IN DISGUISE

On a cold afternoon in a season that should be trying harder to turn into spring, Jenna is looking out the window, watching the rain falling on the street below. She's supposed to be circulating around the living room of an apartment on the Upper East Side of Manhattan offering canapés to the guests at a bridal shower, but in her mind she's on an elevated subway train, heading toward the Woodlawn station, last stop in the Bronx. She's fourteen or fifteen, and she's looking out the train window at rain falling on the rooftops of old tenement buildings, on the umbrellas of women in kerchiefs hurrying home from the grocery store. Rain is slanting against the red brick walls of the armory on Kingsbridge Road where you're supposed to hide if nuclear bombs fly through the sky and head straight for New York City. It's nineteen-sixty-something. Her mother's dead, she doesn't get along with her father, and if it were up to her, she'd just ride the train all night and never go home.

God, what's wrong with me today? Jenna thinks. *It's just rain. Why am I in such a rotten mood?*

Hoping no one has noticed that she paused by the window for a few moments, Jenna stiffens her back and holds out her tray again, acting properly subservient, but not totally. Megan, her boss, who is catering this party, has often stressed that she is a supporter of women's empowerment and that if doing a good job means acting the part of a mostly invisible but well-paid servant, then so be it. It's just acting, and so you can still take pride in doing your work well.

"Jenna? You did meet him once, didn't you?"

That's Megan's voice Jenna just heard, and she thinks that maybe she also heard her name, but she's not sure if she's supposed to answer. "Hmm?" she says, offering a minimal response that can be ignored if she was supposed to keep silent and just continue to float around the room like a ghost dressed in a waiter's black clothes.

"Mick Jagger. Didn't you tell me that you met him once?"

For a moment, Jenna is confused—what *is* Megan talking about?—but then she figures it out. She's worked for Megan on and off for many years, and they've talked like friends once in a while even though they're not friends, not really. But late at night when you're cleaning up all the crap that people leave behind in townhouses and penthouses and huge apartments like this one in a landmark building named for a railroad tycoon, empowered women who are also exhausted tend to loosen up and talk to each other. To exchange little bits and pieces of their lives.

"Mick Jagger," Megan repeats. "Didn't you tell me you met him once?"

"No," Jenna says as the faces of the thirty or so young, pretty women in the living room turn in her direction, "not Mick Jagger. It was Leonard Cohen."

Why has this even come up? *Maybe*, Jenna thinks, *because the young women are all a little drunk by now*, and she's overheard the conversations they've been having. They've reached the stage in the party where they're starting to tell celebrity encounter stories. They all go to the kind of clubs, eat at the kind of restaurants, where they run into movie stars and television personalities, and so they're playing the game of *Were they nice or were they snotty?*

For whatever reason—maybe she thinks she'll get extra credit for having hired a server who once handed a shot glass to a rock star—Megan has decided to tell the guests that one of her employees secretly travels in exalted circles when she's not serving tiny crackers decorated with bits of lobster and caviar. Normally, Megan would have stayed in the kitchen directing the wait staff and helping out with the dishes that need to be served warm, but she goes to the same gym as the woman who hired her—the mother of the bride-to-be—so she's been gabbing away with her, acting more like a guest than the boss of the hired help.

Hearing Mick Jagger mentioned, a little ripple of intrigue surges around the room because everyone knows who he is, but then, interest wanes. Most of the young women at the party have no idea who Leonard Cohen is—he belongs to a different era, a different time. But then, suddenly, a tall girl with long, golden hair raises her voice and says, "He's Canadian. So am I."

Everyone laughs. "Okay, Evie," the newly engaged and very tipsy bride-to-be says, "hooray for Canada. Maple leaves and Niagara Falls."

"And hooray for Leonard Cohen," Evie says, holding back her golden hair so she can sip from her glass of champagne. She's pretty tipsy, herself. "He wrote 'Hallelujah.' You all know that song. And he wrote poetry. Beautiful poetry. He's a national treasure."

"I think I'd better go back into the kitchen," Jenna says.

"No, tell the story," Evie insists. She plops down on her chair and starts pointing her finger at random people in the room. "Don't diss Canada."

"It's not much of a story," Jenna says. "Really." The blonde, she thinks, looks like she was raised on a northern prairie, a big-boned rancher's child who's learned to disguise herself as a slender stem, a rough beauty whose soul was sent to the wrong set of parents but now rightfully deserves to be sitting here among the elite of the Americas. *Well,* Jenna thinks, *everyone gets where they're going one way or another.*

Megan nods at Jenna, the message being that she's getting impatient. "Okay," Jenna says. "I used to work for a restaurant that was right near a TV studio. Anyway, one night, the delivery guy didn't show up, and the manager asked me if I would walk over to the studio and bring them some sandwiches they'd ordered for the people at the show called *Hot Properties*. The manager said he'd pay me extra for missing out on my tips while I was away from waiting tables, so I said okay. Anyway, when I got there, Leonard Cohen walked in right behind me. I put down this big box I was carrying and laid out the food on a table, and he came over to see what I was doing. I was surprised that he was just kind of wandering around by himself. I'd read some of his poetry, and it meant a lot to me so I wanted to tell him that, but I was kind of dumbstruck at seeing him in person. So all I did was ask him if he wanted something to eat and he said, 'Sure.' Then he asked me if I knew how long the program was because he was really tired, and all he wanted to do was finish the show and go to a movie afterwards so he could chill out." Searching for some detail to add that would be of interest to the mostly blank faces staring at her, she says, "I had read that he was dating Joni Mitchell at the time so I thought maybe she was waiting for him back at their hotel, and he meant that they'd go to the movie together."

That last part—about Joni Mitchell—is something Jenna has just made up on the spot because Joni Mitchell and her music have been going through a revival lately, so maybe her name will mean something to these girls, who are still drawing a blank on Leonard Cohen.

"Joni Mitchell is Canadian too," Evie says. Not necessarily what Jenna was expecting, but good enough.

"She is Canadian," Jenna agrees, but all the other young women are still looking at her, still waiting for her to say something interesting. And Megan is glaring at her; she doesn't want to get blamed if her employee just stands in the middle of the room, holding an empty tray and murmuring about Canadians. So, searching through her memories to come up with something relevant, Jenna decides on *money*. Everyone cares about money, about how much things cost. "When cable TV first became available in New York, *Hot Properties* was one of the most popular programs you could watch, along with MTV. And I remember that I only paid $14.95 a month for the cable box and maybe ten channels."

That story elicits laughter all around. *Fourteen dollars! Ten channels! How unbelievable is that?* Jenna slips away, headed back into the kitchen, and in the living room, the conversation moves on. Later that night, when Megan is paying the servers because that's the arrangement—you work, you get paid in cash—Jenna is the last to get her money because Megan wants to talk to her.

"I could have sworn you said Mick Jagger," Megan tells Jenna.

"I wish I had met him," Jenna says, though that's not true. She couldn't care less about Mick Jagger, but she needs the work, so she has to keep on Megan's good side. Megan pats her on the back, meaning all is forgiven. The party guests liked the food and got drunk enough that they'll likely spend the next morning texting each other about their spectacular hangovers. Everyone will live to party another day.

But as she walks toward the subway, Jenna feels humiliated. She catches sight of her reflection in a store window and sees a wraith holding a black umbrella who knows a couple of quaint, stupid stories about things that happened in New York City a long time ago. The rainy streets could be a movie set; the empty subway station where she waits for the train could be a black-and-white photograph in the back of a book about urban decay. *Jesus*, Jenna says to herself as she waits for the train. *I really have to stop this.*

The apartment she lives in is on the far east side of Manhattan. It's near the exit of the Queens-Midtown Tunnel, on a street that has three narrow, old apartment buildings on one side and a municipal parking lot for city trucks and other heavy equipment on the other. Jenna's apartment is small—just two rooms—but the building is rent stabilized, so she's lucky to have the place because it means she can still live in Manhattan, which is where she wants to be. She's sixty-six years old and has worked in restaurants all her life, so she's got just enough savings and Social Security to hold onto the apartment, along with her side gigs for Megan's catering business. It sometimes feels like a precarious existence, but Jenna thinks she can manage. Anyway, she hopes so.

When she finally gets home, her dog thumps his tail and stands up on his hind legs to put his paws on her shoulder. He's a big, lean dog, gray from head to toe except for a long white stripe on his left back leg that's a healed-over scar. The dog has a past, but Jenna doesn't know what it is because she got him from an animal rescue group who said he was a stray someone found wandering near the West Side Highway. The rescue people were calling him Benny, but Jenna changed it to Slim Shady, not because she was a fan of Eminem (who the girls at the party probably wouldn't have known either), but because when she looked at the dog, that's what she saw: Slim Shady, incarnate.

Now, when Jenna takes the dog out for a walk, the rain has finally stopped. There are more than the usual number of traffic lights on the streets around here, lots of bright red arrows pointing this way and that to direct the cars streaming out of the tunnel. The traffic lights, reflected in the puddles, look like sizzling smears of paint. Every time Jenna and Slim Shady reach a corner, the dog seems confused by whether or not it's safe to step in the puddles, so Jenna has to coax him along. He's a young dog as far as she knows. The rescue people thought he was about ten months old, and she's had him now for about two years. There are times that she finds herself measuring her life against what the length of the dog's life might be because it has occurred to her that he might outlive her, and then what would happen? Who would take care of him? She had never really intended to get a dog, but she was at a street fair in the Village, and there he was, being walked around by the animal rescue volunteers, wearing a red jacket that said "Adopt Me." He kept dragging one of the volunteers over to Jenna, sliding his head under her hand and sighing. She's sure she heard him sigh. That night, she called her brother who lives a few states away and told him she was thinking of getting a dog, but she wanted to know if he would take the dog if anything happened to her. She wasn't all that close to her brother, but they lived the same troubled life when they were kids, which involved more than just the dead mother: There was violence, there were drug-addicted stepbrothers, there was hunger, sometimes no heat or electricity, and many nights when Jenna and her brother ended up sleeping in the basement with a dresser shoved up against the door.

Jenna, the older sibling, took the brunt of the anger that swelled itself up to fill every room of the house like it had a life of its own. So her brother didn't think she was being crazy for worrying about what might happen to the dog if she died, which of course is what she meant; he said he had the same kind of thoughts from time to time. That he worried about things he never told people because they wouldn't understand why he was always waiting for something to jump up out of nowhere and punch him in the face. "Sure," Jenna's brother said to her on the phone. "Get all the dogs you want. If I'm the one who's still around, I'll come get them. I owe you that much. Maybe more."

When Jenna gets home from walking the dog, she watches TV for a while and then falls asleep on the couch. When she wakes up, she glances at the clock to figure out what time it is in Petaluma, California, where her friend Kathy lives. Has lived for the past few years since she moved west to help her daughter take care of her kids. The daughter is divorced, the dad isn't helping out with money, and the story goes on and on like that.

"Hey," Jenna says when Kathy answers. "I know it's late, but I thought maybe we could talk for a while."

"I'm glad you called," Kathy says. "I really could use a break."

"That bad, huh?"

"Oh, it's just the usual. If I knew I was going to spend my golden years as a babysitter, I would have taken a lot more drugs when I had the chance. If my brain was just a little more warped, maybe I would actually like things like dishing out meals for kids who each have specific demands for the milk-to-butter ratio of their mac and cheese while I'm also watching five hundred pairs of socks spinning around in the dryer."

"That many?"

"At least. But what's up with you? Did you work today?"

"Yeah, Megan catered a bridal shower. She asked me to tell the Leonard Cohen story, only she thought it was Mick Jagger."

"Because they're so alike."

"Well, Megan's a ditz. Anyway, no one even knew who I was talking about." Jenna doesn't need to explain about the girl from Canada—she's not the point. "I felt so stupid. I mean, I used to feel like I could run around the city and do anything I wanted. You know, like I was waiting for things to happen, but now they've already happened and there's nothing else. Now the city is full of these girls who care about how big their engagement ring is. Who complain that their summer house out in the Hamptons doesn't have enough closet space."

Kathy laughs. "That's not everybody. It's just the kind of people who hire people like Megan. Besides, those type of girls would have been those type of girls even when you and I were their age. And we did get into some shit back then, didn't we? We had our fun."

"That's what I mean. *Had.* When did that happen?"

"I don't know, but it sure did."

Jenna can hear Kathy light a cigarette and pictures her blowing smoke into the air all the way out there in Petaluma, California. On the news, lately, she's seen that there are fires everywhere in California, that fire season never ends anymore. Cigarettes aren't the cause, though, and neither are campfires, so Smokey the Bear, who used to pop up on TV all the time warning about forest fires, doesn't have to worry about that anymore. Instead, Jenna thinks, Smokey should be out patrolling the power lines, since downed wires and random lightning seem to be what cause most of the fires these days. Also vandalism.

"You know what I came across the other day?" Kathy says. "Those pictures of us my sister took when we stayed at that cheesy motel in Vermont, the year we drove up there to visit her at college. Do you remember?"

"I do. It was early in the morning, and we were sitting on the bed in your room."

"I showed those photos to my daughter. She said we looked like lovers. I think we looked like thieves on the run."

"Either one would have been okay with me."

Kathy laughs again. "Why don't you tell me the Leonard Cohen story? Maybe that will make you feel better."

"No, that's okay," Jenna says. "You know it already."

"You should come out and visit," Kathy says. "Kidnap me. Save me from all these kids and their socks." She pauses for a moment, remembering the same thing that Jenna is remembering because they're friends; they're on the same wavelength. "When we were in Vermont, we should have just driven across the border to Montreal, where Leonard Cohen grew up. That was the real plan, wasn't it?"

"But we didn't have enough money."

"Then we should have been thieves. We should have stolen the money, somehow. If we'd gone to Montreal, we would have made great stalkers. We could have stood across the street from the house where he grew up, walked along Sainte-Catherine Street, like in one of his songs. Picked flowers from the park where he met the guy who taught him to play guitar and pressed them between the pages of one of his books of poetry, like in an old movie. Then we would die, and someone would come across the flowers and wonder what they meant. Anyway, what was the name of that book of his that you always carried around?"

Slim Shady climbs up on the couch and puts his head in Jenna's lap. She looks across the room at her bookshelf, knowing exactly where that book is, the one Kathy is talking about because she still has it. "It's called *The Spice-Box of Earth*."

"I was half in love with him myself, you know. Who wasn't, back then? He wrote beautiful songs, he wrote poetry, and he was gorgeous in that dark, swoony kind of way. Whoever first described a man as having a smoldering glance must have meant Leonard Cohen. Was he really that beautiful in person?"

"I told you he was," Jenna says. "But it wasn't just that."

"I know. Anyway, like you said, it's late, and I suppose I'd better get to bed. Nowadays, I keep the hours of a third grader." Kathy sighs, lights another cigarette. She's really not ready yet to get off the phone. "God, I miss New York," she says. "When we were younger, once you and I finally got off work at night, that's when the fun started. We went everywhere, we did everything. Even riding the subway at four in the morning stoned out of our minds was fun. We'd talk to the cops—do you remember? Tough boys from Brooklyn who had two choices in life: be a fireman or a cop. Ours were secretary or waitress, but we did okay. We had our own apartments, we paid our own way. And you even ended up as the manager of that fancy bar on Columbus Avenue. Not bad, kiddo."

"It's harder for people now, I think. Especially girls. Who can just move to the city at eighteen and even afford to pay rent?"

"Where did you meet Yvonne?" Kathy asks. "Was it at the gay bar in the Village where we used to go dancing?"

"Wow," Jenna says, "that's a change of topic."

"Not really. We're talking about New York and we're talking about love. She was the real deal for you, wasn't she?"

"Yes. For a long time."

"And even so, you said you weren't gay."

"I wasn't. I'm not. And I am. Meaning—"

"I know," Kathy interrupts. "You are who you are."

"I guess that's the best way of putting it," Jenna says.

"Well, you did have some spiffy boyfriends too. I'll give you that. Handsome dudes, all around."

"*Dudes*? Is that what old ladies call hot boys in Cali?"

"If they feel like it. And right now, I do."

Slim Shady has fallen asleep, but from somewhere in a dream, he lets out a deep growl. *Go boy, go*, Jenna says to him in her secret thoughts, thinking he must be out hunting in a forest, with the moon lighting a path through the trees. Or maybe he's fighting an arch enemy. Whatever dogs do when they're running through dreamland, wild and free.

"You know what I'm going to do?" Kathy says. "I am going to go to the library, find a book of magic spells, and witch up some way to make these kids grow up extra fast so I can come back to the city. I promise."

"I bet you think that will work," Jenna says.

"Damn right I do," Kathy tells her. And then, finally, she says good night.

For the next few weeks, the catering jobs Jenna gets from Megan are all corporate events, and everything goes smoothly. No one talks to the wait staff at corporate parties; the job is to wear your black polyester pants and white shirt and float around the room with an expression on your face that means absolutely nothing other than "I am at your service." And you should mean it too. Jenna makes a decent amount of money from these jobs, and she's happy enough about that, but otherwise, she's feeling restless, and she's not sure why. And she's not sleeping well. She thinks that she could take some lessons from Slim Shady, but he's not talking. She expects he would if he could.

One night, when she's wide awake, she's scrolling through Facebook and happens on a post from a group of people she went to high school with. Mostly, they post things about their families and what great times they had back in the day, which Jenna reads with curiosity, as if she's reading an old comic book or something like that because it's like they lived in a whole different world than she did. But this time, someone has posted a notice about the recent death of an English teacher who once taught at the school, a man named Robert Frommer, and they've added a photo of him that must have been taken around the time when Jenna was still one of his students. The smudgy picture shows a middle-aged man in a suit and tie, looking away from the camera as if he's got things on his mind other than having his picture taken. Only a few people have commented on the post and all they've said is "Rest in Peace" or "Sending Prayers." Nothing that really means anything.

Jenna tries to go back to bed, where Slim Shady is stretched out like a long gray shadow. He raises his head when she tugs on the blanket that he's got mostly folded around himself and stretches out his legs. *If I could stretch like that, maybe I could fall asleep*, she thinks, but she doesn't even try. Instead, she goes back to her computer, back to the page with the notice about Robert Frommer's death and rereads the two or three comments. She thinks about writing something, but in the end she doesn't because the only thing she'd want to say is, *I never expected to feel this lonely when I got to be this age, and I don't know what to do about that. You probably would have had some ideas.*

Still unable to fall asleep, she pulls on a pair of jeans and a sweatshirt and wakes the dog to take him for a bonus walk. One thing Jenna has realized about having a dog is that it's like having a good cover story—anybody can be out walking a dog at any hour of the day or night without attracting the wrong kind of attention because hey, a dog's got to do what a dog's got to do when the dog has to do it. So she walks along the wet streets, thinking about Mr. Frommer, which was how a student addressed a teacher in 1969 when she was in his English class. Maybe kids aren't so formal with their teachers anymore—Jenna has no idea about that—she never even knew that Mr. Frommer's first name was Robert until tonight.

She really only has a Leonard Cohen story because of Robert Frommer. Jenna was not a good student; she knew she was smart enough to understand the math and science she was failing all through high school, but she just didn't care. Things at home were so bad that her only goal was to leave, and at that time, in that particular just-past-mid-century era, not having a high school diploma didn't seem as important as finding a different life to live as soon as possible, like it was an emergency, which was how she felt. The one class she had been doing well in was English, but when she started failing that too, Robert Frommer made her stay after school one day and asked her what was going on, so she told him. She doesn't remember exactly what she said, but mostly it amounted to, "I hate everything about my life, I am miserable, and I am going to quit school and go live in the city. I am going to find a job and take care of myself because nobody else is doing that. Not even close."

What she does remember about that afternoon, sitting in the quiet classroom with rusty autumn light falling across the desks and a plastic jack-o'-lantern left over from some past Halloween hanging from a nail stuck in the windowsill, is that Robert Frommer didn't try to change her mind about anything. All he did was ask her if she'd ever heard of Leonard Cohen, and she said yes because there was a song she'd heard him sing on the radio called "Suzanne" that she liked because some of the words in the song made her think about things that you might have around you if you had your own life, a life you made for yourself, things like tea and oranges, boats on a river that you could see through your kitchen window, and the sun pouring down on you like honey if you and a friend were sitting someplace safe. "Okay," Robert Frommer said, "I'm going to bring you a book of poems he wrote, and I want you to write a paper about it. The school curriculum says I have to teach you kids about poetry, and they specify the work of Robert Browning and Carl Sandburg, but I'm guessing none of that gets through to you. I think Leonard Cohen's poems will, so if you'll write that paper, I'll give you a passing grade. And if you pass English, you can graduate. It'll help if you at least have a high school diploma. I know you don't think so, but I think I'm right about that."

The book he brought her the next day, and told her to keep, was Cohen's *The Spice-Box of Earth*. Jenna remembers how directly the poems spoke to her of joy, but also of grief and longing. In particular, she still recalls a poem entitled "Travel," which starts out being about the pain of lost love but then, suddenly, takes a turn to describe how a windy sky can seem like a locket for a lover's hair. So that's what Jenna wrote about Leonard Cohen, that he had some kind of dark sadness in him, but he could turn that into a locket twined in a woman's hair. Into tea and oranges and boats on a river.

To this day, Jenna has no idea why Robert Frommer made a special effort on her behalf. Or why, after he read what she wrote, he not only gave her a passing grade but somehow arranged for her to graduate early with what she's still not sure is a real diploma, but she's held onto that piece of paper, stuck in a box somewhere on a shelf. But Robert Frommer was right about the diploma: It did help her get her first job at a coffee shop in Greenwich Village because, the owner said, he was tired of hiring runaways and kids just drifting through the Village on their way to find some commune upstate or hitch a ride to the West Coast. Apparently, he thought that being able to graduate from high school meant that his new waitress was going to stay put for a while, and she did. Jenna did.

Now, Jenna realizes that she has walked pretty far downtown and ended up in a park near the East River where there is, in fact, a tugboat gliding on the water under clouds that hang like lanterns in the lavender dawn. Slim Shady pads along beside her, yawning every time Jenna looks at him as if he really, really wants her to know that it's sleepy time for good dogs in New York City. She pats him on the head to let him know that yes, she is aware of that fact.

That weekend, Jenna has to work another party for Megan, a charity fundraising event that will require nothing of her except that she keep a servant's pious smile on her face and not drop anything. It's surprising, really, how much skill is involved in doing that all night. But after she puts on her black polyester pants and her white shirt, she has some time to kill, so she calls Kathy again.

"Hey," Kathy says, as her voice drifts in from far away in Petaluma, California. "Two phone calls in one week. We must really be good friends."

"Extra special," Jenna says, "which means that we should go. I mean, to Montreal. We still can, you know."

"You do remember that Leonard Cohen died a few years ago, don't you?"

"Well, that happens. But that doesn't have to change our plans. We can still walk through the park across the street from the house he used to live in. We can sit in a café on Sainte-Catherine Street and watch the world go by. I bet I can even remember some of my high school French—at least enough to order a cup of coffee. I did graduate from high school, you know."

Kathy laughs, and Jenna hears music in her voice. Tea and honey and oranges. "Yes, you've told me that story too," she says.

"So?"

"So, okay, yes, it's a deal. You can start planning. It might take a while, though."

"That's alright. As long as you mean it."

"Yes ma'am," Kathy tells Jenna. "I do."

"Then I'm going to save up some money because I want to buy a few things for the trip. Maybe a slouchy hat. A beautiful pair of leather boots. And I'll buy you a rhinestone necklace and a pair of shades you can wear all night."

"Aha!" Kathy says. "So we'll be thieves in disguise."

"The best kind."

Then off she goes, Jenna, to work. It's the kind of party where wealthy people in beautiful clothes will be spending money to do good deeds. At least, what they hope will do some good. There was a time, Jenna reminds herself, feeling empowered to smile the smile of someone who once stole a woman's heart, she did a good deed too—a small thing, maybe silly, but it's what she's thinking about tonight. It was what happened at the end of the Leonard Cohen story, and how this story will end too. After the poet said that he was tired and wanted to go to a movie, he asked Jenna what was playing in the neighborhood, if there was anything good that she'd suggest he should see. She can't remember, now, what movie she recommended, but she hopes it was something he enjoyed.

JOHN AND PABLO MEET THEIR NEIGHBORS

"Don't forget that we're moving the chemo suite across the hall," the receptionist says to John as he's leaving his doctor's office. "So, when you come back next week, make sure you go to room 112."

"That was my draft number." *Where did that come from?* John is genuinely startled to hear what he's just said out loud. He really believed that number had stopped haunting him years ago. Years and years.

"I'm sorry," the receptionist says with a polite smile. "Your draft number?"

"Vietnam," John says. "One hundred and twelve was my number when they held the draft lottery."

"Oh. That's really something." The receptionist, a pretty young woman who John figures can't be more than twenty-something years old, clearly has no idea what he's talking about. Why should she? The Vietnam War, the draft, the psychedelic craziness and looming terror of that era—*death in the jungle with the high-wire sound of mortar fire screeching through the burning sky*—belong in the nightmares of men John's age, not hers. They are the remnants of another world, a dying generation, long gone from the modern scene. At least, that's how John sees things, how he feels.

Heading home, John has to take a long bus ride down Queens Boulevard, six lanes of killer traffic cutting through the borough, and he is nauseous all the way. He has a small blue plastic bag tucked in his jacket pocket just in case he has to throw up before he gets to his house. Earlier, in the chemo suite, John saw a box of these bags in a corner next to the dispenser of latex gloves, and his eye was caught by the words "lightweight and convenient" printed on the side of the box, as if the disposable plastic bags that patients are meant to vomit into when they can't get to a bathroom are just any other household product, and it's important to be able to gauge their best traits against their competitors'. All the way home, John has his hand in his pocket with his fingers touching the bag just in case he needs it. This has happened in the past but luckily, today, he makes it to his stop without having to be sick. He's on his second of three rounds of chemotherapy, which will have to be repeated after a pause to assess their effectiveness. The chemo is meant to treat the liver cancer he was diagnosed with several months ago. The nurse who is regularly assigned to the chemo suite is watchful and concerned about the people in her care, and the way she discreetly slips the little blue bags into her patients' hands as they leave is like a magic trick that John thinks she is probably proud of, and rightly so.

Walking home from the bus stop, John steps through the puddles left by the morning rain. Now, the weather has cleared. It's a fresh and breezy spring afternoon, with sunlight just beginning to break through the clouds. He's in Rego Park, the Queens neighborhood where he lives in a small two-story house with a brick staircase leading up to the front door and vinyl siding affixed to the outer walls like second skin. The house, which John and his wife bought soon after they were married, looks like all the others on the block, a line of neat, modest boxes built to house families with two working parents and children in school. John is no longer working, he doesn't have children, and he isn't married anymore. He hasn't been for a long time, but when he and his wife divorced, she moved out to California to pursue some post-hippie dream that she couldn't give up and left him with the house. He'd told himself many times that he should move, that he doesn't belong in this kind of neighborhood anymore, but since he's never decided where else he could live, he has simply stayed put. The area all around has changed a good deal in recent years, mostly because of price fluctuations. These houses were relatively inexpensive when he bought his back in the early 1980s, but now, in the post-Covid era, housing prices have skyrocketed as people seek a middle ground between living in the suburbs and finding someplace close enough to ease the daily commute to the office towers of Manhattan. John hasn't paid much attention to any of this, especially lately, because his mind is on other things. Well, just one thing, mostly: whether he's going to live or die. His doctor says that the odds are in his favor, but John isn't so sure. He wishes he were, but he's not.

As soon as John gets home and opens the door to his house, his dog, Pablo, begins to whimper and spin around in circles. John is pretty sure that this behavior is caused by anxiety. After John's cancer diagnosis, he had to have surgery and was in the hospital for over a week. Pablo had to spend that time in a kennel and probably thought he'd been abandoned; now, he must fear that might happen to him again, so every time John leaves the house, he envisions the dog hiding under the bed, worrying. This hasn't made things any easier for either one of them.

Today, after spending a few minutes sitting on the floor with the dog to try and calm him, John pulls himself back to his feet and then climbs upstairs, which requires just about the last bit of strength he has. A window is open in his bedroom, and the scent of spring—new flowers, green grass—drifts in with the breeze that gently lifts the curtains. John collapses on his bed and almost immediately falls asleep with the solid weight of the dog pressed against his back. Pablo is a gray pit bull mixed with who knows what else; his body is squat and strong, but inside, he's a baby. Since he's been sick, John has been especially glad to have the dog around, to sleep and wake knowing there is some other living creature in the house with him. He'll get up later to feed Pablo even though he likely won't be able to eat anything himself.

The following week, when John goes back to have his last round of chemo for a while, he happens to glance at his hand as his picks up a pen to write his name on the check-in sheet and sees the blue and yellow bruises where the intravenous needles have left their stab marks on his skin. For a moment, he can't remember how he got these small wounds and is mesmerized by them.

"Mr. Dunham?" John's attention is still focused on his injured hand, but he looks up when he hears the receptionist address him. "I hope you don't mind," she says, "but after you mentioned the draft lottery last week, I went home and did some research online. I knew about Vietnam of course—well, I knew a little, but I'd never heard about the lottery. It seems like it was a very cruel thing to do to young men. I'm sorry you had to have that experience."

"Well, I was lucky," John tells her. "My number was never called. If it had been, I don't really know what I would have done. There were only two options: show up at the nearest induction center or run off to Canada. It was hard to imagine myself as a soldier but even harder to think about living my whole life as a fugitive." This is a lot more than John usually says to anyone here about anything other than, "Where should I sit today?" or "When should I come back?"

"Well, I'm glad you made it through that," the receptionist says. "I'm sure you'll get through all this too."

As she summons the next patient to her desk, John walks across the hall and through the door that leads to the suite where the chemotherapy infusions are now being administered. There are six patients here today, all tucked into recliners and covered up to their necks by rough white hospital blankets. The room is always cold, perhaps in an effort to stave off infections or because the chemo drugs require a chilly environment. There is a rack on the wall where volunteers have left a variety of crocheted caps for patients to wear so they can keep their heads warm. The caps offer a welcome display of color in this otherwise gray-and-white room. Gray walls, white blankets, silver poles with transparent bags of liquid poison that drip into the patients' veins as they read or nap or listen to music on their headphones.

John usually brings a book with him, but today, he can't concentrate on the story he's been reading about a troubled detective wandering the Scottish moors as he tries to puzzle out the murder he's trying to solve. Instead, he finds himself working through the puzzle of his own life, as if walking through the door of suite 112 is another kind of magic trick, one that sends him back to the time of the draft lottery whether he wants to think about it or not. So, while his body lies back in one of the recliners, his mind wanders off to the library where he went to look up his lottery number. He had to get stoned on hashish to get up the courage to do it. Very stoned.

He was a tall, rangy teenager back then with a ponytail and as much of a beard and moustache as his fine, light brown hair allowed. He was usually dressed in an old pair of jeans, a leather vest, and love beads, all part of the requisite outfit of rebellious youth. That was the outfit he was wearing when he opened the copy of the newspaper where the newest lottery numbers were published. They were based on the birth date of young men eligible for the draft, and when John found his, he realized it was in the range of numbers that had a good chance of being called up. That frightened him even more than he expected. His fear embarrassed him, and it shadowed him everywhere he went. That year, the last number called up for the draft—and, as it turned out, the last number ever selected by the lottery—was ninety-five, but

John had no way of knowing that he would never be conscripted. So he had to find a way to live with the threat of imminent death, which is what he believed would be his fate if he was ever forced to serve in the army. Why shouldn't he have believed that? The body count was on the news night after night, and so it seemed inevitable that if you were drafted, you would be added to the list of dead boys whose names would scroll by on the TV screen, and that would be the end of everything. Period. Done. Dead and buried. And there was no way out, no exemption he could ask for because he wasn't planning on going to college, one of the few ways to avoid the draft. What would be the point? There was a revolution coming, wasn't there? Very soon, society was going to change, and everything was going to be different. John, who marched in anti-war protests and participated in demonstrations of civil disobedience, believed that young people were at the vanguard of a great social upheaval, that enlightenment and flower power and all those things that the music on the radio celebrated would soon make life better for everyone, equally. When John thinks back to that time, it's hard to remember exactly what he imagined was going to happen, but he was sure that it would be something life altering. The war would end—all wars would end. Peace would prevail all over the world and people everywhere would be safe and happy. *Yeah, well,* he thinks now. *Look how that turned out.*

The only plan John was considering when he graduated from high school was to maybe get a part-time job and then try to qualify for a student loan so he could enroll in art school—that is, if the revolution didn't come as quickly as everyone expected because his plan B was to become a cartoonist. He wanted to be the kind of artist whose biting, satirical work was featured in underground papers like *The East Village Other*. He had been hanging around the East Village from the time he was fourteen when he began taking the subway from the Bronx, where he grew up, to Manhattan.

On a cold winter day soon after he read the results of the lottery, he was walking down St. Mark's Place, shivering in his jacket and sneakers, when he happened to run into the dealer he bought hashish from, who invited him to spend a weekend at a commune in Woodstock in upstate New York. John went—and didn't come back for over a decade. Even though by sheer luck of the draw he avoided the draft, he had already become enmeshed in the counterculture and soon found himself following the hippie trail from New York all the way to San Francisco, from one commune to another, one set of inner-city squatters to back-to-the-land farmers growing vegetables and marijuana on communal plots of land along the Oregon Trail. He also had his days with the more radical groups, the violence-prone, self-proclaimed revolutionaries who thought flower power was for girls in mini-dresses and big sunglasses; in their view, the real undoing of American society, the goal they were devoted to, would only be achieved through the use of guns and Molotov cocktails. By the time it became clear that the days of expecting a revolution—either of universal peace or armed-to-the-teeth culture wars—were indeed over, faded and gone, John was about thirty years old and tired of traveling and of living in a constant state of poverty. So he started hitchhiking, standing on the shoulder of a highway in Oklahoma where he had been living in an RV with a couple of friends. He was heading home to New York City. Where else was he going to go?

"Mr. Dunham? Did you fall asleep?"

"Oh," John says, startled to be called back to the present day. "I guess I did nod off for a while."

He blinks his eyes to clear away the blur that clouds them and sees the nurse who roused him unhooking his intravenous drip. "Thank you," he says, but as he stands up from the chair, a wave of nausea overtakes him. He runs into the bathroom and throws up. Then he throws up again—and again. When the spasms eventually subside, John feels like someone has been beating on him for hours.

He's so weak that he barely makes it out of the doctor's office and down the street to the bus stop without collapsing.

Half an hour later, when he finally walks through the front door of his house, Pablo goes through his usual near-hysterical ritual of greeting, whimpering, and spinning as his nails tap on the wooden floor. John realizes that he should take the dog for a walk, but he's also well aware that he wouldn't make it even half a block, so he opens the back door and lets Pablo out into the yard. He doesn't usually do this, but it's an expediency: He'll pick up after the dog when he's feeling better, but for now, this is the best he can do.

Still animated by excitement, the dog runs back and forth around the backyard, jumping and barking as John settles himself in an old lounge chair. He leans back and closes his eyes, listening to the birds chattering in the trees and letting the late morning sunlight warm his skin. Soon, he's drifting off to sleep.

Then, suddenly, he hears a loud crash. For the second time today, he has to struggle to pull himself back into the waking world. When he does, he turns his head in the direction of where he thinks the noise came from and sees Pablo sitting on top of what appears to be a pile of broken lumber. The dog looks bewildered.

John quickly figures out what happened: Pablo has accidentally crashed through the wooden fence that separates John's yard from his neighbor's on the right. The old wood has probably begun to rot, so it isn't surprising that this section of the fence didn't survive the collision with the solid bulk of an over-energized dog.

Lifting himself out of the chair, John is already planning what to do: He'll go next door, apologize to his neighbor for what's happened, and then call some fence repair company to come out and replace the broken slats. He doesn't know his neighbors on either side of his small piece of property, but he's going to have to introduce himself to one of them right now.

But just as he gets to his feet, John hears another loud sound as the back door of the neighboring house bangs open, and a big, heavily muscled man steps out, holding the hand of a child—a girl of maybe four or five. After quickly surveying the damage, the man sees the dog, who appears to be frozen to a spot atop the broken lumber. Letting go of the child's hand, he strides over to where Pablo is sitting and kicks him in the side.

Crying out in pain, the dog runs over to hide behind John. "Hey!" John yells out. "What's the matter with you? Don't you come near my dog again. It was an accident. I'll get someone to repair the fence as soon as I can."

"That's a pit bull, isn't it?" the man yells back. "I have a little girl here. That animal could have attacked her."

"That would never happen," John says. "The dog isn't dangerous. Just calm down, will you?"

"I won't fucking calm down." The man's face is reddening, and he has curled the fingers of his right hand into a fist. "I want all this shit cleaned up right now."

"I already told you that I'm going to call someone to fix the fence. It's really no big deal."

"Well, it is a big deal to me." The man begins to kick at the broken pieces of wood, sending a few slats flying across the yard. Wide-eyed, the little girl pulls away from her father and runs back into the house.

In the same moment, John is struck by another wave of nausea. He feels his stomach contract and, unable to control what's happening, he vomits onto the grass.

"Pussy ass motherfucker," the man says.

"I'm sick," John mumbles, still bent over. He hadn't meant to say anything at all, but the admission just seemed to slip out on its own.

"Sick?" The man's voice is heavy with sarcasm. "Sure. You probably need a fix or something, right? Listen, buddy, this is a family neighborhood. A junkie like you shouldn't even be allowed within a mile of this place. Besides, I thought all you hippie assholes died out years ago."

Junkie? Hippie? If John was feeling better, he'd probably laugh at those words: They're so old and well used that they seem to shine like pennies tossed up in the air. Instead, he just wipes his mouth on the back of his hand and turns to walk away. As he does, he happens to glance down at the T-shirt he's wearing and realizes it's an old souvenir from his Woodstock days with a peace sign emblazoned on the front. *Yup, hippie,* John thinks. *And there actually* are *a lot of drugs sloshing through my veins today.* So then he does laugh, and it feels pretty good.

"What the fuck is so funny?" The neighbor steps over the pile of broken wood so that he's now standing in John's backyard, well over the property line.

"Look," John says. "I really don't feel well. If it will make you happy to stomp around out here for a while, be my guest. Me, I'm going inside to take a nap, and when I get up, I'll make that phone call about the fence, like I said. Nice meeting you."

John walks into the house followed by the dog, who keeps close to his side. Then he locks the door because he's not an idiot, and he wouldn't be surprised if his neighbor tried to come charging into his house. He washes his face and hands at the kitchen sink and then makes it as far as the couch in the living room before he collapses into the cushions and falls immediately asleep with the dog stretched out on the floor beside him.

He wakes up in the late afternoon and does what he said he would: In an old Yellow Pages, he finds the names of fence repair services and calls the first one that's nearby. They come the next day, and John watches from an upstairs window as they remove the broken slats and start replacing them with new ones. He thought his angry neighbor might show up again and make a scene, but it's a weekday, and the man is probably at work. When he comes home tonight, the fence will be repaired, and that, John hopes, will be the end of that.

As he watches the workmen, John sits at a desk in a room he calls his office, though all he usually does there is write checks to pay his bills and file his receipts. Lately, however, he's been coming into the office and sitting at the desk more often because he's started to draw again. He doesn't remember actually making a decision to do this, but he does know that he began to draw when he was in the hospital, after his surgery. He was in pain, he was full of morphine, and he was having strange dreams—more like hallucinations, he thought, than actual dreams. He had taken a lot of LSD when he was younger, and the weird images floating through his brain reminded him of that time. Night after night, he felt like he was watching a movie that had something to do with his life—though maybe not his real life—interwoven with pictures of flowers bursting into bloom and clouds speeding through a sky made of streaming colors. At one point, John felt like he was standing on top of a glowing timeline, with the years lit up like roadside signs at night. The timeline represented all the years he'd been alive, but he couldn't tell if he was standing at the end of it or if there was more to go. He hoped it wasn't the end. Even with all the pain he was in, all the troubles he expected to find himself confronting after his surgery—chemo, damaged nerves tingling with shocks that felt like giant bee stings, weakened muscles wasting away from inactivity—he hoped there were more lights up ahead, more signposts to help him find his way. John thinks it might have been the signposts that he started drawing, but he isn't sure because when the janitors came to clean his room every day, they threw his drawings away. He doesn't blame them: They had no idea what they were.

Now, John is just doodling, mostly. It's a beautiful, sunny day. His yard is full of bright yellow dandelions and there are robins hopping through the branches of the trees. The view is like a child's picture book, but with his old ambitions beginning to stir, John is drawing caricatures of the birds sitting cross-legged on the branches with cigarettes stuck in their beaks and sketches the flowers in the yard below them wearing fedoras and playing banjos.

He's feeling a little better than he did yesterday, so he's just amusing himself. Just having fun.

When the workmen are finished, he goes downstairs to pay them. The new slats are lighter in color and more raw looking than the rest of the fence, but the man who's in charge of the work crew assures John that the wood will weather quickly, and soon, and he won't be able to tell the new slats from the old. "Okay," John tells him. "That's fine with me."

He stands in the sunny backyard for a few minutes, staring at the fence. Then he walks back into the house and upstairs to his office, searching for a marking pen. He finds a black one with a wide tip and goes back downstairs and out to the yard, followed by the dog, who is still shadowing every step he takes. Up and down the stairs, into the house and out again—it doesn't matter. Everywhere John goes, the dog goes too.

Then, standing in front of the fence, John uncaps the marker and begins to draw on the new slats. It doesn't take him long to finish the drawing, which seems to have just slid into his mind through some open window. When he's done, he feels that just having the energy to complete the picture is like another touch of magic in his life. It's like juju, like sticking pins in a doll to reverse a curse. What he's drawn on his side of the fence is another caricature in the style he liked to imitate when he was young. It shows a male figure with a small head, a rubbery nose, and a slap-happy expression on his face, stretching out one disproportionately long leg with an enormous foot wearing a metal-studded shoe kicking a fat, dumb-looking oaf into the air. The oaf has pointy emojis flying around his forehead to show that he's seeing stars. A big dog with long, floppy ears is looking on, grinning at his master's triumph.

"R. Crumb?"

Startled, John turns around and sees a man casually leaning on the fence that runs along the other side of the yard. The man, who John realizes must be another neighbor, looks kind of young, though everyone under forty—maybe even fifty or sixty—looks young to John these days.

"That's great work," the man says, gesturing toward the caricature that John just drew on the fence. "I really like it." As he's speaking, a German shepherd pops his head up over the slats. Pablo runs over and the two dogs, standing on their hind legs with their paws on the fence, begin happily sniffing each other. It's a stretch for Pablo, but he manages.

John walks across the yard to stand beside his dog. He is very surprised that the owner of the other dog knows that he was copying the style of R. Crumb. The cartoonist, who was a leader in the underground comix movement of the 1960s, was one of those artists who had inspired John to think that he wanted to follow the same path.

"Well, I guess I was kind of plagiarizing," John says. "Do you know Crumb's work?"

"I'm a big fan," the neighbor says. "My father had old copies of *Zap Comix* stashed away in the back of his closet, and I found them when I was a kid. They were a real showcase for Crumb's work, and I loved everything he drew—I really did. He had such an original style that I'd recognize it anywhere, like on the fence over there. I wouldn't exactly call it plagiarizing, though. Let's say it's an homage."

"Okay," John agrees with a laugh. "I'll let myself wiggle off the hook that way."

"So, listen," John's neighbor says, gesturing at the caricature of an oaf, a dog, and a hero getting his revenge, "did that really happen? I heard something about it from the fellow who lives in the house behind mine. He looked out of his upstairs window and got a glimpse of you and your other neighbor over there having some kind of heated discussion. He also told me that the other guy is a total jerk. Someone to be avoided."

"It did really happen," John says, "only I was on the losing end of the argument."

"You mean your vicious dog here didn't defend you by biting the guy's arm off?" The neighbor reaches over the fence to scratch Pablo's ear. The dog whimpers with pure happiness. He pushes his anvil-shaped head against the neighbor's hand, hoping for more attention. "These dogs get a bad rap, even mixed breeds like your buddy here, but they're usually sweethearts. What's his name?"

"Pablo."

"Well then, Pablo my friend, meet Rocky." At the mention of their names, both dogs wag their tails vigorously and continue their energetic meet-and-greet. "I'm Mike Harvey, by the way," John's neighbor tells him. "Doctor Harvey, actually. I'm your new local veterinarian." Mike Harvey extends his hand across the top of the fence, and John reaches over to share a quick handshake. "Maybe you've noticed the animal hospital that just opened a few blocks away? That's me—us, actually. My wife's a vet too, and she works there with me. We thought it would be a good idea to live nearby, so here we are. We just moved in next door to you a few weeks ago."

"Nice to meet you. I'm John Dunham." John is trying to remember if he's seen movers around anytime recently. He doesn't, but he's been in such a fog these days that he could have walked right past men carrying furniture from a van into the house next door and not even registered what was going on.

"So," Mike Harvey says, "have you lived here long?"

John doesn't feel like running the exact calculation in his mind, so he just says, "Oh, it's been a while. I'm retired now, but I used to work as an installer for BQ Cable. They were the first company that started bringing cable TV to Queens. That's how I ended up here—same reason as you—to be near work."

"Wow!" Harvey says. "You were one of those guys who answered the call when everyone was bouncing around, yelling, 'I want my MTV!'"

"Yeah, something like that," John says. "It wasn't exactly like my secret ambition in life was to work for the cable company. I just happened to see a help wanted sign on one of their trucks and I needed a job, so . . ."

So why am I talking about this? John hears himself saying things out loud that seem to be speaking for themselves without consulting him, in the same way he started babbling to his doctor's receptionist about his draft number. But now that he's mentioned the job he got when he came back to the city, that help wanted sign and everything about the day he saw it is showing up somewhere behind his eyes as clearly as if it's all happening again. Even as he goes on talking to Mike Harvey, John is remembering an icy December day, walking down the broken front steps of an East Village tenement and seeing the cable TV truck parked across the street. John had been hanging out there for a few weeks along with the girl who later became his wife, the girl who was happy when John got the job with the cable company and they finally had enough money to rent this house and then to buy it—until she wasn't happy anymore. But John was. Maybe not happy, not really, but happy enough. Being a cable installer seemed like something that would tide him over until he could start drawing again. At least, that was his intention, but once he got the job, drawing took a back seat. He's still surprised that he remembers how to use pencils and markers and ink. Maybe it's muscle memory or some brain cells deciding it's time to let him recover the art that they've been keeping safely hidden for him all these years.

"Well, I'd better get going," Mike Harvey says after a while. "I hope that asshole next door doesn't bother you again. If he does, give me a call. I'll let Rocky loose on him. He's a very good boy, but he's also trained to show his guard dog instincts when I want him to." Whistling to his dog to follow him, Harvey starts to turn away, but before he leaves, he says, "I'm not too proud to admit that I'm looking for new clients, so why don't you bring Pablo by for a checkup later this week? I'll give you the good neighbor discount."

"I'll do that," John replies. "Thanks."

He walks back to the lounge chair and stretches out again. The dog lies down beside him on the carpet of new spring grass. Now, behind his eyes, John sees the image of his neighbors—the oaf and the good guy—and finds himself wondering what they think of him. The oaf probably has him pegged as a wimp, a weakling who owns a dog that resembles a small tank as a substitute for having any real strength or swagger of his own. The good guy likely thinks he's just some lonely old man with a hobby and a pet. There may be a little bit of truth in both conceptions of who he is—but just a little. He is weak right now from the chemo, and there are times when he is lonely, but there is another version of himself that is more real to him and more important.

So here is the version of John that he is thinking of right now: a young man, tall and lean and strong, stripped down to a pair of cut-off jeans as he stands amid the corn rows on a commune somewhere, someplace. It's late August, a hot, brilliantly sunny day, and there's another dog with him, a big happy fellow who follows him as he walks down the rows. Soon, that version of John is going to help with the harvest and then join in a feast with a dozen other wandering souls who've found a haven here, on this commune, if just for the summer. Or maybe some of them, maybe including John, will decide to stay through the winter until they travel on. Whatever choice John makes will turn out to be okay because in the mind of that young man, he's already faced the worst, most frightening experience he could ever have—sitting in a library on a rainy afternoon and opening the newspaper to look up his number in the Vietnam War draft lottery. The number that every boy coming of age back then believed to be the signifier of his death.

And now, fast-forward many years to find a man, decades older, relaxing in a rusty lounge chair with a dog generations removed from the old friend who was with him in the cornfield. Maybe the young man was foolish in some ways—even many ways, truth be told—but he did manage to survive his trials and travails. And maybe the old man will survive his too, or maybe he won't. That's the way it always goes, right? Maybe yes and maybe no. And after that—well, after that, who can tell? Come what may.

MOON IN THE MORNING

When Anders wakes up in the morning, the moon is still in the sky. Today, it's in the right-hand corner of the window frame; in two or three days' time it will be gone, on its way to continue its endless travels around the blue globe that holds it captive. Then it will be back, a slice at a time, until it shows up in his window again, round as a plate, bright and beaming. It's just the luck of the draw that he has this view for a few days every month or so, but it never meant much to him until recently. Until, for the first time that he can remember, Anders doesn't have a great pool of figures and shapes swimming around in his thoughts, with colors and tints and hues blending together to fill in the outlines of pictures he wants to create. Anders is seventy years old now, so this has been all he's known for what feels like forever—certainly, since he was a young child, when he felt compelled to draw the pictures in his head with the pencils that were all that was available to him, or later, to paint, when he was finally able to buy the necessary supplies. But for the past few months, no pictures have come to him; there are no images in his head, no swirling colors. It feels like the essential machinery of his life has suddenly shut down, as if his heart has stopped and his thoughts are as blank as an empty slate.

Frightened and filled with anxiety, Anders came up with a way to at least keep working, hoping that if he kept to the disciplined daily schedule he's followed for most of his adult life, which was to work at least a few hours at a time, he would jump-start his imagination. So, for no real reason other than the subject was right there in his view, Anders has begun to paint what he saw in his window on that first day that he woke up with no idea what to do, and that was the moon, still visible in the pale morning sky.

Sometimes, even when Anders thinks that he should be able to see it, the weather obscures the moon. It hides behind clouds, behind the turbulence of a stormy yellow sky, the mist of a violet dawn. But that's alright; he doesn't really need to see the moon in the morning anymore because he's fixed the image in his head. The part of him that he thinks of as his painter's mind functions like a camera, storing images that resonate with him for reasons he may not understand for years and then, suddenly, and seemingly out of nowhere, appear as part of a composition he's working on, sliding into place just when he's worried that he might be stuck. The few time in his life that Anders has had a gallery show and his paintings have been reviewed, critics have applied the label of contemporary realism to his work, and he is fine with that, though as he's gotten older, his pictures have become more abstract. The moon paintings are some combination of both styles that he hasn't yet tried to categorize for himself, perhaps out of some superstition that doing so will interfere with the continuation of whatever mysterious process is at work somewhere inside himself that has replaced the constant flow of pictures and images with the morning moon, as if it is a placeholder. A thing waiting for something else to appear.

For most of his life, Anders worked at night because during the day, he had to make a living. His art has never supported him. There was a time in his twenties that he was briefly famous—he had a show at a Soho gallery that the *New York Times* called "a revolution in contemporary realism, a depiction of daily urban life that challenges the viewer to reimagine cityscapes bathed in light and color." But that was his one great success. From then on, he struggled to gain attention for his work, though he has won some awards, received a few prestigious grants. To support himself, Anders has had a succession of different jobs, most of them involving some sort of craft. He's worked for a company that made stained glass windows, operated a kiln that produced ceramics for the retail trade (vases, garden gnomes, crockery and mugs), and even did a stint in a woodworking shop carving rosettes for guitars. His most recent job, and the one that lasted longest, was at a leather goods shop in Greenwich Village, where he sat at a bench and stitched sandals over and over again, year after year. The place closed down during the Covid pandemic and has not reopened, so Anders is now barely scraping by on Social Security. Besides his financial insecurity, he also has a lot of time to fill because he doesn't have the stamina that he used to and can't stand or even sit at his easel for more than an hour or two at a time. So he's tried to adjust his routine. He paints during the day now and tries to get a decent night's sleep, but his sleep is poor. This change in the schedule he's followed for many decades may be part of why he's struggling with his work these days, though of course he has no real way of knowing if that is true.

This morning, he begins his new routine by getting up and feeding his cat. The cat, who curls up beside Anders when he goes to bed, is a much better sleeper than he is, and often in the night when Anders is awake, he tries to listen to the cat's soft, rhythmic breathing, hoping he can follow it to dreamland. Now, as soon as he sits up, the cat runs into the kitchen and sits by his dish, patiently waiting to be fed.

Anders has almost always had a cat. This one, a dark marmalade—mostly black and brown, with tufts of orange here and there—is named Billy. Anders found his first cat many years ago, scrounging for food by the garbage cans outside his building. It lived to be sixteen, and when it finally died, he found another one just two days later, in almost the same spot. This has happened to him several times now, most recently with Billy, who was a scraggly kitten when Anders retrieved him from behind one of the building's trash cans on a snowy night. It was fairly unusual to come across feral kittens in the middle of winter, but there he was, sitting silently in the snow, too weak to even cry. Anders picked him up and brought him upstairs because he assumed that was what he was supposed to do. By now, he has come to expect the appearance of one cat to replace another. This would no doubt be a strange and unsettling occurrence if he was the kind of person who believed in signs and portents, but he isn't. Not really. This business with the cats is, he thinks, just something that happens to him. Something he accepts.

After he feeds Billy, Anders goes out to do some shopping, which is also part of the new routine he has fashioned for himself. Every day he goes to the supermarket to buy something for dinner, but first, if the weather permits, he gets coffee from a food cart and carries it to a bench in a nearby park. Today, the weather is pleasant. It's spring, and though the sky is gray and cloudy, it's warm enough outside for him to sit for a while. Here, in the park by the 59th Street bridge, he has a view of the East River, and the noise of the traffic on the highway that snakes along the edge of the river on the east side of Manhattan isn't too bad. Luckily, even though his apartment is close by, he doesn't hear the traffic noise. Anders's small apartment is in the back of a building on one of the few streets in the area that has not been visited by redevelopment, and it looks the same way it did in the early part of the twentieth century: a few brick tenement buildings sagging against each other, each with narrow vestibules, mailboxes with bent doors, and iron railings out front where those garbage cans are kept, the ones where he keeps finding cats.

Anders has lived in the same apartment since about a year after he came to New York from Canada. He was the youngest of seven boys, all with wheat-colored hair and gray eyes, who were born in a small town in the province of Alberta. His father owned the local hardware store and all the boys worked there with him at one time or another. All except Anders. He looked like his brothers, who looked like their father, but he was different. He was the artistic one. Maybe some long-repressed gene, passed down from people who left their handprints on cave walls, suddenly emerged to dominate his life. He started drawing before he even started school, and when it was his turn to spend his afternoon hours in the store, he simply sat in the back and kept on drawing. His father was a well-meaning and tolerant man, so he let the boy be. When Anders had just turned seventeen, he got on a bus to travel to the nearest town that had a library where he could look up information about youth hostels in New York City because he had formed a plan, which was to go to New York, get a job, and take classes at the Art Students League where many of the painters he admired had studied. Back in the late 1960s, that's what you did when you needed to know something—you went to the library, you wrote letters, you waited for responses to be returned to you in the mailbox. Those things took time, so Anders started acting on his plan far in advance.

He left home when he was eighteen and hasn't been back since. He missed his family at first, but not really; he liked them all well enough but never felt that he belonged with them. There were times when he had wished he did, but he seemed to have no say in the matter. He was who he was, so he had to leave. The Art Students League didn't work out, though; what he found out after a few classes was that trying to study art was like trying to fit into his family—he had his own ideas about things, and he had to follow his own instincts. He couldn't learn from a teacher. Also, he felt a great deal of resentment toward the other students, many of them from families wealthy enough to pay their way through school and socially connected enough to open doors in the art world that Anders would have to break through himself. It was his intention to do just that, but he felt like an outsider in an insider's club, and it bothered him. All the time.

The youth hostel, which was on the outskirts of the Village, was a better fit. He got a lot of useful information from the other young men and women staying there, such as how he could find an apartment by waiting at the news stand on Sheridan Square for the weekly edition of the *Village Voice* newspaper to be delivered so he could be among the first to find the new listings for cheap rentals. That was how he found his place. It has two rooms and a kitchenette. The smaller room is where he lives, where he has a sleeper sofa, a TV, a chair—all the basics. The larger room is his studio. It doesn't get a lot of light, but that doesn't matter to him. He makes do.

The one important role that the Art Students League played in his life was that it was there, in one of his classes, that he met his first girlfriend. It was a long and serious relationship. She quit art school soon after he did but for a different reason: She told him that she realized that she would never be an important painter. She was good, she could probably sell paintings here and there, but she was never going to be the sensation that she had always expected to become, so instead, she enrolled in the City College of New York—which was as close to free as you could get in those days—to study art history. If she couldn't be an artist, at least she could immerse herself in art, just in a different way. This was an important decision for her, but also for Anders, who realized that while she was doing the right thing for herself, it was not a path that he could ever follow. There was no second best for him, there was only the work he wanted to do.

That girlfriend was followed by another and then another. For someone who did not consider himself particularly attractive and who had thought it likely that he would spend his life alone, he was surprised to find that when one relationship ended, another one soon began. It was something like the thing with the cats—inexplicable. And yet, it was the way it was.

The last relationship Anders had, which had lasted for almost two decades, ended about a year ago. The woman was considerably younger than him, and it was her choice to leave. Perhaps Anders was not in love with her, but he had been comfortable in her company, comfortable to have entwined his life with hers, but clearly, she needed more from him than that. The breakup was a shock to him. At first, he thought he would be fine—after all, he had based his life on two things: his need to paint and his ability to take care of himself—but more shocks were coming because, though it seemed unimaginable to him, he found that he was lonely. Worse than that, he was actually becoming fearful about being alone.

How could that possibly be? When he tried to review how he had incorporated this principle into his life—the *I can take care of myself, I am fine alone* thing—he came to the surprising conclusion that he had been fooling himself. From his Art Students League days, he had gone from one relationship to another with little alone time in-between, so there was ample evidence that he had been deluding himself. Or maybe it was just something about being the age he was, owning the knowledge that at seventy, he was likely to be living by himself from here on out. From here to the end. This has begun to cause him a great deal of anxiety, real anxiety that comes upon him suddenly and leaves him shaking. Sometimes it wakes him from sleep in the dark and empty hours of the night when he finds the bed drenched in sweat and his heart pounding like a wild machine. These are terrible feelings—terrible. He doesn't like to think about it, but deep down he suspects that this fear, this anxiety, also has something to do with the lack of ideas for new paintings. For the placeholder pictures of the morning moon.

Still, before the breakup, he had paid for a spot in the spring Washington Square Outdoor Art Exhibit, which was coming up soon. The cost was steep, and he doesn't want to waste the money, so he plans to exhibit a selection of his older work along with some of the morning moon paintings, which, lately, have taken an unexpected turn. When he began this series of paintings, Anders was simply painting different phases of the moon in the morning sky, but almost without realizing what he was doing, he began adding other elements to the paintings. First there were rooftops, a line of rooftops leaning against each other at the bottom of his canvas. These were the rooftops of old tenement buildings, like his own. Then the rooftops vanished and people appeared, blurry men and women seen from the back. They all seemed to be emerging from the bottom of the canvas so that an observer looking at the picture could not tell what they were standing on. Perhaps it was the horizon. Perhaps the edge of the Earth. And then the people vanished too. What replaced them—what Anders began to paint below the morning moon that felt to him like a series of received images that had flown into his mind from who knows where, took hold of his hand, his paintbrush, and directed him to include in his pictures—were the prairies of Alberta.

Anders had not been back for more than half a century and yet, there on his canvas, was the scene that he looked at every morning when he woke in his bedroom in the house where he lived with his family in a small rural township. From the window of the room he shared with two of his older brothers, he saw the wide, empty prairie: miles of yellow, green, or brown grass, depending on the season. Sometimes what he saw were unbroken fields of snow. The wind was like the prairie's breath, blowing clouds across the blue bowl of the sky. Sometimes wildflowers bloomed on the prairie, sometimes golden eagles floated on the spring breezes. When he was a child, Anders was indifferent to this view, but it seems to have embedded itself in his memory and has now reappeared, demanding his attention. Demanding that he paint it, over and over again, beneath the morning moon.

On the first day of the art show in Washington Square, Anders carries his paintings downstairs and stacks them carefully in the back of a van he's rented. Each canvas is wrapped in plastic and foam board to protect it on the trip downtown. Once he arrives, it's impossible to find a parking spot, so he has to leave the truck in a nearby garage. Next, he has to wheel the paintings into the park on a flatbed dolly and set up each picture for display on standing gridwall panels that he keeps in a storage locker along with the dolly, the foam boards, and other items he needs for the various art shows where he exhibits his work over the course of a year. He also sells his paintings on a website that a former girlfriend had set up for him but which he hasn't updated because he hasn't yet figured out how to maintain it by himself.

Just getting the paintings out of the truck and hung up for display is hard work. Tiring. So when he's finally done, he settles himself down in a beach chair he's brought along and tries to look approachable. He has a stern face—various girlfriends have told him that—so he does what he can to adjust his expression to make it seem like he would be an easy person to talk to about his work, which people tend to want to do at these kind of art shows. Generally, the questions are not intrusive. People want to know what the title of a particular painting is, what kind of paint he's used (oil, mostly, though sometimes acrylics), how long he worked on a particular piece. In just the first few hours, Anders sells two paintings—one of the morning moon alone in a lavender sky and one older piece, a moody seascape of a windswept beach with a lone cat, modeled on Billy, walking along the shore. The cat is an unexpected element in a seascape, which is what the woman who buys the painting says to Anders: "I don't think I will ever stop being surprised when I see this picture hanging in my hallway. A cat, of all things. A cat walking by the sea."

The day is warm and breezy, with the fresh scent of blossoms in the air. Late in the afternoon, in the hour when the feel of the park is beginning to change from a pleasant urban oasis of art and greenery to something edgier, something a little more fluid as parents and children leave the playgrounds to head home for dinner and art patrons are slowly replaced by weed dealers and buyers looking to score, a man stops by Anders's paintings and examines them, one by one. The man, who looks to be about the same age as Anders, is tall and rangy, with gray hair long enough to be flattened against the back of his neck by the blue baseball cap he's wearing.

Finally, the man raises an arm and points to one of the pictures hung on the top of the middle panel of Anders's display. It's his most recent work. "Is that Alberta?" the man asks.

Anders is startled. How can this person possibly recognize that the painting he's fixed on—rows of yellow wheat stretching out toward the horizon with a crescent moon, looking as thin and pale as an old sheet of airmail paper hanging overhead in a cloudless blue sky—was painted from Anders's memory of the fields outside the town where he grew up?

"Yes," Anders says. "How did you know?"

The man shrugs. "I couldn't tell you that. The thought just came to me."

There's a way the man speaks, a flat, drawn-out sound to his voice that Anders is pretty sure he recognizes. If he's right, this man, like himself, is far from home. "Are you from Alberta?" he asks.

"Near Milo," the man says. "Do I maybe know you? Did you grow up around there?"

"I did," Anders said. "My father owned a hardware store in town."

"Stuttgart's?"

"Yes."

"I guess maybe that explains it then. My dad used to take me to that place from time to time, when he needed a hammer and nails or something like that. Maybe I saw you there, once. I remember my father telling me that Mr. Stuttgart had a whole bunch of boys, and they used to work in the store."

"That was us," Anders agrees. "Me."

The man nods, then holds out his hand. "My name is Terry Benoit."

"Anders Stuttgart."

The two men shake hands, then Terry Benoit steps back as if some ritual has been carried out and concluded. "Well then," he says. "Strange to run into someone from Milo after all these years. Who'd have thought?"

"Not me," Anders says.

The man lets his gaze linger on Anders's face for a long moment and then gestures toward the painting. "I like the painting, but don't think I could afford whatever you're charging."

"Fifty bucks," Anders says. He has priced his paintings a lot higher than that, but there's something going on here, some feeling he's having that he can't quite name that makes him almost want to hand over the painting for free. Saying "fifty bucks" was as close as he could come to not doing that.

"Sold," Terry Benoit says. "But I live out in Queens, and it's too big for me to carry on the train. Maybe I could come back later with my car."

The two men make the necessary arrangements. Benoit gives Anders two twenties and a ten and says he can get his car and be back by six o'clock. That's an hour past the time when the exhibitors are supposed to pack up and leave, so they agree to meet at a nearby bar.

Good as his word, Benoit shows up at the bar right on time. Anders is already seated at a table, drinking a beer. "Listen," Benoit says, "can I buy you another? Maybe sit and talk a while?"

"Sure," Anders says, gesturing at the chair across from where he's sitting.

At the bar, a place called the Quiet Lamb on West 4th Street, not far from the park, music is banging through the rafters. Songs about whiskey and women and traveling on lonely roads. A waitress brings two tall glasses of Guinness, and the men clink them together.

"How long have you been living in New York?" Benoit asks.

"Forever," Anders says. "At least, it feels that way."

"Yeah, me too. It wasn't my plan, really, but when I was twenty, I met this girl. I guess that's always part of the story, right? You meet a girl and whammo, everything changes. She was a cousin of a friend of mine, and she'd come to visit. Anyway, she was from Hoboken, over in Jersey, and I ended up moving there. We got married, I went to welding school, and that's pretty much my story. My wife died a few years ago, but I'm still working. I'm the oldest guy in the shop where I work, but it keeps me busy." Benoit has already finished his Guinness and impatiently signals the waitress to bring another. "I thought women were supposed to live longer than men," he says. "I couldn't stay in my place after she died, so that's how I ended up in Queens. I take the ferry across the river every morning to go back to Jersey, to work."

It's a sad story, and Anders is saddened by it, but also disturbed. Is there some meaning to the fact that out of all the people wandering around New York City on a pleasant spring afternoon, this one man out of millions happened to randomly walk up to him in Washington Square Park and turn out to be connected to him through their boyhood in a shared province of Canada? Canada, far to the north, far away. Anders can't shake the feeling that he's supposed to understand something here that he's not understanding. Are he and Terry Benoit like refugees from the same small town who happen to meet in a refugee camp after long years of struggle and travail? That happens in movies, but does it happen in real life? Or is the universe twisting and turning around him in some way, suggesting how he might ease his loneliness by offering him a friend—a man who is clearly lonely enough to want a friend—since both he and the universe understand that Anders is too old to meet another woman who would want to take him on? Or is the opposite thing happening—something bad instead of good, meaning, is he supposed to understand Terry Benoit as an example of what happens to boys who leave their families, who risk their future for love—or for art—and then are left to live alone, sad and drunk, riding ferries, walking to the supermarket, feeding their cat? Actually, Anders can't understand why he is even having thoughts like this. *The universe twisting and turning around him.* Where did that idea even come from? Maybe it has something to do with how anxious he's been feeling lately because he feels the anxiety coming on now. Coming on hard and fast, rising like heat inside his body, like a fire igniting in his skull.

"I have to get going," Anders says to Terry Benoit. "It was nice meeting you." He leaves some money on the table and gets to his feet. He feels like he's fleeing, like he's running away. "I hope you enjoy the painting," he says to Terry Benoit and then gets out of the Quiet Lamb as quickly as he can.

To try and calm himself, Anders walks back through the park. The night sky looks like dark foil pierced by tiny diamond stars. The smell of marijuana drifts through the trees, wafts along the paths that radiate out from a splashing fountain at the center of the park. Before Anders headed off to the bar, he locked up his paintings in the back of the rented van so he can set up in the park again tomorrow, which means he's going to have to take the subway home. On his way to the train station at Astor Place, he passes an art supply store on West 8th Street that he's familiar with and decides to stop in. He's still working on the prairie pictures and needs a particular color to pair with the pale morning moon that appears in this painting. He thinks what he needs is cerulean blue, a cool hue that will cool the color of the prairie grasses so that they look like water. The moon might be an oyster carrying a pearl.

Anders goes into the art supply store and begins wandering down the aisle where the tubes of oil paint are displayed. There's a particular brand he usually buys, but he's thinking that he might try experimenting with another, so he stops to examine a book with samples of how the color looks on different types of paper and canvas. He's deep into thinking about how the slight variations in tint may affect his picture when he suddenly hears three loud cracking sounds. He thinks he's hearing a backfire from a car outside or maybe fireworks, though he can't imagine why anyone would be setting off fireworks at this time of year. He's still holding the book of paint samples when he looks down and sees that there is blood on the page in front of him. One drop of blood and then another and another.

"Oh my God!" someone cries out, and then, as Anders later tries to recollect what happened, things get a little blurry. He remembers a store clerk rushing up to him and herding him toward the back of the store and into an office, where he's told to sit down in a chair. Someone else wraps some kind of scarf or bandage around his head as the room fills up with policemen and emergency medical personnel. Anders is still holding the sample book, but someone takes it from him. A gurney is brought into the office, and Anders is told to lie down on it. "I'm fine," he keeps saying because he thinks he is until he realizes that the side of his face hurts; it feels like it's burning. And there is blood all over his clothes.

He is wheeled through the art supply store and out into the street, which is filled with police cars. Then the gurney is lifted into an ambulance, which goes screaming past all the traffic lights, heading toward a nearby hospital. Finally, trying to make sense of what's happening—Anders feels like he's in a fog, like some kind of filmy curtain has been pulled down in front of him, separating him from the world outside—he looks up at the EMT in the ambulance who's sticking a needle in his arm and asks, "What happened?"

"You're okay," the EMT says. "The bullet just grazed your cheek. I'm giving you some pain medication right now and hanging a bag of fluids. Just relax."

"What bullet?" Anders asks. "What are you talking about?"

The EMT sighs. "Some crazy kid," he says. "This is the second time in a week that we've been on one of these calls. All of a sudden, kids are back into graffiti, and they've been trying to steal spray paint anywhere they can get it because in New York, you can't buy it legally until you're eighteen."

"What?" Anders says. "Graffiti?"

"Yeah," the EMT replies. "Remember the seventies? Kids tagging subway cars, dangling from rooftops to wildstyle the sides of buildings? Well, it's all back. Fun times all around," he concludes with a sour expression on his face.

Anders is taken to Bellevue. It's Saturday night and the emergency room is a crazy place. He's transferred to a bed in a corner cubicle and hooked up to an intravenous drip. Still feeling numb with shock and light-headed from the pain medication he's been given, Anders has to make a real effort to pay attention when a doctor shows up and walks to the side of his bed.

"Well, I think you're a very lucky fellow," the doctor says as he examines the side of Anders's face. "It's just a graze wound. A quarter of an inch one way or another and we'd have a very different story here. Looks like God decided to spare you tonight. He must feel that you deserve a blessing."

God? A blessing? Anders isn't sure that's what he actually heard, but then decides that yes, he did. To Anders, this young doctor—Stephen Maxwell is the name on the plastic ID card pinned to the pocket of his white coat—looks like a millennial club kid, slick and handsome, with an expensive haircut and sparkling white teeth. God is about the last thing he'd expect Dr. Stephen Maxwell to be spouting off about. Anders can't think of anything to say in reply other than, *I don't actually believe in God*, which would likely lead to a conversation he doesn't think he could sustain right now, so he just keeps quiet as Maxwell goes about cleaning Anders's cheek and applying a bandage.

"Okay," Maxwell says. "You're good to go. We've given you an antibiotic, and I'm going to write you a prescription for more that you should fill tomorrow and take for about a week. Leave the bandage on for a few days and take a bath if you can instead of a shower so you don't get it wet. Come right back here if there's any sign of infection, but there shouldn't be. I think you're going to do just fine."

"Thank you," Anders says, swinging his legs over the side of the bed. He still feels a little dizzy but doesn't want to let Stephen Maxwell see that in case he starts saying something like how God might want him to stay in the emergency room and rest for a while. That's not what Anders wants. He wants to get out of here as soon as possible.

A nurse comes in to unhook him from the intravenous drip, and then he has to sign a sheaf of papers before he's released, which takes a while. Still, he's surprised to see how late it is—nearly eleven—when he looks up at the clock above the exit door as he's leaving the hospital. Maybe all the events of the night didn't really go by as quickly as they seemed to him. Or maybe, in his head, it felt like time had stopped, when in reality, it was still slipping on by.

Outside, on the busy street bathed in the fluorescent glare of the light pouring out from the enormous hospital complex, Anders hails a cab and carefully climbs into the back seat. His apartment is not far from here, but he doesn't trust himself to walk just yet. He doesn't feel entirely steady on his feet.

"Sir? We're here."

Anders hears someone talking to him and opens his eyes. Apparently, he's fallen asleep during the short ride because he has no memory of the movement of the taxi, no memory of being transported through the streets of Manhattan from the hospital to his building, but here he is. And there is the iron railing, the garbage cans, the front door that leads to the narrow vestibule where the mailboxes are, the ones with the bent doors.

"Sorry," Anders says as he hands over the money for the ride. Then he gets out of the cab, walks across the sidewalk, and enters his building, where he climbs the stairs to his apartment. The cat, Billy, is waiting for him right inside the door, but as soon as Anders crosses the threshold, the cat lets out a yowl and runs away. Anders follows after him and soon finds the cat sitting in the dark, pressed against the back of the sofa that folds out into a bed. His eyes, round as coins, look full of fear.

"Hey," Anders says, holding out his hand, "it's me." Hearing his voice, the cat seems to relax a little, but not much, so Anders goes into the bathroom and scrubs his hands and face, trying to wash away the smell of the hospital, which he guesses must be what has the cat so spooked. As he does, he glances at his face in the mirror, and what he sees looks pretty awful. Ravaged. Tomorrow, at the art show, he's going to have a harder time than usual trying to look like a regular nice guy. Time and circumstances are not being kind to him, he thinks. Time and circumstances, both coming at him like raised fists.

"Better?" he says to the cat when he goes back into the room. He sits down on the sofa and holds out his hand so the cat can sniff his fingers. But Billy stays where he is, making soft noises in his throat. The sounds may be a growl, or they may be something else.

The next thing Anders knows is that he's blinking as he opens his eyes, which feel moist and sticky. He must have fallen asleep again, because he's still sitting on the sofa, but the cat is gone. Anders has been dozing in the dark because he didn't even turn on a light when he first walked into the room, but he does now, leaning over to reach a lamp on the table beside the sofa. It's something he found at a flea market long ago, a lamp with a tan shade decorated with the silhouette of black bears. The lamp casts a warm light, and in its glow, Anders sees the cat sitting in the doorway between this room, where he lives his life when he's not painting, and the studio, where the rest of his life—the most important part—takes place.

Once the lamp is turned on, the cat walks toward Anders and then jumps up on the sofa. He's holding a leaf in his mouth and drops it in Anders's lap. It still looks like a living thing, this leaf, green and vibrant, newly plucked from a tree blooming in the new season, this new spring. Anders can't imagine where the cat found it, because all the windows are closed, so it can't have blown in that way, and if it had been stuck to his shoe it wouldn't look so perfect, so clean, without even a single tear. It's a real mystery, another strange experience in a night of unexpected twists and turns. But wherever the leaf has come from, Anders understands that Billy means it as a gift. It's something the cat does from time to time, bring him odd bits and pieces that he finds—well, who knows where? Anders wonders if the cat does this because he thinks it's a means of paying his way. Or maybe the small items Billy brings to him are gifts of love. But maybe, right now, the cat is still a little worried that Anders, who has come home unaccountably late and smells of strange and unknown places, may not be who he appears to be. Maybe the cat is still afraid of him, and the leaf is a test, given by one creature to another, to see if the one who came through the door is still the same as he has always been. Who is the one presence he trusts in the whole world—which, for the cat, exists in the space of these two small rooms. So Anders picks up the leaf and puts it in his shirt pocket, which is what he always does with the trinkets that the cat brings him. Perhaps this familiar gesture will reassure Billy that all is well, which seems to work because when Anders next reaches out to pet the cat, he finally begins to relax. Anders can feel that: He feels the tension leave the animal's body as it accepts that everything is still the way it should be, and that he is safe. "Good boy," Anders says to the cat. "See? I'm still me. There's nothing to be afraid of."

Which, of course, is not really true. It's not true at all, and Anders knows it. In this world, there is a lot to be afraid of. Real things, but also things you make up in your mind, and things that are just part of your nature. For example, Anders used to think that the bravest thing he ever did was leave home, but becoming an old man, an old person who's probably going to be alone for the rest of his life, is much worse. Much more frightening. But here he is. This is his life, and this life is the sum of his choices, plus all the random things that happened to him along the way and the things he did. The work he did—the work that will continue until the end of his life, through the life of the last of the cats, which may be Billy, though maybe not.

In the morning, though he feels stiff and sore, Anders gets himself out of bed, gets dressed, and takes the subway downtown, where he retrieves his paintings from the van and sets up his display in the park. It's a warm and lovely Sunday, and many people come to visit the art exhibition. Some stop by Anders's paintings to admire them, some ask about the bandage on his face, and when he tells them what happened, they offer sympathy, they say yes, they saw the story on the news, and it's awful that Anders got caught up in this new wave of urban crime. They talk about graffiti, ask whether Anders thinks it's a legitimate form of art, and Anders says yes, he believes it is, though he finds a way to make a joke out of the idea that there are better ways for an artist to obtain materials than to rob an art store. This is city talk, New York talk, gab and chatter that passes the time, that connects people to one another as they stroll through a landscape of trees and playgrounds budding with the welcoming signs of spring. Anders sells several paintings, most of them from the series depicting the morning moon. A woman who buys one of these paintings tells Anders the story of how she first saw the moon in the morning sky when she was a child living in the mountains of West Virginia and was astonished by it; she says that it was the first time she ever understood that the division between night and day was not absolute, that one thing can blend into another, that not everything she thought she understood about the world, or was told by others, was always going to be true, and she was going to have to figure things out for herself. A lot more things than she expected.

That night, after Anders has returned the rented truck and brought home the paintings that remain unsold, he spends some time in his studio, making sure that he has everything he needs to start work again tomorrow. As he sorts through his paints and brushes, he realizes that he never did get to buy the cerulean blue he wanted, so he thinks about trying to make do with what he already has. It also occurs to him that he actually hasn't looked for the morning moon in some time; except for the past two days that he spent at the exhibition, he's been painting steadily, working from memory without even catching a glimpse of the subject of his recent pictures. There's no real reason for that, he just hasn't bothered to look out the window in the morning, hasn't checked to see if it's one of those days when the moon lingers in the sky long after dawn.

Anders finds that he has a tube of phthalo blue and thinks he can try that for the picture he has in mind of the watercolor prairie under a pearl-pale morning moon. He takes the tube out of the drawer where he found it and places it by his easel, so he won't forget. He doesn't think he will, but just in case, it's better to have it waiting for him than to try to remember, in the morning, what he had planned to do the night before. As he leaves the room and turns off the light, he has another thought: Here is a way he could find out whether or not he'll be able to see the moon tomorrow morning. He knows that the moon is in different phases and different places in the sky throughout the month, and he could easily look up the information online—so much more easily than, say, riding a bus to a library or waiting for a letter with a list of youth hostels in New York City to arrive in the mail—but he doesn't think that he will do that. Instead, maybe he'll take the bath that was suggested to him. Maybe he'll watch some TV and let his cat—who seems to have accepted him back by now—curl up beside him and dream about whatever it is that cats dream. The moon will simply appear in the morning, or it won't. Right now, though certainly all this may change at any moment, Anders feels that he can just wait and see.

NORMAL PEOPLE

Lissa is on the train, riding New Jersey Transit to the station near her ex-mother-in-law's house on Concannon Drive in Fords, NJ. She hasn't made this trip in many years, but she's on her way this morning because this is the one day that the realtor selling Katherine McInerney's house has set aside for designated friends and relatives to claim any keepsakes they may want. Katherine died a few weeks ago, and this is what she specified in her will. After the house is sold, the proceeds will be split among her children, who used to number eight: five boys, three girls. Only five are still alive: two of the girls—grown women now, of course—and three of the boys, the younger ones, all men in their forties.

Lissa was surprised when she had received the letter from a law firm telling her that she was on the "designated relatives" list. Her ex-husband, Chris, the second oldest of the eight siblings, had died several years ago, but they had been divorced for over a decade before that, so she would not have expected Katherine to include her among the relatives. Still, she had been fond of her mother-in-law and felt genuinely saddened when she heard about her death.

In truth, Lissa hadn't really planned on making this trip because she couldn't imagine that there would be anything she'd actually want to take from the house, though she changed her mind when she woke up this morning and realized how beautiful a day it was going to be: warm and sunny, with the fragrance of June scenting the air. Something about all that brought back a random memory of the day that Frank McInerney, Lissa's father-in-law at the time, had installed an awning above the back porch of the house. Frank, who passed away a few years before Katherine, had been a dockworker, Katherine a housewife, and money was always tight, so for them to have spent several hundred dollars on an awning to keep the porch cool on summer days when their adult children with families of their own came to visit was a major investment, one they were both very proud of. So: summer days, a striped green-and-white awning over the back porch, pitchers of iced tea, hot dogs and French fries. Those were nice memories, and though God knows, there were many more of a very different nature associated with that time in Lissa's life, they had spurred her to think, *Oh, why not go?* Maybe she'd find some small memento that she'd like to have around to remind her that sometimes, there were happy days that she could remember spending in the house on Concannon Drive.

Lissa arrives at the station just before noon. As she waits for the train door to open, she sees her reflection and can't help comparing it to the young woman who used to stand here, with her handsome, dissolute husband, who was—as she well knew—already plotting how to get through lunch with his parents so he could hurry back to the city to start drinking and then score enough dope to keep him entertained for another lost night. What Lissa remembers of herself is that she was pretty—maybe not head-turningly so, but pretty enough. Now, what she sees is a much older version of that woman, with shorter, shoulder-length hair—still dark, thanks to regular coloring—and features sharpened by time and events that have chipped away at her talent for convincing herself that things happening right in front of her are not as bad as they seem. These days, she is a better judge of situations like that, though it is, as she readily admits to herself, a little late in the game to have come to that realization.

She also sees in herself one of those women who carry a little dog around like an accessory tucked into a purse. Lissa's little dog, Bodhi, is some kind of mixed-breed terrier that she saw in the window of a strip mall pet store a few years ago. He was sitting alone in the back of the window display, surrounded by puppies playfully bouncing around in a pile of shredded newspaper. His head was down, staring at his feet, and he looked malnourished, so something struck her heart; something made her feel that she couldn't simply walk away. When she went into the store to ask about the dog, the owner insisted that he was four months old, but Lissa guessed that wasn't true. A few days later, the vet she took him to—after paying $95 for the dog, an amount that tested her carefully managed retiree's budget for the month—told her that the little brown terrier was at least two years old. Who knew where he had come from or what his life had been before, but whatever had happened to him had left him with a bad case of anxiety. Her neighbor—who said he did not mean to sound like he was complaining because he was a dog owner himself—told her that the dog cried all the time when she left the house, so Lissa started taking him with her whenever she could. She bought a shoulder bag that had a front compartment designed to hold the dog snugly while letting his head stick out from under her arm, which was not quite as embarrassing as an actual purse, or having him wear a rhinestone collar and a fake Burberry jacket, which is the kind of thing she saw on other little dogs that women carried with them on the subway or in the supermarket. Lissa would never have expected to be this kind of woman, but a lot of things have happened to her that she never expected, so there you go.

Now, she takes a cab from the station to Concannon Drive, and when it lets her out, she stands at the edge of the front lawn, looking up at the house that she used to visit every other Sunday or so during the twelve years that her marriage had lasted. This is a quiet middle-class neighborhood of two-story homes with bay windows and vinyl siding in shades of white and gray, sitting on quarter-acre plots where families raise children who play in the backyard and housewives plant flowers along the side of the driveway. Some of the houses are shaded by maple trees, some have birdbaths surrounded by a row of shrubs in full leaf. The house that Lissa will be entering any minute has a statue of the Virgin Mary near the front door.

First, she has to take a deep breath, as she is momentarily overwhelmed by the feeling that she is looking at a double landscape, meaning that while she has a whole collection of memories about this place spinning around in her mind, she is also experiencing a peculiar sense of never having been here before. It's as if the memories are from another life—maybe somebody else's, somebody different who was playacting the part of dutiful daughter-in-law, contented wife. What she thinks now is that she must have been very good at it because for a long time she fooled everyone, including herself.

Still, she can't just stand out front all day, so she goes up the walk and rings the bell. The door is opened by a young woman in professional young woman's business attire who introduces herself as a representative of the real estate company handling the sale of the house. The young woman finds Lissa's name on the list of people welcome to go through Katherine's belongings, and she is invited in.

The house looks the same as when Lissa was last here. The same patterned sofa and matching easy chair, the same well-used dining room table with decorative plates arranged on a wooden rail above the door leading to the kitchen, the same framed picture of Jesus with eyes that follow you around the room.

"When we had dinner here, I always made sure I sat with my back to that picture. It still gives me the creeps."

Lissa, who has been staring at the picture, turns around and sees her former sister-in-law, Elaine Matsumoto, standing in the living room. Lissa walks over to her and gives her a hug. "It's so nice to see you," Lissa says, and means it. She hasn't seen Elaine for many years, but out of all her former sisters- and brothers-in-law, Elaine was the one she felt a real kinship with. They were both about the same age, both had been raised in New York, not New Jersey, and both—for many reasons—did not easily blend in with a family of Irish Italian Catholics. "Is there anyone else here?" Lissa asks.

"Not right now, thank God," Elaine says. Then, noticing the little dog, she laughs. "And who do we have here?" she asks.

"This is Bodhi," Lissa replies. "Actually, it's Bodhisattva. It means 'someone who is able to reach nirvana but delays doing so out of compassion in order to save suffering beings.'"

"Well holy shit," Elaine says. "That's a lot for that little piece of fluff to carry around, don't you think?"

Now it's Lissa's turn to laugh. "It was just the first thing that popped up in my mind when I was trying to think of what to name him."

"Your hippie past come back to haunt you?"

"Maybe something like that," Lissa says, laughing again.

Elaine knows a lot about Lissa's past because they talked about it; Lissa knows about Elaine's too. And each also knows a great deal about the other's ex-husband, because both men were the subject of many conversations Lissa and Elaine had, sitting on the steps of the back porch, furtively smoking cigarettes that their mother-in-law disapproved of. What Lissa told Elaine was that Chris was the best-looking guy she had ever met, that she knew he drank a lot and seemed to have no real direction in life, but she was kind of a wanderer too. She didn't drink, but she did like weed, and after she left home at eighteen, she had lived the life of a go-along-to-get-along hippie, renting a tiny place in an East Village tenement building so old that it still had a tub in the kitchen. She scratched out a living by waitressing in a succession of downtown coffee shops and restaurants, but living hand-to-mouth didn't matter because everyone she knew lived that way: It was the era of sex, drugs, and rock and roll, of be-ins and protest marches and maharishis.

Chris had been mostly working part time in music studios where bands rented rooms to rehearse. He was the handyman who fixed broken pipes and blown fuses but could also fill in on guitar or drums when someone didn't show up for rehearsal. By the time Lissa and Chris met and got married, they were both thirty-six years old and they made a pact to try to become what they both thought of as normal people because they knew that the time of happy hippies had passed, and so had the years of lazy jobs that you only showed up to when you were in the mood. They thought that what they needed to do was stand up and fly right, which required transforming themselves into people with regular nine-to-five employment, who didn't blow all their money on just hanging out and getting high, who bought real furniture in a store instead of finding stuff on the streets. People who had savings accounts and health insurance and plans for the future. Lissa kept her side of the bargain—she took a computer course, learned Word and Excel, and got a job with a social services agency where she actually felt like she was doing something useful. Chris, on the other hand, not only kept his love affair with Jack Daniel's tuned up but added first heroin and then crack into the mix. He had signed on with the maintenance crew of the city's housing authority, but that didn't last long. He went through all the money he earned each week, then everything Lissa made, and screamed at her when she tried to withhold at least enough to pay the rent on the apartment they had moved to in Queens. That way of life dragged on and on until Lissa finally left. When she did, she had the impression that Chris really didn't care.

Elaine had quite a different experience. She had moved to New Jersey when she was in her early twenties and joined the state police, where she met and married a fellow officer, Dennis McInerney, the oldest brother in the family. Elaine turned out to be a first-class sharpshooter who won marksmanship honors in national police competitions. She was not only the first and only woman in the nation to achieve that kind of success, she was also the first Asian American. It wasn't any kind of professional jealousy or the idea (offered around by his cop buddies at their post in Trenton) that tough-guy Dennis felt emasculated by his tiny, barely-made-the-height-requirements-of-the-state-police wife that broke up the Elaine-Dennis marriage, it was his chronic infidelity. They had two children, and for the kids' sake, managed to remain on good terms even past the time that they both retired. Dennis died soon after. Along with Mary, the middle sister in the McInerney family, those are the dead: Chris, Dennis, and Mary.

Now, though, that's all behind the two women who have met, by happy happenstance, in their former mother-in-law's house. Lissa lets the dog out of the carry bag and he runs around, sniffing all the new corners he can find. Together, she and Elaine wander through the house, looking through the bedrooms, the den, the sewing room, the kitchen. Mostly, this makes both women feel melancholy. The relentless passage of time has left its cold and loveless mark in the stillness of the air, on the cloudy mirrors, the shadows on the walls. Reluctant to even touch anything but feeling the obligation to choose at least one item to carry home as a keepsake, Elaine takes a piece of costume jewelry—a gold pin in the shape of a peacock with outstretched feathers—and Lissa choses a little Capodimonte basket with pink flowers around the rim, which she decides she can use in her kitchen to hold the packets of artificial sweetener that she uses. She remembers seeing the porcelain basket every time she came here with Chris and always thought it was ugly, but now . . . well, it just seems like something that deserves to be saved from the junk pile.

"Okay," Elaine says to Lissa. "I think we've done our duty, so I'm going to head home." But then, looking toward the door in the kitchen that leads out to the back porch, she pulls a pack of cigarettes from her purse and says, "How about one for the road?"

"Sure," Lissa agrees. She calls to Bodhi, and the two women head outside, followed by the dog. There's still a table and chairs along with a barbeque grill set up on the porch. "Oh boy," Lissa says as she settles into one of the chairs. "This brings back memories."

Elaine nods. "It does. We did have some nice days here."

They sit on the porch, smoking Marlboro Lights and watching Bodhi happily run around in the grass, which is dotted with bright yellow dandelions. An early summer breeze rustles through the trees; sparrows alight on the wooden fence that separates this house from its neighbors.

"Why was she always so nice to us?" Lissa says. It's a thought, a question, that came to her as she walked through the dead quiet rooms of the house. "I mean, you and me. She was always so kind to both of us, but I'm sure you heard the stories too—about how horrible she and Frank were to their kids. The constant beatings—even the girls got smacked around and beaten with a belt."

"Dennis said his mother used a wooden spoon like a weapon. And even when they were adults," Elaine says, "she took every opportunity she could to belittle her children. Nothing they accomplished was ever good enough. Maureen is a pediatrician, for God's sake, and she told me that Katherine still managed to make her feel like she was stupid. That's why she moved to California, so she had an excuse to never come home and visit her parents. And when Frank was alive, when he got mad at his sons for something, he got that look in his eye . . ."

"Oh yes, I remember," Lissa says. "'Push me one more inch, and you'll see that I can still break your arm if I feel like it.'"

"And he did too. Remember when Michael was a teenager—I think you and Chris had just gotten married, right? I don't recall what Michael had done, but Frank's way of punishing him was to break his arm in two places, and Katherine had to lie about what happened when she took him to the hospital. Frank didn't even go."

"So why was she so sweet to us? She treated us better than her own daughters. I remember the first Christmas that we were married, Katherine actually hung a Star of David on the Christmas tree. It was a little weird, but I knew that she wanted me to feel included. Like I was part of the family."

"I know. When Dennis first brought me here to meet her, I was sure she was going to faint, but nope, she was nothing but lovely to me. And when we were getting divorced, she told me that Dennis was never going to find anyone that was in the same class as me. Can you imagine?"

"Maybe it's because she wasn't responsible for us," Lissa says. "I mean, when we met her, we were already adults. We were who we were. She had nothing to do with our values, our behavior, or anything else, so she could, like, relax. No one could ever hold her accountable for how we turned out. Besides, think about how she was raised—it was a different world, everything was different. When she grew up on the Lower East Side of Manhattan, it was barely the turn of the twentieth century. There were still stockyards where the UN is now. Everyone was an immigrant, all the adults barely spoke English. Where they had come from—Ireland, Italy, Eastern Europe—children worked in the fields or in factories, and if they didn't do what their parents wanted, they got beaten within an inch of their lives. She probably thought that since our parents—yours and mine—were born in the United States, they had raised softies, so it wasn't our fault if we came across as smart alecks with crazy opinions about things."

"You know what?" Elaine says. "You're one smart chick."

Lissa sighs. "I think I stopped being any kind of chick a long time ago."

A few moments later, the young woman from the real estate agency steps out on the porch and says she's going to go out and grab something for lunch. Lissa and Elaine stay where they are, sitting on the back porch, enjoying the pleasant weather, chatting and smoking Elaine's cigarettes. When they hear the front door slam open, they're surprised by the loud sound, but assume that the young woman has returned.

"We're still back here, on the porch," Elaine calls out.

They hear heavy footsteps pounding through the living room and the kitchen. Then, the door to the porch flies open.

"Wow. Look who it is. The Jap and the Jew."

Lissa and Elaine narrow their eyes, exchange a quick look. "Well, hello to you too, Kevin," Elaine says to her ex-brother-in-law. Like Elaine and her ex-husband, Kevin is also a cop, but city, not state. He spent four years in the navy, and now he's on the job in Newark.

"Yeah, hi, Kevin," Lissa says. Kevin is her ex-brother-in-law too, the second youngest in the family. He's thin, with pale blue eyes and light brown hair, like all the brothers, like their father. The sisters look pretty much the same, except, by the vagaries of fate or just scrambled DNA, they were all born with chestnut brown hair, like their mother.

"What are you two doing here?" Kevin says. "Slumming in the boonies?"

"We were invited," Elaine says, blowing out thin tendrils of cigarette smoke. "I came out of respect for your mother. So did Lissa, I'm sure. She obviously wanted us to have some remembrance of her."

"Right. Like you actually care. Like you gave a shit about her when she was alive, but it's fine and dandy to come here now and pick through her bones."

"Okay," Elaine says, stubbing out her cigarette in a seashell sitting on the table. Getting to her feet, she says, "If it's going to be like that, I think I'll just get going, Kev. So, sorry about your mother and I wish you the best, et cetera, et cetera. Lissa, want to walk me out?"

"Sure," Lissa says. She calls to the dog, who runs up on the porch. Instinctively, Lissa lifts him up into her arms.

"What's the matter?" Kevin says. "We could have a nice little family meeting here, just the three of us. Share some memories, have a few laughs."

He's swaying on his feet as he stays positioned in front of the door, seeming to be intentionally blocking it. Elaine stands completely still and Lissa, sensing that she should just follow her sister-in-law's lead, remains exactly where she is.

"Kevin," Elaine says, finally, "you're drunk. I know you are—I can smell it."

"So what?" he says. "I'm off duty, and you're retired, so you don't get to say anything to me about what I do. You're not a big fucking deal anymore, Miss State Trooper. Miss big-shit marksman—or is it markswoman? Fuck me if I'm being politically incorrect."

The relationship between Kevin and Elaine has always been an uneasy one, partly because there's always tension between state troopers and city cops, partly because these two people simply never liked each other. Years ago, when one of the other brothers or sisters was around, they would run interference, but there's no one here to do that now. Certainly, Lissa doesn't feel equipped to calm these waters: Kevin was never particularly fond of her either.

"Bye, Kev," Elaine says. With Kevin still blocking the back door, Elaine motions to Lissa, then turns and walks toward the porch stairs, meaning to go around the side of the house and out to the street. "I'm done with this."

"What's your problem?" Kevin says, his voice rising. "Too chickenshit to face off with me? Don't tell me you left that baby Glock at home."

"I never leave my gun at home," Elaine says in a quiet voice. Too quiet.

"Then why don't you pull it out and see if I can't get it away from you faster than you can yank it out of that stupid ankle holster you're so famous for? It's just a pussy-ass way of showing off. Everyone knows the draw's too slow to do any good."

"You don't really want to find out if that's true," Elaine says.

"Maybe I do," Kevin tells her. Then, in one swift motion, he moves away from the door, steps toward Lissa, and grabs the dog from her arms. Lissa is too startled to utter even a single word of protest. "Are you going to play hero if I twist the head off this stupid piece of shit?" he spits out at Elaine. Then, turning to Lissa, he says, "I hate little dogs. Another girl thing that just makes the world a lousier place than it already is."

Lissa is so startled that she's finding it hard to form coherent thoughts, but there is one that suddenly lights up in her mind like a big neon sign, and it's that Kevin sounds just like Chris when he was at his worst, drunk and stoned and gripped by the same poisonous rage that went so deep, reached so far back into the past, that there was no remedy—at least, none that Lissa could ever come up with. Eight siblings: six with perfectly normal, productive lives—more or less—and two, Chris and Kevin, as broken and bleeding as the walking dead. The wounds were invisible at first, but boy, as time went on, whatever kept them functioning began to peel away like burnt skin.

"Why are you even carrying this thing around?" Kevin says to Lissa. As Bodhi begins to whimper, Kevin tosses him up in the air and catches him, holding the dog under his front legs so that his back legs are dangling in the air. "I thought you were better than that."

What does that mean? Lissa can't think of anything to say to Kevin that isn't likely to make the situation worse, so she decides to simply tell him the truth. She knows what it is, even though when she adopted the dog she told herself it was because she was doing a good deed, because she thought it was unlikely that anyone else would want him, and then eventually, he'd be put down. "I got him because I'm lonely. I need some living thing to keep me company; I'm getting old and I'm all alone and I don't know what else to do about any of that."

There's a pause, a brief but undeniable silence that hangs in the air because something's been said that no one in this family ever says. But then it's gone. "Oh, boo-hoo," Kevin finally replies, twisting his mouth into an ugly sneer. "Poor fucking you."

"Listen to me," Elaine says, drawing Kevin's attention back to her, "I am going to reach into my back pocket and get my phone. Then I'm going to call your captain. I know him—Jack Beason, right? I am going to call him and tell him that you are threatening me and my sister-in-law, and I need a patrol car to respond to this address with all possible urgency. That will be the end of your career and your pension. Do you want that? Because here's my phone."

Kevin looks toward Elaine, who now has her cell phone in her hand. In that moment, without even thinking about it, Lissa lunges forward and pulls her dog out of Kevin's arms. He steps toward her, but as she cradles the dog in one arm, she raises the other and lifts up her hand. Her fingers open like a fan. "Don't come near me," she says. "Don't you fucking touch me."

Kevin hesitates for a moment but then steps back. "You're both such crybabies. You can't even take a joke."

"Fuck you, Kevin," Elaine says, glowering. She pushes past him, and Lissa follows, holding tight to her dog. When they're back outside, Elaine opens the passenger-side door to her car and tells Lissa to get in. "I still hear things," Elaine says as she slides in behind the wheel and starts the car, "and what I hear is that Kevin has already been suspended twice. They shouldn't let him back on the streets at all because he's way out of control." Once they've turned the corner on Concannon Drive and the house is out of sight, Elaine has something else she wants to say to Lissa. "Look, Kevin's one thing, but Chris—well, Chris. I never realized how bad things had gotten with him. I really didn't. I know that this comes a little late, but I am so sorry about what you must have gone through with him."

"He was very good at hiding it from everyone," Lissa replies. "It's nobody's fault."

The dog is still whimpering and looking around as if he's waiting for someone to strike him. "It's okay, little boy," Elaine says, reaching over with one hand to stroke the dog's ear. "Everybody's safe now."

There was something there, something in that small gesture of comfort that it seemed necessary for Lissa to repay. All she has is a confession. "I kept thinking things would get better—that I could *make* them better, but by the time I admitted to myself that wasn't possible, I felt stuck. Trapped. I had no friends left, and I had to hide money from Chris just so I could pay the rent every month. It took a long time for me to decide that I had to finally take a chance on saving myself. I had health insurance through my job, so I talked him into going to rehab, and then I moved out of our apartment. When he dropped out of the rehab program, which I guess I knew was going to happen, he wanted to come live with me in my new place, but I wouldn't let him. After that, he used to call me every once in a while. He told me he'd moved back to Jersey, got a job as a custodian in some apartment complex, and had stopped getting high, but I knew it wasn't true—the not getting high part, anyway. It was about a year later that he overdosed. I still miss him, sometimes. There was a time when I really did love him, but by the end, that guy wasn't there anymore."

Elaine turns away for a moment as a private look—pain, introspection, something like that—passes across her face. "Yeah, it was sort of the same with me. I mean, about Dennis. No matter how much it hurts inside, it just seems easier to keep going along. The alarm clock rings, you get up for work, you come home exhausted, the days are crazy and full of so much crap that dealing with the other stuff in your life—like your marriage—requires more effort than it seems possible to find anymore. And then—*poof!*—you just wake up one morning and realize you're already gone, and you're going to have to start your life all over again."

That seems all there is to say. They continue on in silence for the rest of the short ride to the station, where they exchange a brief hug, and then Elaine drives off into the summer afternoon.

The train back to the city is delayed by debris on the tracks, so it takes much longer than it should have for Elaine to get home. When she finally reaches Penn Station, she has to change for the subway out to Queens, so by the time she reaches her stop she finds herself walking home in the early evening. The sky is lavender; the horizon is darkening, deepening into blue.

Lissa lives in a small studio with a terrace, high up in an apartment tower with a view of the Manhattan skyline. After she left Chris, she was able to save some money, so with her small pension and Social Security, she is now able to pay her rent without worrying about it each month. She thinks about that now, as she opens the door and steps inside—it's a plus in her life, one less thing to worry about, although the list of troubles that may come always remains on her mind. That do come, no matter what. Still, at least she's home now, and for the moment, all is well. She puts the dog down on the floor, and he runs to his food bowl, waiting for dinner.

"Are you okay now?" she says to him and imagines that he would say yes. Who knows what he remembers about the things that frighten him, how much he will remember—if anything—about what happened to him today?

After she feeds the dog and eats her own dinner, some leftovers from last night's takeout (which she does not feel bad about, not one bit; she never liked to cook and is fine with ordering in even though so many of the TV shows she watches portray that as some sort of decline in the quality of life for older women), she goes out to sit on the terrace where she watches the lights coming on in the towers of the city. She takes her knitting with her, as she does most nights when it's warm enough to sit outside. Lissa's mother died when she was twelve, and her father, who had zero ideas about how to take care of a child by himself, sent her to spend that summer with his sister, Lissa's aunt, who was also at a loss when it came to knowing how to comfort a grieving child. All she could think of doing was to find a way to occupy Lissa's time, so she taught her to knit, which was the one thing she herself loved to do. All summer, they sat in rocking chairs on the porch of the aunt's house in a suburb of New Jersey that seemed to have been designed to inspire nothing but a sense that life was an endless round of meaningless days. Lissa did learn to knit, but she hated it, and she grew angrier and angrier with each loop she was instructed to wind around her needles. That was the summer she changed, the summer she became another person, uncontrollable and beyond the reach of anyone who tried to make her behave like the nice, well-mannered girl she would have become—maybe—if her mother hadn't died and her life hadn't taken an unexpected turn.

After that, when she was sent back home because school was starting, most nights she just walked out of her father's apartment in the Bronx and took the subway down to West 4th Street in the Village, where she roamed around, got into the hippie scene, listened to music in coffee shops and cafés. She was a lonely, angry teenager, but the music soothed her, the people she met shared their ideas—all new to her—about how life could be. That's how things went, mostly, until she met Chris, until they made their ridiculous pact to be normal people. The problem with that, of course, as Lissa now knows all too well, is that neither of them was normal to begin with. Whatever that means, it wasn't them.

But a few years ago, Lissa happened to pass a craft store and saw a skein of glittery black yarn in the window that she thought would make a beautiful sweater. *Which I bet I remember how to make*, she thought, so she bought the yarn and yes, it all came back to her. There was some trial and error involved, and it took a lot of time, but in the end, she was able to knit a long-sleeved sweater with a V-neck that almost looked like the work of someone who had been doing this for a long time. After that, when it became apparent to her that she had some natural skill, she watched YouTube videos that taught her a variety of advanced knitting techniques. Soon, she was able to produce beautiful, elaborate pieces, and even though she sometimes feels that what she's doing—all this knitting—is an old-lady pastime that she should be embarrassed about, she's managed to turn her new avocation into a little business for herself. These days, she knits sweaters and scarves and sparkly evening shawls that she sells on Etsy or in consignment shops where they sell quite well. She even made up a name for her creations, Night Owl Designs, after one of those cafés in the Village that she used to hang around in. She spent hours and hours there, in the Night Owl Café, drinking Coke and eating potato chips, all she could afford. When she decided on the name, she ordered labels to sew into her knitted pieces from a woman who has her own small business hand making labels for handmade clothing. The labels Lissa has the woman make for her show a little owl with oversized eyes sitting on a branch. The owl is winking.

Now, as Lissa works at her knitting, Bodhi follows her onto the terrace and stretches out beside her. A few minutes later, though, he's on his feet, looking up at the sky with rapt attention as a pair of small brown bats go swooping by.

Whoosh. Whoosh. The bats fly by in silence, but in Lissa's mind, she hears the way the wings of the bats might sound as they glide through the deepening twilight. The first time Lissa saw bats flying past her terrace, she thought she was imagining things, but then she searched online and found that yes, brown bats are common around here. They live under bridges, in trees, in parklands all through the boroughs. She enjoys seeing them because it's like knowing a secret about the city. The city is full of secrets, of course, but this is hers.

As she works and her mind wanders, Lissa finds herself imagining that she's a character in a scene that has a kind of Southern Gothic feel to it. And this is what she imagines: that she is a woman in a pensive mood, sitting all alone with her knitting, perhaps with the memories of her mysterious past. With a pet dog at her feet and bats flying through the gloaming of a century that's long gone and far away. It's an image that makes her smile, maybe just because it's so different than the truth. In fact, the year is 2023 and she's in New York City, living a life like any other, more or less. Walking down the street, Lissa thinks that you'd never pick her out in a crowd, never dream there was anything special about her, anything important. But looking back, Lissa does think that she has some stories she could tell if anyone wanted to listen. Stories about good things that happened to her as well as bad. Stories from when she was as wild and free as she would ever be. And if no one wants to listen, she can tell them to herself. Maybe that will help, as the days turn into nights and the nights, sometimes, seem to go on forever—especially if, as you get older, you find it hard to fall asleep. But then it's always morning again, and the story goes on.

OUT OF SEASON

After the Labor Day weekend, it finally felt like summer was winding down in Provincetown. Most of the tourists and summer residents were packing up and leaving, stopping first to have their farewell cup of coffee and a plate of cinnamon toast at their favorite breakfast place. "Goodbye, goodbye, hope to see you next summer," they'd say to the young girls who had worked as waitresses this season, then maybe they'd walk over to the gift shop next door to buy one last souvenir before heading down Route 6 toward the Bourne Bridge that meets the highways leading home. But since none of this was on Neil's agenda, he bought his morning coffee at the fishing dock near his motel, then went back to his room and sat on his deck, which had a view of the salt marsh stretching out toward the horizon. As he watched the hazy sunlight slowly brighten, he saw a great blue heron picking its way over the flat terrain of flooded bullrushes and mud, then suddenly take wing. Following the bird's path through the sky until it finally disappeared into the far distance, he thought, *Another tourist flies away.*

He lazed around until early afternoon, when he went back to the dock to grab some lunch from a vendor selling sandwiches to the fishermen, then walked up Commercial Street, the main route through town, and went to the library where he read the newspaper and used one of their computers to check his email. Opening the program, he saw that he had a message from his neighbor, who was feeding his cat while he was away. The neighbor wrote that the cat was doing fine and attached a picture of the gray tabby sunning himself on the windowsill in the living room of Neil's apartment. *Thanks so much!* he wrote back, adding the appreciative exclamation mark to show that he was really grateful for the help.

When he left the library, he sat outside for a while, resting on a bench near a kite shop that had a sign on the door saying it was going to close for the season at the end of the week. *Thanks for another high-flying summer. See you next year!* was hand-lettered in rainbow colors on the bottom of the sign. Neil remembered seeing this same sign—or some version of it—in the windows of kite shops on Commercial Street for as long as he had been coming here, which, by his calculation, had to be for something like fifty years. His first visit was when he was in his early twenties when a group of friends, on a lark, had driven up to Provincetown from New York City and brought him along. By that time, this old fishing village at the tip of Cape Cod had become well-known as a gay mecca, as well as a favorite retreat for artists and writers. A city boy who knew the ocean only from subway trips to a crowded beach at the edge of Queens and had never seen the sunrise over a landscape of endless sand dunes or climbed the winding stairs of a working lighthouse, Neil had fallen almost instantly in love with the place. After his first visit, he had come back almost every year. He'd come with friends, with a particular boyfriend, and now, on his own.

The past two years were the first he'd ever missed making his annual trip, and that was only because of Covid. There had been a major outbreak of coronavirus in Provincetown, so tourists and travelers had been discouraged. This year, though, with the pandemic declared over, the town had welcomed people back, and it had been packed all season, which was the reason that Neil had decided to drive up at the tail end of the holiday weekend and stay on for a while after the town emptied out. He was happy enough to miss the crowds of people elbowing each other on the sidewalk or being stuck in his car, dodging the endless line of vehicles crawling down the narrow streets. Besides, he loved it here at any time of year. Spring and summer were beautiful on the Cape, but even in the colder months, he was happy enough to walk along the lonely beaches, content to sit in a quiet bar drinking the afternoon away. *And speaking of drinking*, he said to himself, *the Sailor's Inn is just across the street.* He didn't have to convince himself that a cold bottle of beer sounded great right about now.

The Sailor's Inn was one of the local bars that stayed open year-round. In the summer, the place was famous for its drag shows, but the last one, a rousing finale featuring a trio of well-known drag performers, had concluded late last night; now, the small stage that had hosted the show was curtained off, and only about a half dozen men were seated around the bar. Neil settled himself at the far end of the line of stools so as not to appear to be intruding on the group, who all seemed to know each other. Still, he couldn't help overhearing their conversation, which was sprinkled with joking references to how one of them had jumped onstage last night, joining the performer in singing a melodramatic rendition of a weepy old standard. The bartender, who was included in the friendly chatter, pulled himself away from the group to walk over to Neil and ask what he'd like to drink. Looking at the special brews listed on a blackboard behind the bar, he ordered a summer shandy.

The bartender brought out the bottle and told Neil that he was drinking the last of the selection since they didn't keep summer shandy in stock when it was out of season. Hearing this, one of the men called over to the bartender and said, "Hey, Joey, you should give the fellow a freebie."

“Oh yeah, Mitch?” the bartender, Joey, replied. “Why’s that?”

“End-of-summer celebration,” Mitch replied. Looking over at him, Neil saw an older man—*Well no*, he told himself, *You can’t say that anymore because you’re an old specimen yourself*—wearing a dazzling Hawaiian shirt and a kerchief around his neck. “Now we get to have the town to ourselves for a while,” Mitch concluded.

“I’ll tell you what I’ll do,” Joey said. “Let’s have a contest. Who-ever wins gets free drinks for the rest of the afternoon.”

“Deal,” Mitch said. “Right, dear hearts?” The other men at the bar laughingly agreed.

“Alright, then,” Joey said. “Here’s the contest. Each of us is going to tell the story of how we ended up with our cat—or cats, since I know some of us have a whole herd. Then we’ll vote on who wins.”

“How do we decide?” one of the men sitting at the opposite end of the bar asked. “Are we voting for the funniest story, the strangest—or who lies the best?”

“All of the above,” Joey ruled.

“Wait a minute,” someone else chimed in. “Why do you assume that we all have cats?”

“Because this is a gay bar and every queer over fifty has a cat,” said Joey, smiling as he picked up and polished a glass that didn’t need the attention.

“What makes you think you know how old we are?” the same fellow protested.

“Because, like Mitch said, summer’s over, and all the young cuties are back in Manhattan or Miami or wherever they fly in from on their summer fairy wings.” Joey then turned toward Neil and said, “How about you, Summer Shandy? You’re welcome to join in. I assume you’ve got a cat?”

“Ha!” yet another fellow sitting at the bar chimed in. “Good one, Joey. That’s a super sly way of asking if he’s a fagele.”

“A what?” Joey asked.

“*Fagele*. It’s Yiddish for little bird. It’s what my grandmother used to call gay boys. Meaning, my family decided that I was the one who killed her when she found out about me—never mind she died five years later."

"You know, we could change the contest to come up with the most amusing slur we've ever heard," Mitch said.

"Too gloomy," Joey declared. Then he turned back to Neil. "So do you want to tell your story first? And what's your name, by the way?"

"Neil. And I do have a cat, but . . ." Here, Neil paused, while everyone laughed out loud and one or two raised their glasses in a joke salute. "His name is Otis, but actually, there's nothing all that interesting about how I got him. I inherited him from a friend when he moved."

That was half a lie: Neil had taken in the cat when the friend he was referring to had died after a long struggle with a particularly lethal cancer. During his last days in hospice, he asked Neil to take in his cat because he had no one else—no friends or relatives—who would do him this one last favor. Contrary to the theory about gay men and cats being floated at the Sailor's Inn, Neil did not consider himself a cat person, but over time, he had grown fond of Otis. The cat had been very frightened when Neil first brought him to his place, a small one-bedroom condo in a quiet building on a quiet street in Queens. Otis hid in the bathroom for almost a week, only coming out at night to drink water and sneak some quick bites of the food Neil put out for him. The first time he left the bathroom in daylight, he took nothing more than a few wary steps into the hallway before he ran back to his hiding place. Two weeks later, he finally made it all the way to the living room. Now, the cat slept with Neil, curled up in the crook of his arm. Sometimes, with the cat tucked in beside him, Neil found himself thinking about an article he once read about the results of a survey of pet owners that asked what they would say to their dog or cat if their pet could talk—but only for thirty seconds. Neil had assumed people would ask, *Do you love me? Do you know that I love you?* But surprisingly, what pet owners most wanted to know was if their dog or cat was suffering any kind of pain or illness that wasn't apparent to them. *Does anything hurt you?* was what they wanted to ask Ruby or Willow or Scout. *Is there any kind of help you need from me?*

While Neil was still mulling over the circumstances that brought a cat into his life, the contest at the bar was underway. "Alright then," Joey decreed, "let's hear from everybody else. And since I'm sure we've all done this, no one gets points for being the good-hearted dumb fuck who adopted a cat left behind by the people who fed it all summer and then decided not to take their adorable little kitty home with them because, by Labor Day, it had turned into a grown-up pussy."

After everyone laughed at the joke and eventually got to tell their cat story, a unanimous vote that included Neil, who was allowed to cast a ballot, declared the winner to be a carpenter from nearby Wellfleet who described how he found his cat after last summer's Gay Pride parade. The annual event was important for the town because it attracted hundreds of visitors each year to watch participants in elaborate mermaid costumes; or dressed as lobsters, movie stars, ballerinas on roller skates; or as Pilgrims, locally celebrated as the first tourists to set foot in Provincetown. The cat that the carpenter found—actually, a calico kitten—was wandering around by the Pilgrim Monument, a tall granite tower just outside Provincetown. Someone had managed to wrangle the kitten into a Pilgrim costume that included a black dress with a white apron and had even tied a tiny bonnet to her head. The carpenter passed around his phone so that everyone could see a photo of the kitten on the day he brought her home. Accepting the first of his free drinks, he said that he's kept the costume in case the kitten wanted to try it on again "when she's all grown up."

Neil stayed around for another half hour or so, when the group sitting at the bar began to break up. Some were headed home;

others left to meet with other friends. As they departed, it was time for the kitchen in the back to open up for the early dinner service. The bartender carried a blackboard outside that listed the menu, and a few new people began wandering in—mostly couples, now—seating themselves at the tables in the area near the curtained-off stage where meals would be served. The bouncy afternoon music that had been playing in the background was changed to soft jazz, and the lights were dimmed. A waiter appeared to take orders.

It was too early for Neil to be hungry, and he didn't feel like eating alone at the bar, so he, too, got up from his stool and headed for the door. Joey and Mitch both called out goodbye as he walked away, which suddenly—and unexpectedly—caused a wave of deep, painful sadness to wash over him.

What's the matter with me? he asked himself, but really, he knew: He was lonely. An afternoon spent in the company of people who were all friendly with each other, all telling funny stories and cracking jokes, had made it impossible for him to ignore that these days, loneliness weighed heavily on him, weighed him down. Though he'd made himself own up to being one of the older men who'd been sitting at the bar that afternoon—how could he not, seeing his somewhat grizzled, gray-haired reflection in the mirror above the ranks of bottles—it was still difficult to accept that getting older was bringing with it a great load of sad and troublesome memories that he didn't feel he could keep carrying around but also had no idea how to put down.

Among those memories was his unresolved relationship with his parents. It seemed like eras, epochs of time, had passed since he'd lived at home, but he still wondered about how things would have been between them all if he'd managed to come out to them rather than have them suspect who he was and argue with him about it in a roundabout way. Openly, what they objected to was his long hair, the Deadhead music wailing from his bedroom, and the fringed jackets and bell-bottom jeans that they considered effeminate. He left home before they got any further than that and rarely saw them in the years that followed. But he managed to get by on his own. He worked his way through one of the city colleges in the time when tuition for city residents was still free, and after he graduated, entered a training program to become a paramedic. He worked on ambulances for many years, which he enjoyed, but eventually took on an administrative job, running the ambulance service for one of the city's largest public hospitals. He continued in that position long past the time when he could have retired, leaving only when his own health problems intervened. First, there was a hip replacement, and after that, a fractured vertebrae that never healed properly after years of lifting patients onto gurneys became almost crippling unless he kept to a regimen of prescribed pain medication. So, though it wasn't what he wanted, he finally did retire—which turned out to be just a few months before Covid shut down the world.

He managed to get through the isolation of the pandemic by finding ways to keep himself busy. He became a volunteer at the same public hospital where he had been working, which was soon overrun with indigent patients who had nowhere else to get help. Through many long months, in all kinds of weather, with his back aching and his legs feeling like they might buckle under him from the strain of being on his feet for hours on end, he stood outside the hospital with nurses and translators, helping the blocks-long line of desperately ill men, women, and children fill out forms that required information they were often reluctant to disclose. "You're safe here, we won't tell them anything," he repeated day after day, hating the federal immigration officers who often showed up to prowl for people they could deport.

When he wasn't at the hospital, he was watching the news. Keeping the television on was like having access to a twenty-four-hour-a-day town hall meeting. Even if he couldn't sleep in the middle of the night, he could tune into someone discussing some aspect of the pandemic. He lived alone, but he didn't feel alone because people seemed to be talking to him all day, all night. *We're in this together* was the message, constantly beamed at him from the TV, from the governor's briefings that interrupted local programming, and from the men and women, grim-faced but always reliably present, reporting the news around the clock.

But when the virus had been mostly defeated and the world was opening up again, Neil had no more work to do. The hospital gave him a certificate commending him for his volunteer efforts and sent him home, back to his apartment in the quiet building on the quiet, tree-lined street. It was springtime then, a season of sunshine and blooming flowers. For the first week or two that he was home, Neil was fine: He slept late, drank his breakfast coffee on the small terrace outside his living room, and shopped for groceries to restock his kitchen cabinets with items that had disappeared from the store shelves during the pandemic's darkest months. But there came a morning when he woke up with no plans in mind and, he realized, no one to call, no one to hang out with. His friends had always been people he knew from work. Neil was hardly the only gay man or woman among his varied group of colleagues over the years, and no one seemed to care one way or another. They were all good, loyal friends—until, seemingly overnight, they were not.

Maybe, Neil thought, that was because he had worked for so long that he'd ended up being older than most of the people he'd been friendly with and now had little in common with them beyond the boundaries of their jobs. And maybe Neil himself hadn't made enough of an effort to keep in contact during the pandemic when all the rules of friendship and socializing no longer applied. This trip to Provincetown had been an effort to shake himself up, to show himself that even on his own, he could still do the things he liked, still keep active and take pleasure in his life. But as he walked along Commercial Street heading back to his motel, he had to admit that he hadn't achieved his goal. He had enjoyed the time he'd spent in the Sailor's Inn, but the loneliness that had crashed down on him when he left was only getting worse now with each step he took. It was like a physical sensation, like wind passing through his body, sunlight darkening at the edges of his vision. These were dreadful feelings, and he had no idea how to shake them.

He was just a block or two from his motel when he had to stop on the corner to let an SUV towing a pair of jet skis on a trailer go by. The driver was having a hard time navigating the turn, so as Neil waited, he walked over to a nearby art gallery and looked in the window, where he saw a painting that caught his eye. What he saw was several rows of small lonely-looking cottages standing on a grassy bluff darkened by shade and shadow, with a ladder of wispy white clouds lying across a pale sky. For the few moments he paused in front of the gallery to look at the picture, he forgot about how badly he was feeling.

But he was soon brought back to reality as the door of the gallery opened, and a young woman walked out holding a large box full of files. She carried the box over to a car parked at the curb and then turned back.

Seeing Neil looking at the picture, she said, "I'm really surprised by how everyone stops to look at that painting, even though it's just a copy."

"A copy?" Neil said. "Wow. Should I have seen the original somewhere?"

"Well, I thought you might have. It's called *Corn Hill*, and it's by Edward Hopper. You probably know some of his other paintings."

Neil started to say no, but then remembered something from a long-ago art history class. "He painted *Nighthawks*, right? A couple of people sitting at a counter in a diner, late at night?"

"Yes, exactly. That's probably his most famous painting—the one everyone knows."

Something else Neil remembered from that long-ago class filtered back through his memory, and he recalled a discussion about the troubling sense of alienation that the picture was famous for. The landscape he was looking at in *Corn Hill*—the empty sky, the dark-roofed cottages standing alone on the blurry-looking dunes—gave him the same feeling.

"If this is just a copy," Neil said, "I don't think I would have known it from the original." Then, laughing at himself—which felt like just the relief he needed, even if it was only momentary—he said, "I mean, not that I'd probably even be able to point out what a bad copy looked like."

"Well, this is a really *good* copy. It's part of a special end-of-season show we had on for the past few weeks. We asked local artists to paint their version of Hopper's Cape Cod pictures. He painted quite a few of them."

"I had no idea," Neil said, having already used up all the information about Edward Hopper that his art classes had provided to him.

"Oh, sure," the young woman continued. "Hopper came up here every summer for about thirty years and painted dozens of pictures based on places around this area on the outer Cape."

Curious, Neil asked, "Did he actually live in Provincetown?"

"No. He had a cottage up on the dunes above Fisher Beach in Truro, which is just about twenty minutes away. It's still there, as a matter of fact." The young woman pulled open the door to the gallery and said, "I'm really sorry, but I'd better get back to what I was doing. I've got to get all these files out of here because we're trying to close up for the season."

"Well, thanks for the lesson about Edward Hopper," Neil said. "It was interesting."

He left the gallery and headed out into the empty street, where the SUV and its cumbersome trailer had long since driven away. He walked back to his motel, but when he got there, he found that he didn't feel like going up to his room just because he had nothing else to do. Instead, he thought he might go for a drive. Maybe he could find Edward Hopper's cottage up on the dunes above Fisher Beach in Truro; he had a general idea of where it might be because he'd been to the area once or twice in the past. Besides, he thought, smiling to himself, maybe on some other summer afternoon in the Sailor's Inn, he could start a drinking contest about who had made a pilgrimage to the homes of famous artists on the Cape.

He got in his car, but before he left, he Googled "Edward Hopper in Truro," and the results showed him pictures of an ordinary-looking cottage set back among a line of grassy dunes. The only thing that stood out about the dwelling was that it had a large window on one side divided into four panes of glass. He couldn't find an exact address to plot into his car's GPS, so he simply entered "Fisher Beach" and followed the directions that appeared on the screen, which took him to a parking lot at the edge of a high bluff. There was one other car in the parking lot—an old yellow VW Beetle—but whoever the owner was, they were nowhere to be seen.

A sign at the end of the parking lot directed him to a path leading down to the beach. He walked along, following the shoreline but glancing up at the dunes from time to time as he looked for Hopper's cottage. He was beginning to worry that he'd somehow gotten turned around and was walking in the wrong direction when he came to a place where the tumbled rocks of a broken jetty had created a narrow promontory that jutted out into the water. As he rounded this spit of land, he saw two things at the same time: a cottage high up on the dunes with a window divided into four panes of glass, and a woman in a blue cotton dress standing on the beach below, looking up as she shaded her eyes with her hand.

Surprised to see someone else here, Neil wasn't sure what to do. He didn't want to startle the woman or seem like he was lurking around, so he decided that the best thing to do was to offer a friendly hello.

"Hi," he called out. "I didn't want to scare you."

Hearing him, the woman turned around and smiled. "That's very nice of you," she said. "Thanks."

Then, looking up toward the cottage, she said, "I guess I'm not the only one who decided to make this pilgrimage today."

"I don't know if that's exactly what I'm doing," Neil told her. "It's just that someone in a gallery in Provincetown told me Edward Hopper had lived around here, so I thought I might see if I could find the place."

"Well, you did," the woman said, smiling again.

She seemed nice, Neil thought. A nice person standing on the beach in the late afternoon sun. Feeling like he wanted to continue the conversation, he said the first thing that came to his mind. "That must be your car in the parking lot."

"If you mean the yellow Beetle, then yes, that's my car." Holding out her hand to Neil she said, "I'm Emily Warren."

"Neil Jensen." They shook hands and the conversation moved on. "If that's really where Hopper lived, it doesn't seem like anything special. Just an old cottage stuck back there in the dunes."

"I kind of thought the same thing the first time I came here," Emily Warren said. "It doesn't even look like it was very comfortable to live in."

"So you've been here before?" Neil asked.

"A couple of times," Emily Warren replied. "I guess I've always been trying to see what he saw. I mean, I know what he's famous for is painting lonely people in lonely places, but he also said that when he was up here on the Cape, what he was really trying to capture was the special quality of the light."

"Really? The light?" Neil said, puzzled.

"I don't know how to describe it, but I think I understand what he meant," Emily Warren said. "Sometimes, you look at the dunes and they seem bleached out, like what you're looking at is a flat, one-dimensional landscape. A sad, lonely, Edward Hopper kind of place. And yet, at other times, the sunlight seems so bright and luminous that you can almost feel it shimmering all around you. Either way, I think that when you're standing here, on the beach, with the dunes above you stretching out to the horizon, the light can make you feel like you're in an in-between time, you know? Like this is an interlude in your life—a time after everything that's ever happened to you and before everything that's going to come." Suddenly, Emily laughed and shook her head, as if she had just snapped out of a spell. "I'm sorry," she said. "I think I just got a little carried away."

"Don't apologize. I probably would have thought I'd trekked all the way here for no reason if you hadn't told me what you just did. I appreciate it."

"Well, thanks for saying that. It's very kind of you."

A soft breeze came up and blew a few strands of Emily's long brown hair across her eyes. As she raised her hand to brush them away, there was something about that gesture—something Neil hadn't thought of for a long time—that caught him off guard, so much so that all he could do was mumble a stilted goodbye when Emily said she had to be going. He watched her walk down the beach and soon disappear from view, but that wasn't really what he was seeing: In his mind's eye, he was watching a young man who had a habit of making that same gesture brush the hair from his eyes—only his hair was corn-silk blonde and he liked to wear it long enough to sweep back behind his ears.

The man's name was Michael—never Mike—and he was a radiologist at St. Vincent's Hospital, a place long since demolished by the developers who seemed to be remaking all of New York City into condominiums and office towers. Neil had met Michael O'Connell when the ambulance Neil was working on was diverted to St. Vincent's on a busy Saturday night. That was when both men were in their twenties, and they soon began a love affair that lasted for over a decade. Sometimes they lived together, sometimes they didn't because the relationship had its ups and downs. The ups were wonderful, but the downs were nearly unbearable for Neil, and they worsened as time went on. The problem was Michael's drinking, which Neil told himself he could live with in the early years of their relationship when Michael cared enough about his job to remain sober when he was at work. But the rest of the time, he drank as much as he wanted to when he wanted to and because he wanted to. He did have periods of sobriety, but during those intervals he was often unfaithful, as if he were making the point that being sober wasn't going to be a magical cure for anything. In the end, it was Michael who broke things off, saying that he couldn't go on trying to be the person he knew that Neil wished he was. "I can't control my impulses," he told Neil, "and I don't want to. You think you never knew that about me, but you did because I told you. And year after year I kept telling you that I have to do what I want, even when it hurts you."

With these memories swirling around in his mind, Neil didn't realize how long he'd been standing on the beach until it began to get dark. He trekked back along the shore and climbed up the dunes to the parking lot where he retrieved his car—the only one in the lot now—and drove back to the motel.

Once again settled in his room, he ordered a pizza—*Even at the end of the world,* he thought, *there will always be someplace to order pizza*—and tried to find a movie on one of the cable channels that he felt like watching. Tomorrow would be the end of his vacation. He would pack his bag and drive back to the city, which seemed, at the moment, a million miles away.

The next morning, he woke up early enough to get a last cup of coffee near the fishing dock and drank it on the deck outside his room. Looking out at the salt marsh, where a tall white egret was picking its way through ribbons of haze, he thought, *What if I didn't leave? What if I decide to move up here for good?* That, he decided, was probably a fantasy that many people toyed with at the end of their sojourn in some lovely vacation town as they closed the door of their summer rental, then drove along the main street for the last time that year, passing a kite store and their favorite breakfast place with the perfect cinnamon toast. But it was just a dream, not something that anyone might likely do.

Still, as Neil left the motel, got in his car, and started the drive down Route 6, heading for the Bourne Bridge that would take him to the highway leading back to New York, instead of feeling the bonds to Provincetown loosening, Neil found himself thinking of a day when he might really pack up his apartment, put his things in suitcases and boxes, and take a last walk through the empty rooms. *Goodbye, goodbye,* he'd say to the bare walls and the long years of life he'd be leaving behind. The glorious ups, the woeful downs. Then he pictured himself in some pleasant cottage high on a dune above the beach, with golden afternoon light streaming in through a four-paned window. His cat would probably be frightened to have his life upended again, but he had come to trust Neil, so eventually, he would come to accept his new surroundings. He would settle in, and Neil wouldn't even have to fantasize about some kind of magical intervention that would let him ask the cat, *Are you okay? Do you feel safe and well?* He wouldn't have to ask because he knew by now that he could tell.

SUMMER IN THE MOUNTAINS

It's early on a soft summer morning in Woodstock, in the Catskill Mountains of upstate New York. David Graeber wakes up in his room in the Maude Macy Hotel, just off the main street that runs through town, and feels desperate for coffee. That's how he feels every morning, so last night he made sure to fill the coffeemaker with the Arabica blend he stashed in his backpack. He's only here for the weekend, so the backpack is all he has with him except for his guitar, which is locked in the trunk of his car.

Yawning, he pulls himself out of bed and pads into the tiny kitchenette to turn on the coffeemaker. As he waits for it to brew, he looks out at the room, which is outfitted with the sort of hippie décor advertised on the hotel's website: There's a purple cotton bedspread with a swirling, psychedelic pattern hung on the wall; a black-and-white Janis Joplin poster on the bathroom door; a small brass incense burner holding the lingering scent of patchouli on a table by the bedside. The hotel is, however, a bit grubbier than he had anticipated and in what seems to be poor repair. But he's willing to be forgiving about that because it was built in 1870 as a boarding house and has been standing on this street—once a road traveled by wayfarers journeying through the mountains—for such a long time that he supposes he's lucky that the pipes are producing hot water for the shower and that the electricity seems to be keeping the coffeemaker bubbling steadily and the air conditioner rattling along.

By 9:00 a.m. he's ready to get going. He makes his way down the stairs to the front door—there is no reception desk here and no staff; the key to his room was left under a flowerpot on a table at the end of the hallway—and out into the day. It's high summer, and Woodstock, with its association to the Woodstock Music Festival, which was actually held miles away in the town of Bethel, is crowded with tourists. But David has never been here before, so he strolls up and down Tinker Street, which is at the heart of the town. Nearby, he lingers for a few moments on a small footbridge that crosses a narrow creek. Gazing down at the clear, slow-moving water burbling over the rocks and leaf litter, he finds himself bemused by the fact that he's even thinking of words like "creek" or "burbling," or that when he looks toward the horizon there's a mountain in his view. David, who has lived his entire life in New York City, is not much of a traveler, so, while he is familiar with cityscapes and even beach scenes, creeks and mountains are generally out of his purview. The only trip he's ever taken outside the United States, for example, was a week-long vacation spent in Paris with a girlfriend decades ago, when he was twenty-three. He did not enjoy it. He knew that he was supposed to be enchanted, but all he felt was out of place and uncomfortable. At the time he thought that maybe it had something to do with being Jewish, being the grandchild of refugees from Eastern Europe, or just his own inability to appreciate what the girlfriend kept telling him was beautiful architecture and romantic vistas—but whatever it was, he had been more than happy to get home.

He's up in the Catskills right now because he's made arrangements to visit his cousin Joe, who lives a few miles away. He isn't expected until lunchtime, though, so he continues his stroll along Tinker Street, where shops and restaurants are lined up tightly, one after another. Everywhere, peace signs and colorful psychedelic banners abound. In a souvenir store, David buys a T-shirt that proclaims "Woodstock: Home of the Happy Hippies" on the back and on the front, has a free-hand drawing of a guitar. He also buys a box of rock candy as a gift for his cousin, who has always been partial to that particular treat. The candy will also serve as an early birthday present: Joe will be seventy-two in September. David is only three months younger, so he will turn the same age before the end of the year.

In David's mind, Joe's life has taken a strange turn. Until recently, David would have thought of himself as the only member of the Graeber family who disappointed them with the way he lived his life. Instead of going to college, from the time he was eighteen through his early thirties, he had worked as a roadie sometimes but mostly played guitar in a variety of rock bands. He managed to eke out a living, but once he had to face the fact that he wasn't destined for fame and fortune, he took a job managing a rehearsal studio where bands rented space by the hour to work on their repertoire. He always enjoyed his work, and it kept him connected to the music world, but the staid, secular Jews of his family—including his two sisters and numerous cousins—all followed more conventional paths. That included Joe—until a few years ago, when he retired from his job as a high school English teacher and told his wife he was leaving her and moving to Woodstock to live in a cabin near a forest preserve. Through all this upheaval, Joe and David had kept in touch, though David had never pressed his cousin for an explanation of his actions, and Joe had never offered one. But David expects that he will hear more about this subject today—a lot more, probably.

Around noon, David returns to where he's parked his car near the hotel and starts the drive to Joe's house. David follows along the route that his GPS tracker sends him, which winds along a steep, narrow road that climbs one hill after another. Halfway through the drive, the road edges along a valley so deep that, looking out the window, all David sees are the tops of tall trees below him, ablaze with sunlight. The treetops look beautiful, magical—but also somewhat fearsome, because if he drives just a few feet off the road, David and his car are likely to plunge into an abyss that will swallow them up in an instant.

Finally, David arrives at Joe's cabin, which turns out to be far less rustic than he expected. It's constructed of smooth, dark planks and has a wide porch looking out on a field of wildflowers. As David exits his car, the front door opens and two huge brown dogs rush outside, barking like crazy. Joe, appearing on the front porch, waves his arms and calls out to David.

"They're friendly," Joe says. "Don't worry. They like having visitors."

David nods and walks up the dirt path toward the cabin, escorted by the dogs, who are radiating happiness. He looks up at his cousin waiting to greet him on the porch and is struck by how much they have begun to look alike. Two old men, still tall and straight-backed, but totally gray now. Joe's hair is beginning to thin, but David's is still long, worn in a ponytail gathered at his neck by a black rubber band.

On the porch, the two men embrace with familiar ease. Not just cousins, they have had an enduring friendship that began in childhood and has been sometimes close, sometimes distant in stretches of years and years, but never severed. Now, on this bright summer day, they are happy to see each other.

Joe shows David around the cabin, which again surprises by being clean and modern inside. It has two bedrooms, a full kitchen, satellite TV. "See?" Joe says. "Contrary to what you've probably heard, I am not living like a hermit. I go into Woodstock at least twice a week to do some shopping, go to the library and so forth, and drive all the way to Kingston once in a while to go to the supermarket there, or to the movies when there's something playing that I want to see."

"I haven't heard much of anything," David tells him truthfully. "There's nobody left, really, that I was ever close to. I mean, I talk to my sisters on the phone once in a while, but that's about it."

"Yup," Joe says. "It's sad."

It is, David thinks, then silently adds, *That could be said about a lot of things.*

Joe ushers David back outside where there's a small table and two chairs set up on the porch. Here, true to his non-hermit standard of living, he has laid out a rather fancy spread for lunch: bagels and lox and whitefish spread with salad and dill pickles. And a six-pack of a local microbrew with a label that shows a laughing moon clinking bottles with a smiling star.

As the two men begin eating, Joe casually feeds bits and pieces of his meal to the two dogs, who sit beside his chair. "Their names are Captain and Sailor," he tells David, "but don't blame me—that's what they called them at the shelter where I got them, and I didn't want to try to teach them to respond to something new. Janet would faint if she saw them—she never liked dogs, especially big ones." Seeing the look of concern blooming on David's face, Joe laughs. "For heaven's sake, that's not why I left. If I had insisted, I could have had a dog. She would never have stopped me."

"I wasn't going to ask," David says.

"I'll tell you anyway, because it's no big secret. Maybe it didn't make a lot of sense to Janet or my friends or my kids—and by 'kids' I mean my two forty-something-year-old children who I don't owe an explanation to anyway—but my reason made sense to me: I just didn't want to talk anymore. I don't mean that I wanted to go silent or anything crazy like that—I just got tired of the endless drone about nothing that went on all day between Janet and me. Between me and just about everyone else, if I'm being honest. Blah, blah, blah, blah, blah, blah, blah. *What should we eat for dinner? Should we buy a new couch? Should we talk to our accountant about this year's tax returns? Should you go to the dentist? Should I go to the rally for a new bike lane in town? Should we invite the neighbors for dinner, see the grandchildren, wash the car, pull down the window shades, pull them up?* There came a time when I just couldn't answer these questions anymore. I didn't care one way or the other, and I just didn't want to talk about these things or anything else because they didn't matter. They don't. And I just got tired of thinking about all that crap day after day, night after night. Now, I can read all day or watch TV or take the dogs for a hike through the woods, and I don't have to say anything or think about anything I don't want to think about. Here, I can just rest my mind. And wait."

"Wait? For what?" David is genuinely puzzled.

"Who knows? To get sick and die, I guess. That's certainly what's going to happen sooner now than later. I'd just rather do it in a place like this, without having to talk about that too. Like when my father died—do you remember that?"

"Yes. He had pancreatic cancer."

"And everything anyone said or did for three years, any plans anyone made, all revolved around my father's illness. I don't want that for myself. I couldn't stand it."

"Joe," David says, "are you sick?"

"No," Joe tells him. "That isn't what this is about. It's what I said—I just want some peace and quiet. Not all the time, though—I mean, I've got neighbors down the road who I have dinner with once in a while. And I'm certainly glad you're here. But hey, I've been doing all the talking. How about you? Are you still with that band?"

David had forgotten that some years ago, when the cover band he's been playing with for almost a decade had a gig in a club near where Joe lived in New Jersey, he had come to see them. "Yes,"

David says. "We get a booking maybe once or twice a month now. Sometimes more, if there's a fair or a festival somewhere around."

This is a subject where David can sympathize with Joe in one way at least: The band is not something he really wants to talk about. Or even think about, truth be told, because he's beginning to have his doubts about why he's still playing the top ten songs from the era when FM rock radio had its debut. His band's playlist includes almost nothing that was released after 1975, and while he used to feel that what he and his bandmates were sharing with their audiences—mostly people their own age—was a collective secret about how wonderful those long-gone, drug-infused, mystical, magical days really were, David is beginning to believe that none of this is true. Time, music, life itself—everything has moved on, and there is no point in pretending that constantly trying to recapture the fleeting moments of joy he remembers from his younger days is doing anything to help him now. If it even helped him then. He was married once, when he was twenty-six, to a beautiful girl whose greatest romance in life was with heroin, in a time when that seemed romantic to David too. He had tried it a few times and loved it so much that he knew he had to stop; his wife never did. They parted five years later when she wanted nothing from him but money to get high. What happened to her after that makes for a sad story that he does not like to dwell on very often.

Enough of this, David thinks, so he changes the subject. "Let me ask you, Joe—doesn't it ever feel weird to be spending summer in the mountains? I mean, remember when we were kids, we all always went to the beach?"

Joe smiles happily, broadly. "The Burgers' Bungalow Colony in Rockaway! I remember that place. Your parents and mine always rented those little white stucco bungalows next door to each other, the ones on the sand street, because they were cheaper. Your dad and mine came out on the train every night."

“And every night when it wasn’t raining, my dad would change into his trunks and go swimming,” David says. “He loved that so much. To use one of his favorite expressions, that was living in the lap of luxury. He’d work all day cutting coat patterns in that factory in Brooklyn and then take the A train out to the beach.”

“And after my dad drove a taxi in the city ten hours a day, all he wanted to do when he got home was listen to a baseball game. I think the only thing he ever prayed for was that the Yankees would win the pennant.”

“But do you remember how it always seemed weird that some of the families in the neighborhood spent the summer in the mountains while ours went to the beach?”

Joe laughs. “When I was a kid, I thought you had to choose. Like sign a form or make a declaration or something like that—we’re beach people or we’re mountain people. You couldn’t be both.”

“Well, it was really all because of anti-Semitism. I never realized that until years later when I started reading about it—back when we were kids living in the Bronx, just about the only summer places nearby that Jews could rent were in Rockaway, out in Queens, or up here in the Catskills.”

“It feels like a million years ago.”

“I think maybe it really was.” David reaches out for another bottle of beer. “So, anyway, how did you end up here?”

“Janet and I drove up to Woodstock on a lark maybe ten, twelve years ago. And . . . well, I don’t know. I just got a kind of vibe from the place. It always stuck in my mind that I would like to live here, and now, here I am.”

“You don’t feel like everyone in town is trying too hard? Keeping the hippie stuff alive and all that?” David asks.

“I don’t even notice it much anymore,” Joe replies. “Mostly, I just like being out here in the woods, watching the seasons change, seeing all the different kinds of birds and spotting deer walking by outside my windows. Last year, I even saw a bear with two cubs. And just about a mile from here, there's a ridge where you can stand and see way out across the Hudson Valley. It's beautiful. Next time you come, bring along a pair of boots and I'll take you hiking."

"Okay. I will." David isn't being disingenuous—he finds that he is really hoping there will be a next time. He thinks he might enjoy hiking in the woods with his cousin and the two big dogs who, after caging their allotment of snacks, have been happily snoozing the afternoon away, lying together on the porch behind Joe's chair.

The two men go on talking for a while, and then David decides it's time to leave. It won't be dark for a few hours yet, and he feels the urge to go for a drive, to see what there is to see around here. Joe suggests a route that will take him to a town called Alderville where there's a restaurant he recommends. David types the name of the restaurant into Waze and sees it will take him about forty-five minutes to make the trip.

"One thing to be careful of is that there are a lot of Hasidim living around here," Joe says. "It's Saturday—*Shabbos*—so they'll be out visiting each other, and since they can't drive, they'll be walking along the side of the road, so watch out, especially for kids."

David feels like he's being warned about the habits of reckless wildlife, but he realizes that Joe is serious. "I knew there was an Orthodox community in Monsey, but I didn't know they had moved up here too."

"I guess they feel it's safe. That's one thing that hasn't changed—people in long black coats and fur hats are still targets for sickos."

"I'll be careful driving," David assures his cousin. "And I'll keep in touch. You too, okay?"

"Sure. An email a week helps keep cousins in the pink." Joe laughs again. "Or something like that."

David walks back to his car, and as soon as he opens the door, he sees the box of rock candy sitting on the passenger seat. He feels relieved to have found it now so that he can go back to the house and give it to Joe instead of coming upon it later and regretting the mistake of not presenting his cousin with this small gift. And Joe does seem touched that David has remembered his birthday, so the two men share one last hug before David returns to his car and drives away.

The road to Alderville is not as narrow as the one David took to reach Joe's house, but indeed, he does pass several groups of Orthodox Jews walking on the rocky shoulder. *Where are they going?* he wonders, because he doesn't seem to be driving through any villages, and there are no signs directing a traveler to a religious community or even a synagogue, but it's not like he's going to stop and ask. As he passes by these people and sees them in his rearview mirror, falling away behind him, he thinks of crows and ravens. Tall black birds walking in the dappled sunlight of a weekend afternoon.

When David arrives in Alderville it seems like an odd place to him. It's an old town that was built around a small collection of tanneries and lumber mills that closed down in the late 1800s and then had a brief revival as a summer resort community until a nearby railroad spur that used to bring visitors here was destroyed in a spring of heavy rains. Now, as he locks up his car and walks the few short blocks that comprise the town center, David can hear leaves rustling like crumpled paper, birds calling out from the trees, but otherwise, all is quiet here. Most of the shops seem to be shuttered or boarded up. But finally, at the edge of town, he finds the restaurant that Joe recommended, where a few people—young, artsy looking—are sitting at tables outside, eating burgers and drinking beer. There is also an art gallery, a bookshop, a store that sells expensive pottery and decorative glass items, another one displaying beautiful hand-sewn dresses made of satiny fabrics and beads, plus—of all things—a kosher supermarket. *So odd*, David repeats to himself. *Art and fashion over here, religion right next door. I wonder if they all get along or just ignore each other?*

David walks into the restaurant, which is larger than he expected. It has tables on one side, booths on the other, and a big display case of cheeses and pies. The wide planks of the floor gleam with polish, and there is a long, curving bar made of dark mahogany that looks as well-stocked with name-brand liquors as any in the supposedly hippest neighborhoods back home, in the city. Music is being piped in through speakers up high on the walls, and, as David takes a seat at one of the tables, the song that starts playing is Bonnie Raitt's "Angel from Montgomery." This is one of David's favorite songs, and he'd love to add it to his band's repertoire, but the other members of the group think it's too country for their usual audiences. More than once, David has expressed his opinion that some songs have universal appeal, but so far, he's been on the losing side of that argument.

As David settles himself into a booth, a young woman pushes open the front door and stomps over to the bar with heavy steps. Her hair is dyed a midnight shade of black and her bare arms are decorated with darkly inked tattoos, which seem to match what is clearly an angry mood that she is more than ready to share.

"Well," she says to the bartender, another young woman who has a similar look about her, minus the fiery demeanor, "Josh promised he'd drive me down here for dinner tonight, but do you see him anywhere around? No, of course not! And it's not even that he's working! He's in the middle of some damn video game tournament that seems to involve half the world, and I am sick of it."

"I know," the bartender says, sympathetically. "It's a lot to deal with."

"It's *always* a lot to deal with, which is my point."

"Just give it some time. I'm pretty sure Amy and Leslie are coming in later so you can hang out with them. Let Josh stew in his own juices for a couple of hours, and then see how it goes."

"Mmm. Maybe. Anyway," the young woman says, suddenly brightening a bit, "do you have the mac-and-cheese burgers tonight? That'll help."

She gets her request and tucks into her meal. Someone turns up the volume on the music, which goes banging through the rafters. Now, David can't hear the rest of the conversation going on at the bar, and he's sorry for that. It's been like eavesdropping on the first act of a play, and he finds himself very badly wanting more clues to what will happen next. Will the young woman forgive her boyfriend? And what are they doing anyway, living up here in this odd little mountain town? What kind of work does Josh do? And his companion, the mac-and-cheese lover: Is she an artist who sells her wares in one of the nearby shops, or does she do something else?

David realizes that he could go on considering dozens of questions like these, but the more he does, the sadder they make him feel. So the most important question is: Why are these inconsequential musings having such an unhappy effect on him? *Probably*, he thinks, *because they serve to point out that the young woman is, indeed, just that—young*. The future stretches out before her, full to the brim with a seemingly infinite number of choices she can make about herself, her relationship, the place where she wants to live. For David, though, this moment and his thoughts about it feel like they will stay in his memory forever, like tiny pieces of time trapped in amber, while for everyone else—the young woman, the bartender, the few others in the restaurant, the friends who may or may not arrive—all that is happening now is likely just a passing scene, soon to be forgotten.

David eats his meal and then leaves. The sun is beginning to slip below the horizon as he arrives back in Woodstock, and the moon is on the rise. Like ancient counterweights, they exchange day for night as they slide past each other in the sky. Stars begin to appear, tiny points of light strewn across the darkening horizon.

David parks his car in the lot behind the hotel and begins to walk toward the entrance on the street but then turns back to get his guitar. Fifty years ago, he drove all the way from New York to the Martin Guitar Factory in Nazareth, Pennsylvania, to buy this guitar, which is made of honey-colored Alpine spruce with a rosewood back and sides. He has two electric guitars—a classic Fender Stratocaster and an Epiphone Les Paul Special—that he uses when he's playing with his band, but the Martin is his treasure. Its warm, woody sound has been a comfort to him all through the years, at those times when he's sat alone and played the songs he loves, just for himself. Feeling happy, woebegone, or somewhere in-between, the guitar has always provided the background music for his life. So tonight, he carries it up to his room and plays for a while, finishing one song and beginning another, just strumming whatever comes to mind. Yesterday, when he left the city, he had debated whether or not to bring the guitar with him, but now he's glad he did.

After he puts the guitar away, he watches television for an hour or so, thinking that he'll go to bed soon so he can get up early and head back home. But after he's decided that it's time to turn in, he doesn't quite feel like he'll be able to fall asleep yet, so he goes to sit on the balcony outside his room, hoping the soft night air will lull him into feeling drowsy. Instead, once he steps outside, he suddenly feels even more wide awake.

The balcony that runs around the front of this old building is narrow and seems to pitch forward, as if it is leaning down to the sidewalk. David's room faces a quiet street where the road out of town begins, but on the opposite corner it intersects Tinker Street, which seems to have closed down for the night. There are no cars driving by, and though the traffic light that David can see continues to blink red and green, no one passes by to obey its commands to stop and go. There is, however, one store right on the corner—the souvenir shop where David bought the T-shirt before he started his drive to Joe's house—where the lights have been left on, and its bright windows bloom with electricity.

Looking out into the night, David is aware of the symbolism set out before him: There is a quiet street, a lonely road, a shaky perch where he sits and waits, and, not far away, there is a light burning in the darkness. But what he is waiting for, he could not say. And what everything else taken together might mean for him remains, at least for now, unknown.

ABOUT THE AUTHOR

Eleanor Lerman has published eight award-winning collections of poetry along with several celebrated novels and collections of short stories. One of the youngest individuals ever to be named a finalist for the National Book Award, she also won the inaugural Juniper Prize from the University of Massachusetts Press and the Lenore Marshall Poetry Prize from the American Academy of Poets, among other accolades. In addition, she has received a Guggenheim Fellowship for poetry as well as fellowships from the National Endowment for the Arts for poetry and the New York Foundation for the Arts for fiction. She has lived most of her life in New York City, which is the setting for the majority of her fiction, and now lives in Long Beach, on New York's Long Island.

Author photo © Jeff Tiedrich

Looking for your next great read?

We can help!

Visit www.shewritespress.com/next-read or scan the QR code below for a list of our recommended titles.

She Writes Press is an award-winning independent publishing company founded to serve women writers everywhere.